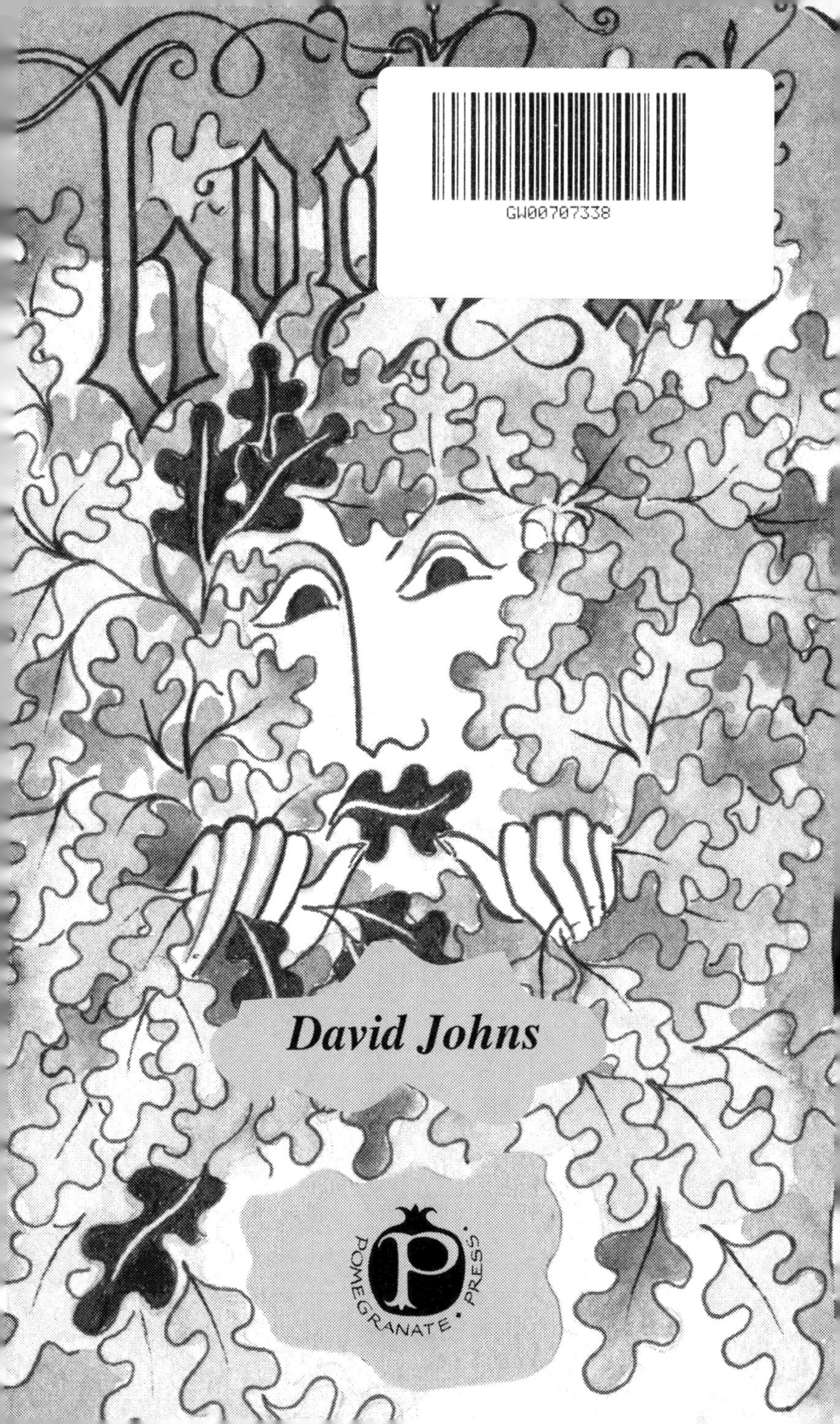
GW00707338
David Johns
POMEGRANATE PRESS
P

Published by Pomegranate Press,
Dolphin House, 51 St Nicholas Lane, Lewes, Sussex BN7 2JZ
www.pomegranate-press.co.uk

Also by David Johns: The Eye & Blade Trilogy
The Frozen City
A Flight of Bright Birds
Shadows in Crimson Colours

ISBN 0-9548975-2-8

British Library Cataloguing-in-Publication Data.
A catalogue record for this book is available from the British Library

Printed and bound by CPI Antony Rowe, Eastbourne

Contents

1 A Summons to the Castle

From the shelter of the drey Ranulph watched the hunting party return through the forest. Beneath him the dogs fanned through the trees, their muzzles raking the undergrowth, hugely concentrating, their movements a sort of haphazard progress as they were constantly urged on towards the great bulk of the castle. Their handlers, following close behind, filled the cold air with yells and curses, all the time cracking whips to keep the beasts from the hooves of their masters' horses.

He grinned. They were so close that he could almost smell their bodies hot from the hunt, and yet they passed unaware. The handlers, their skins a greyish brown leather, their tunics rough homespun, were the colour and stuff of the forest they moved through, but the huntsmen, richly arrayed in fine brocades frosted with silver, resembled birds of paradise flown accidentally from the tropics to this northern place.

'Faster!' rang a commanding voice, and Ranulph, before he crossed his arms in front of his face and closed his eyes as tightly as he could, had a fleeting glimpse of a large man dressed all in black sitting astride a huge black stallion with a blaze of white on its forehead and wild, bloodshot eyes.

'Faster, wheyface, or I'll have your head sliced off your shoulders!'

The hunt coursed by, and yet Ranulph sensed that not every rider had gone. His ears were as acute as his nose, and there had been a set of particularly heavy hoofbeats among the rest that had drummed closer and stopped beneath his tree. He scarcely dared to look, but nevertheless lowered his arms to his nose and squinted above them.

Below him, breathing heavily, Baron Fulke swayed comfortably in his creaking leather saddle. His shoulders were broad, his hair thick and black. Steam rose from the great horse towards Ranulph's drey, a hideaway built in imitation of the squirrel's home but far more dense. No man's gaze could penetrate it.

But was he really so confident? At this moment the burly horseman swivelled his head and looked up into the tree. Ranulph felt a chill shiver of fear run through his body. Something he had never been able to discover connected him to the fearsome Baron Fulke. They had never once met. All he knew was that the Baron had forbidden anyone, on pain of death, ever to allow him entry at the castle gates. That made him a kind of outlaw, but not for anything he himself had ever done. Not, at least, for anything he *knew* that he had done.

Now they seemed to stare at one another eyeball to eyeball, although he was sure that he could not be seen – and yet not so sure as to prevent the sweat pricking his forehead. Those eyes seemed to pick their way through the webbed branches, relentless and ruthless. The head inclined slightly, quizzically. The Baron was puzzled.

And then a squirrel shot down the tree trunk, froze for a second when it saw horse and rider and bounded away into the undergrowth. The Baron gave a snort and kicked the stallion with his heels.

'Home, Tarquin!' he boomed.

What did the Baron know about Ranulph that he didn't know about himself? Was it anything to do with the terrible sickness which had swept through the land a few years past and which had never entirely gone away? They called it the Pestilence. Could it be that, in some way he could not understand, he was responsible for bringing evil upon the village? Nobody would ever tell him.

When the hoofbeats had died away he crawled from his nest of woven branches and dropped soundlessly to the forest floor.

Hunting animals was a fine sport, but his was a finer thing still: to watch, to learn, to copy the ways of the animal.

A passing woodman, hugely burdened with cut branches, almost collided with him and gave a sour scowl.

'Idiot!' he growled beneath his breath, perhaps outraged to see a healthy lad of fourteen not engaged in meaningful toil. 'Get out from under my feet!'

Ranulph stopped in his tracks, reminded that there was, indeed, work to be done. His guardian Grete, a mountainous deaf-mute whose huge presence always seemed voice enough, had demanded wood for the fire, and now he must scrabble and forage on the forest floor until he had enough to last them through the night. Muttering evilly to himself, he plunged into the trees.

It was more than an hour before he had gathered enough wood. Daylight was fast fading. There was a flurry of snow as he made his way home, the air filling with a swarm of white insects which fussed and fluttered around him, settling on his head and shoulders and finally on his nose, only to be dislodged when he thrust out his lower lip and blew upwards.

Home was a stone lodge pressed against the high wall of the castle, close by the gate which the hunt had entered. He pushed aside the heavy skins that hung across the doorway, dumping the wood on the floor without ceremony.

Grete, massive and unsmiling, her blond hair pushed under a headscarf of heavy wool, strode forward to meet him. There was something she wished to tell him, he could read it in her eyes, but she simply gathered kindling wood and fed the fire which smouldered in the centre of the earthen floor. It spluttered into life and sent smoke and sparks through the roof vent towards the glinting stars.

Everything inside the lodge was illuminated by the flickering light of the flames: on one side Grete's bed, a pile of straw and a few rough grey blankets, on the other Ranulph's cot, its wooden endboards ornately carved with birds and flowers.

Apart from a scattered collection of pots and bowls, these were all they possessed. And yet, by some standards, they were rich enough, with a sound roof above their heads and four solid walls around them. Few others of their class could boast walls of stone. It was something Ranulph accepted without understanding, just as he accepted without puzzlement the fact that all their food, dull but filling, came from the kitchens of the castle. Grete had only to fetch it and heat it. Which other peasants had such treatment?

This evening their meal was a thin, cabbagy gruel with some tough fragments of an unidentifiable meat floating in it. He prodded at the meat with his spoon and began to eat, breaking off pieces of coarse bread and dipping them in the liquid to soften the staleness.

'What is it, Grete?' he asked aloud, knowing she could not hear him. Something had happened.

The fire began to fail. The wood he had brought was damp, and the flames became a thick, choking smoke which seemed reluctant to move upwards through the vent, curling itself around Grete and Ranulph instead. It obscured the taste of their food – perhaps, he thought, for the better.

As they finished their meal in a gloomy half-darkness, Grete prodded his arm and began to make gestures with her hands and face. It was a private language which he had learned by heart over the years, yet he could not believe the message he read.

'I'm to visit the castle?' he asked, at once excited and terrified. He used her own sign-language. 'I shall be allowed through the gates?'

Yes, it was true. He had been summoned. He must go in the morning. Someone would come for him. That was all.

'I don't want to go,' he told her, but Grete only shrugged her large shoulders. What must be, must be.

Ranulph crept beneath his blanket and imagined himself curled beneath the hollow roots of the great oak that lay near the hermit's hut in the forest. That was his favourite place, more private even than the drey. The drey he had built himself, and he took great pride in it, but the tree roots were a part of the forest. The hollow had been created by a great storm, which lifted the oak from the ground. Other trees, greater than the oak but long since dwarfed by it, had held it tilted like an accusing finger pointing at the sky. It had continued to grow, the hollow enlarged by the scrabbling of animals and the scouring of rain and wind.

Ferns, grasses and a thicket of saplings now concealed its entrance, and Ranulph's discovery had been the purest accident. Lying there with his ear pressed to the ground he could hear the earth speaking to him, its voice rising through the damp soil, through the rock, the sands, the clay, telling of great mysteries. Sometimes he visited the hermit and spoke to him, but his mysteries were cloudier and wrapped in the language of the church.

'I shouldn't be talking to you at all, boy,' Brother Walt had told him on one occasion. 'My vocation is to live apart from men.'

'Then why do you do it?' Ranulph challenged him with a grin, knowing that the old man was always pleased to see him.

'Because you don't count. You're somewhere between man and the beasts with your wild ways and your knowledge of the earth. God allows it. St Francis preached to the birds, after all.'

Ranulph had accepted the explanation as a rare compliment, and he grinned again to think of it now. From beneath his blanket he could hear Grete grunting and snorting, strange nocturnal animal noises which contrasted with the silence of her days. An occasional fizzing sound suggested that the snow was falling again, the flakes drifting through the vent to the smouldering ashes of the fire.

And then the howling began, distant, like the wailing of lost souls. Wolves!

Ranulph shuddered and wrapped his blanket tighter. No more of the hollow roots: he was pleased to have the four stone walls protecting him.

And that long stretch of wall which was part of the castle's defences: was he really going to pass through that in the morning? He fell asleep befuddled by fear and wonder.

*

'Where are you boy!'

The call came for him all too soon after first light the following morning. The castle steward stood outside the lodge in a curling mist, stamping his feet to keep the cold at bay.

'Coming, Master John.'

He pulled his tunic straight and brushed himself down with hands black from charcoal he had been using to draw crude images on the lodge wall – spirals and stars and a giant crescent moon. Even as he pushed through the animal hides and felt the chill air bite at the back of his throat, Grete was rubbing at these images with her sleeve, fearful of charges of witchcraft. What was it that possessed him?

'What's the matter, boy?' demanded the steward, leading the way to the castle. 'Are your legs as lame as your brain? Hurry along!'

Ranulph knew the steward. He had seen him about the village, strutting and commanding and enjoying all too well the power he had over the people. And if Ranulph had little love for the villagers, who shunned him and treated him as an outsider, he had even less for this man with his rat-like face and bullying voice.

They passed through the massive gateway and crossed a cobbled courtyard. Through a window he saw two soldiers lounging by a roaring fire. They leapt to their feet as the steward strode into the room, shuffling awkwardly into soldierly positions, rigidly upright, the stiffness of their bodies echoed by the spears they clutched.

'Slovens!' spat out the steward.

He opened a low door at the back of the room, ducking his head under the arched lintel.

'Stay there until you're called for,' he commanded Ranulph, who was too confused by the strangeness of it all to do more than give him a wild-eyed stare.'And you two make sure he doesn't go anywhere.'

The door slammed to. The room was hot and foul-smelling. At the steward's departure, the soldiers began to relax, and one of them grinned malevolently: 'Aren't you the idiot boy who lives with the mute witch outside the wall? What on earth can the baron want with you?'

Ranulph shrugged, trembling despite the heat. The other soldier looked uncomfortable.

'Be careful of your words,' he hissed to his companion. 'It doesn't pay to cross the likes of him.'

The first soldier hawked into the fire and lapsed into a sullen silence, which seemed to spread wider and wider. Ranulph shifted his weight from one leg to the other, not daring to sit down and afraid to make any other movement.

Eventually the small door opened.

2 The Baron's Sport

'This way!' commanded the castle steward, and Ranulph had to sprint from the room to catch up with him. They continued in silence, walking briskly along a cold narrow passageway which made sharp turns every so often to left and right. The steward at last pushed open a large oaken door and motioned him inside.

'Wait in there,' he ordered roughly.

Light poured in from a large arched window high in one wall. There was a low bench inside the room and a small table inlaid with lozenges of coloured glass on which the outlines of strange, unearthly creatures had been engraved. They reminded him of the gargoyles on the church tower, whose open mouths gushed with water after a cloudburst.

He was running a finger round the outlines of these weird beings when the door swung open and a girl of his own age walked in. He leapt to his feet and almost fell to his knees before her. She was young, but she was already a lady. He saw it in her clothes, which were very fine — a dress of the lightest sky-blue, which clung to her slender body, with a girdle of crimson silk and a brooch of matching colour at her breast. But he saw it even more in her bearing. She was used to comfort. She was of good breeding. She was like a graceful bird, a summer swallow, beautiful, moving without effort.

'Please sit down,' she said, her voice soothingly soft. 'You're Ranulph, aren't you?'

He sat down, heavily. He felt horribly coarse and awkward. Surely his clothes must stink.

'I'm Elizabeth. You know of me?'

He shook his head, bewildered. His tongue seemed to hang heavy in his mouth, like an iron clapper inside a bell.

Now, for the first time, she seemed to notice his appearance.

How could she not have known him for a peasant from the first? He had the shabby clothes, designed only for warmth. His skin was weatherbeaten. His hair was crudely cut.

'You don't live in the castle?' she asked.

'No, my lady.'

'My lady!'

She laughed, but immediately brought a hand to her lips. It was delicately gloved. She seemed suddenly embarrassed, uncertain. There was something she didn't understand.

'Where do you live, Ranulph?'

'Outside the gates, my lady.'

She stood quickly and, a look of suspicion on her face, opened the door. There was nobody outside.

'You are Ranulph,' she asked, 'son of Richard, Baron Fulke's brother?'

He clutched the edge of the table in his hands, his heart pounding. In that moment he seemed to understand so much that had been a mystery for all his conscious life.

'I've never known whose son I was,' he breathed. 'I have no parents. Grete has raised me, outside the walls.'

'Dear God!' cried Elizabeth. 'I fear that I'm being used and that something dreadful is about to happen.'

'What is it?' He was on his feet in a second, ready for defence or for flight. 'What is it you fear?'

Elizabeth put a gloved finger to her lips.

'I'll tell you all I know,' she said, motioning him to sit beside her. 'I am here to be betrothed to Baron Fulke's son, Simon. He is only nine years old, but we shall marry when he comes of age. My family is related to his. That's how I knew of you. I've known about you for many years.' She smiled at him, confidingly. 'I always hoped we'd meet.'

'And where's the danger?' Ranulph persisted.

'The danger is to you,' she frowned, 'if you are the Ranulph

I think you are.' She looked closely at his features. 'Yes, I can see that you are. Poor Ranulph! I had expected to meet you as soon as I arrived at the castle yesterday. I asked after you, but received only a long silence in reply.'

'Danger,' he persisted.

'Richard was Fulke's older brother. His wealth is destined to come to you, his only son. Fulke holds it in trust.'

'I,' he asked weakly, 'have wealth?'

'In law, yes,' she said gently. 'But the number of men who would swear to it has probably fallen away almost to nothing. The Pestilence has taken them off. I never guessed the injustice which had been done to you. I'm truly sorry for it.'

They heard a noise beyond the door. It grew closer.

'Ranulph,' she said, reaching out a hand and taking his. 'I don't know why I was asked to meet you in this room. Do you believe me?'

They sat like two conspirators, their fingers clasped.

'I believe you, Elizabeth.'

She raised her fingers to her brooch, which was made of the most delicate metal, and deftly snapped it in two.

'Take this,' she urged him, giving him the part that had come away, 'as a token of my good faith.'

Their hands clasped once more. At that moment the door was thrown open and two large men brandishing swords strode into the room and seized Ranulph by the arms. He scarcely had time to slip the crimson shard of brooch into a pocket.

'Molester!' cried one of them.

'Violator!' shouted the other.

He was aware only of Elizabeth's eyes, brimming with tears, as he was jerked away from the bench and dragged from the room, his feet banging against the floor behind him as they hurried along the passageway, up a steep flight of steps and into the great hall.

*

Huge tapestries, their deep reds and blues interlaced with veins of glistening gold, were the first things that met his eyes as he was swung into a standing position, his arms held painfully tight by his deeply breathing captors. His nose, trained in the wilds, could smell their sweat. The tapestries covered two walls of the baronial hall to the height of two men. Above them he saw coats of arms, crossed pikestaffs, the mounted heads of huge wild boar. And further up, much further, the walls met massive oaken beams which streched the width of the building, half obscuring the v-shape of the roof timbers.

'What's this?' rang a voice he recognised from the previous morning's hunt. At the far end of the hall, reclining in a large wooden chair whose arms were carved in the shapes of terrifying beasts with scaly backs, arched wings and bared rows of sharp teeth, was the menacing form of Baron Fulke himself. 'Have we found a trespasser?'

He was dragged forward again, his feet swishing against the rushes which lined the stone floor. Two greyhounds, their thin, dark ribs almost bursting from tautly stretched skin, leapt to their feet and, snarling, frisked angrily at his heels. Averting his eyes from the glowering Baron, Ranulph looked wildly about him as if for help. All he saw were a few elegantly dressed lords and ladies who stared at him with amused smiles on their faces, and a bustle of humble workers in rough homespun who went about their business – stoking the great fire, replacing the rushes, bringing jugs and dishes – all the time prudently keeping their eyes averted.

'A violator!' exclaimed one of the two men, suddenly pushing him in the back so that he tumbled to the floor at the Baron's feet. 'Caught in the act of assaulting the Lady Elizabeth.'

The Baron's face darkened: 'What are you doing here, boy?'

'I was summoned here, sire,' he managed to get out.

'Ha!' that thunderous voice boomed. 'And you think I wouldn't know if you had been?'

Ranulph's brain was clear enough to tell him he was somebody's victim.

'The castle steward brought me here, sire,' he said simply, his body tensed for a kick from one of those large boots which hung so close to his face.

'Fetch John steward!' commanded the Baron to nobody in particular. Then, in a quieter voice, he turned to one of the two swordsmen. 'Tell me more, cousin Saward. How did this happen?'

'The lady Elizabeth hadn't been seen since Matins. Norbert and I searched the castle and found her in a side room, flinching from the lustful embraces of this creature.'

'For which crime,' his companion stated flatly, 'we demand the death sentence.'

The Baron raised his eyebrows: 'Indeed?'

God spare me, thought Ranulph, shifting into a kneeling position suitable for prayer. He closed his eyes tight. *This man may kill me, and there is nobody I can turn to for mercy.*

'You called for me, sire?' he heard the steward say, somewhere behind him.

'This lad – you brought him here?'

'I don't recognise the boy, sire,' the steward said.

'Enough,' replied Baron Fulke. 'You may go.'

Ranulph opened his eyes. If the Baron could see the terror in them, so be it.

'That's not true!' he stammered.

The blow came not from the Baron's foot but from one of the two men behind him. It sent him sprawling on his face.

'Cur!' exclaimed the man called Saward. 'And liar!'

'He must die,' repeated Norbert.

Ranulph looked into the Baron's face and saw that the man was pondering. He knew from the expression that the Baron was himself no part of this plot – a plot which seemed to have his death as its inevitable conclusion. But it was not a kind face. It was the face of power. No peasant expected justice from such a man. He regained his kneeling position and closed his eyes once more.

'It would surely not,' he heard Norbert say in a low voice, 'be entirely displeasing to you if the boy should die.'

'Die, no doubt,' the Baron murmured. 'But this is my brother's son. To kill him would be another matter. Could I not have had him killed years ago were I of that mind?'

'But now,' urged Norbert, 'you have ample reason. The crime of rape demands a sentence of death. You have the witnesses.'

The Baron gave a short laugh: 'Witnesses,' he said, 'who might not be regarded as neutral. If I inherit my family's wealth it will, on my death, pass to my son and his wife – the lady Elizabeth, your kinswoman.'

'Of course,' agreed Saward. 'But none of us is without self-interest. The execution of this youth, for a monstrous crime, would be to the benefit of all of us.'

Dear God in heaven, Ranulph repeated over and over to himself. He wished he knew the words that people used in church, but he had been only once in his life and could not possibly have learned the words. He thought of the bright pictures on the walls, particularly those which showed the procession of the damned through the fiery gates of hell. *Dear God in heaven, have mercy!*

'Stand, boy,' ordered the Baron, and immediately he felt himself lifted from his knees. 'You know who I am?'

'I know, sire.'

'You remember seeing me before?'

'I saw you only yesterday, sire, with the hunt. I was in the forest, watching.'

'Not my meaning, but no matter.' Ranulph saw that the Baron was still deep in thought, even as he spoke. 'You enjoy the hunt, eh?'

'It's a fine thing, sire.'

'Indeed, Ranulph. A fine thing!'

The use of his name startled him. But the calculation which he now saw in the Baron's eyes frightened him much more. The smile on those lips was not for him. He knew then that he would not escape. The Baron was about to condemn him.

'Mercy, sire!' he pleaded, close to fainting away.

'Oh yes, boy, you shall have mercy,' grinned the Baron.

'Death!' urged Norbert again, taking a step forward, but Baron Fulke waved him away. He stood for the first time, a giant of a man, and yelled deep into the recesses of the hall: 'Call Fragonard scrivener!'

Ranulph looked on helplessly, only half conscious it seemed. He saw a table brought forward, and then the appearance of old Fragonard, a learned man with a white beard and a dome of a head completely devoid of hair. He saw that everyone gathered round the table, and then he himself was propelled forward, to stand close by the Baron.

'You shall have justice, boy,' the Baron said, in a voice loud enough for all to hear. 'I could have your head taken off your shoulders for what you have done. Instead, I shall give you a chance.'

Was he supposed to offer thanks? He could not. He knew that something ill was planned for him. He saw the hungry dogs at his feet and thought how much better their life was than his. At least they had their master's favour.

'You like the hunt, eh? Then you shall take part in one. Write all of this down, Master Fragonard, so that the law shall be seen to be upheld. We shall have rules for our hunt. And write in English if you please, scrivener. None of your dog-Latin or mysterious French. We all wish to understand it.'

Those who can read, Ranulph thought. *But I shall have to remember it, point by point. My life will depend upon it.*

'The lad Ranulph,' the Baron began to dictate, 'having been discovered committing an act of gross depravity upon the person of the innocent Elizabeth,' – here he drew breath luxuriously, as if savouring the moment. (*God save me*, prayed Ranulph silently, *God save me, God save me, God save me.*) – 'shall be hunted unto death.'

The Baron paused again while the scrivener wrote, the goose quill squeaking on the parchment. He dropped a hand to Ranulph's shoulder, for all the world as if he were a kind uncle bestowing a kindness.

'The rules of the hunt are these,' he continued, breaking off every so often to allow old Fragonard time. 'The said Ranulph having been released from this castle once this document is signed, the Baron's men shall pursue him with dogs, by horse and on foot, from the moment the sun has reached its highest point in the heavens.

'Should he escape and not be found by nightfall, select agents of the Baron's power shall continue to hunt the said Ranulph throughout the length and breadth of the kingdom without cease until such time as he is caught. He shall then be killed forthwith and his body brought back to the castle for presentation to the Baron.

'The successful huntsman shall be rewarded with gold equivalent to ten years of a steward's fee.'

Ranulph held on to the edge of the table to prevent himself falling. His head swam. He saw the gratified smiles on the lips of the two men who had seized him. A boar's head on the wall seemed to gaze down on him with helpless pity, one victim acknowledging another.

'But justice shall be administered with full rigour. Any man sent out by the Baron to hunt the said Ranulph shall bear the Baron's seal, a stag's head transfixed by an arrow. And this seal must be shown to the said Ranulph before he meets his death so that, in the short time remaining to him, he may make his peace with his God.'

Old Fragonard continued to dip the point of his quill in the ink and sweep his letters across the page. It was a slow process, far too slow. Ranulph was calculating how long he had to flee before the huntsmen would sound their horns and start off in pursuit of him.

'And because God in his mercy may protect any man,' the Baron added, a note of generosity in his deep and resonating voice, 'and because we would not seek to presume the ways of Almighty God, the said Ranulph shall have the means to be spared.'

Ranulph saw a sudden scowl cross the face of the swordsman Norbert, but nobody dared to interrupt. The Baron crossed his arms in front of his broad chest and smiled benignly upon the nephew he was sentencing to death.

'The hunt will be abandoned, and the said Ranulph's life will be spared, if he shall bring back to Baron Fulke the most holy relic in Christendom, a phial of the blood of our Lord Jesu Christ. Amen.'

With this pious flourish the Baron completed the rules of his manhunt. As soon as Fragonard had finished setting it all down, the Baron added his bold signature to the document, beckoning Ranulph to do the same.

'But I can't,' he pleaded.

'Your mark, boy. That will do.'

In this way Ranulph was made to sign his own death

warrant. He stood quietly by as Norbert and Saward wrote their names as witnesses, then allowed himself to be shepherded out of the hall, down a long corridor and across the courtyard to the main gate.

'Bonne chance!' called Baron Fulke in a barbarous French accent as he ran through the gate and set off like a hare across the open fields to the shadowed security of the forest.

3 Flight

Brother Walt kicked at the dust which floored his hut, watching the cloud settle over his sandalled feet until he seemed to be growing out of the ground, to be a very part of it.

'Phouah!'

He shook his feet angrily as if to proclaim his separateness. Then he jumped up and down several time, waving his fists at the air in what might have been regarded as a tantrum had he not been a grey-haired old man and had there been anyone to see him. There was not. His hut – his hermitage, as he liked to call it – sat alone in a clearing in the forest a full two miles from the castle and its accompanying village. Visitors were rare.

The walls of his hut were circular, and he now began to pace round them like a trapped animal.

'It's no good, Lord,' he said aloud in a thin, reedy voice. 'I'm just not cut out for it. I get lonely, Lord. I need someone to talk to. I know this is a weakness, but you made me, Lord, so you must know it, too. And if you willed my weakness, who am I to fight against it?'

The logic of this seemed to please him, for a little smile played briefly about his lips.

'I've tried talking to the birds, Lord. *Nothing*! Finer company in a charnel house. Flit, flit, tweet, tweet! They hardly know I'm here. And they all look the same to me – seen one, you've seen them all.'

He kicked at the dust again but kept marching through the cloud, allowing it to settle on the embers of the past night's fire.

'As for that goat!' This he repeated in a shout for the benefit of the poor creature, which was tethered in the clearing in front of the hut and was cry for milking: 'As for Hosea's Wife!'

He kicked at the ground with all the fierceness he could muster, creating such a fog of dust that within seconds he emerged choking into bright sunshine. Hosea's Wife looked up from the grass she was chewing and, seeing her master standing part-blinded by dust and harsh light, took the opportunity of reminding him of his duties. The butt took Brother Walt off balance, and he landed in a heap on the ground with the goat beside him, her face pressed to his, the two horizontal pupils of her eyes fixed on the wide and furious pupils of his own.

'Whore!' he roared. 'Daughter of Satan! Outflow of Beelzebub's bum!'

When the goat prepared to renew its attack, however, he rapidly forgot the insults and shuffled with maximum haste (and minimum dignity) to a point beyond the animal's reach. There, as his adversary strained at her tether, he collected himself, stood up and brushed himself down. To be attacked by a goat, however grand her Biblical name! Frowning, he attempted to settle to what he hoped was a state of prayerful calm. A mere nanny goat!

To calm himself, he took stock of the day's tasks. First he would milk Hosea's Wife and breakfast on that. Then he would clear his small patch of land, well ahead of the spring sowing: it would be some weeks before the earth warmed sufficiently for him to till it, but a hermit had to keep himself occupied, if only to take his mind off his troubles. How he hated that goat! Then he would gather what herbs and roots he could, though the season yielded little.

Next, if he were to eat that day, he would have to catch a fish from the river whose waters could be heard singing through the trees behind the hermitage. It was, no doubt, a pleasant enough life for a contemplative. Alas, he was no contemplative. He would happily have traded it all for a seat in a warm alehouse, a frothing jug before him and a serving maid behind him, running her soft and pliable fingers through his sparse grey hair.

He set to milking the goat, tempering his aggression in the interests of safety. He whispered to her, and as he tugged at her teats his soothing insults grew more and more imaginative until they had become a pure, if obscure, poetry: 'Blasted bag of bone and skin, Devil's kin, evil's in your gamey stink, scraggy pink belly skin, Devil's kin . . .'

It was as he was coaxing the last few white droplets from their warm reservoir into his rude wooden bowl that he became aware of a movement in the forest. Could it be the hunt? He stood with excitement, though he must pretend a solemn concern for the prey in such circumstances, crossing himself very visibly before the passing bowmen for the demise of the unhappy creature which they so colourfully pursued.

The movement drew closer, yet it was not accompanied by the usual shouting and barking. A lone animal? If so, why the urgency, and why did it run towards him? Seconds later his questions were answered as Ranulph came crashing through the undergrowth and fell exhausted at his feet.

*

'If this is a trick, boy . . . Brother Walt frowned, having listened to Ranulph's panting tale of his seizure in the castle, the false charge against him and the Baron's invention of his terrible manhunt.

'No trick, sir, no trick. If only it *was*!'

'And why . . .

'I thought you would hide me,' Ranulph stammered, not waiting for the question to be asked.

The old man's expression of alarm intensified ten-fold: 'Here? Oh, no, that would never do, boy. I could never allow that. This is a house – poor though it is, and lowly –- a house of prayer, of quietude. Why, I shouldn't be talking to you now if I adhered strictly to my calling. But the Lord, may His mercy be upon us, himself never ignored the pleas of the outcast and the fallen . . .'

'Sanctuary, then! They would never touch me within the walls of your hut.'

The mere suggestion seemed to set the old man's body into motion. It shook, as if no longer able to contain the hugeness of his alarm.

'Sanctuary? Never! I mean, look . . . They'd only have to lean on it and...and there'd be questions and priests and . . .'

His eyes rolled heavenwards. Ranulph had imagined that nobody could face greater danger than himself at this awful moment, but the hermit's fear seemed to match his own. The old man stumbled towards his hut, crossing himself and mumbling a few words in what must be Latin. He entered his hut and beckoned Ranulph to follow.

'It's really no good staying here,' Brother Walt said as they squatted in the semi-darkness, their voices hushed and conspiratorial.'But you're a boy who knows the forest.'

'Yes.'

'You'll know places to hide.'

'But the dogs will sniff me out!'

'Not if you're clever. They won't expect it, you see. They'll never imagine that you're still in the neighbourhood. The Baron will plan on your running as far as you can before nightfall.' He paused, and a little smile touched his lips. 'Yes, I can see the sport in it.'

'You traitor!' Ranulph accused him, clenching his fists.

'Now, now boy: no spleen. If the hunted understands the hunter then there's a chance he'll outwit him. A small chance, true . . .'

For a full minute they sat in silence, Ranulph growing ever more impatient and agitated. He imagined the sun rising swiftly in the sky outside.

'Tell me,' Ranulph demanded, 'where I shall find a phial of the blood of our Lord Jesus Christ. It will save my life.'

'That's difficult for an old man like me to say, isolated as I am from the world.'

'You *must* know, you're a religious man!'

'Ah, so simple you are, boy. I have seen relics, but never anything as precious as that.'

'Where have you seen them? When was it?'

Brother Walt smiled: 'There's a wonderful place a few days' journey from here called Lindisfarne. It's a hallowed spot which is also known as Holy Island. I paid a visit to the priory there when I was a young man with bright visions. There they have relics.'

'So, perhaps . . .'

'But nothing quite so precious, I think. Don't pin your hopes on such a thing. Think how best you may escape.'

A silence fell again. Ranulph's brain was in turmoil. His head throbbed with the pounding of his blood. He wanted to rush out of the hut and dash away into the forest and across the fields and moors beyond, through a country he had never seen, but he knew that it would be madness. He could never outrun the Baron's horses.

'Listen, boy,' Brother Walt said at last. 'You must go to the river. It has the cold of winter in it, but it's shallow and you won't suffer too much. Wade upstream awhile so that the dogs lose your scent. Then you must double back and hide. Make sure that your path doesn't cross the path you've taken thus far. And then stay out of sight for several days.'

'For days! So close to the castle?'

'Until they're convinced that you're far away. Now don't

tell me where you're going to hide, because I don't want to know. But I'll leave some food for you by the fallen oak. You can collect it by night.'

With this offer, he rose and ushered Ranulph to the door. He raised two fingers over his head as he left, muttering more incomprehensible Latin, then kicked at the dust around the entrance to obliterate the hunted boy's tell-tale footprints.

'God go with you,' was all he said by way of a farewell.

*

He heard the hunting horn while he was still in the river, his legs numbed by the chill water. They were coming for him! It took a greater courage than he had ever needed in his life to turn towards those cruel men with their dogs and their horses and find a new route back to the hollow beneath the tree. Every second brought them closer.

A noise from a thicket startled him and he fell to one knee, watching and listening. It was only a deer which, as it approached, sniffed at the air and, scenting man, turned and ran. Ranulph shook his head: 'If only you knew how easily I understand you, brother deer,' he said quietly to himself.

The horns were loud in his ears by the time he found his hollow and slid between the leaves and branches which arched over the entrance. There was too much light! He scrambled outside and collected small branches and last year's leaves, stuffing them into the crevices. Did his work look unnatural? He fussed at the camouflage until he heard, he could swear it, the sound of hounds breaking through the undergrowth. He tumbled into his hiding place in terror, lying still and silent, listening.

Yes, he could hear the hounds. They were not a quarter of a mile away, following the trail of his original flight. His imagination drew pictures in his mind of their snarling mouths and great yellow teeth, and he shuddered. But he remembered Brother Walt's words: he understood these hunters and he would manage to outwit them. Nobody knew the forest better than he did.

A voice suddenly sounded close by, a voice calling a dog to heel. They must have fanned out. They were combing the very spot! He could hear the ground beneath the feet of his pursuers, the crunch of dried leaves and breaking twigs. One of the dogs gave a little suppressed yelp of excitement. Two men spoke together, just too far away for him to make out the words. Surely the hammering of his heart must be heard above the ground. The dogs were sniffing, closer and closer.

'Dear God in Heaven,' he prayed silently, his hands pressed closely together. 'If I am spared this death I shall go to Mass once every week for the rest of my days.'

And then a deer broke cover a few yards from his hide, and the air was full of the commotion of yapping hounds and the furious cries of their masters calling them, unavailingly, from the pursuit of their habitual quarry.

*

In the utter darkness of early morning he awoke from a merciful slumber and for a second imagined himself blind. He had slept with his face pressed to the earth, and now he had to spit crumbs of leafmould and soil from his mouth as he uncurled himself and stretched his stiffened limbs.

He was hungry, very hungry. Brother Walt had promised food by the fallen oak. Dare he risk it? His stomach made the decision. He crawled from the hollow as silently as he knew, as silently as the animals he had watched. He paused, sniffing the air and listening. The sniffing was more affectation than use, maybe, but he knew a solidarity with the animal kingdom which he had never felt with the world of men.

By the oak, as promised, pushed beneath the huge girth of the lower trunk, was a leather pouch which contained two unevenly baked fish and a leathery root – dry, uncooked and a challenge for his teeth greater than anything he had yet experienced. It had no flavour that he could recognise, and he would have as soon chewed the pouch. Nevertheless, parts of the fish were good, and he soon cleaned the bones of their flesh.

He took the meal seated in the shadows cast by the moon, his back to the fallen tree, facing the density of the forest. Above him, stars performed their mysteries in the heavens; around him, the trees breathed deeply and silently, and the creatures of the night went about their business unaware that human ears could hear them.

And then he was startled by a voice, distant but clear. He listened hard. Brother Walt. Who was he talking to? Creeping to the end of the trunk, to where the great roots now clawed at the sky, he peered across at the hermitage. The voice came from within. Curiosity prompted him forward, but with huge care lest he disturb the goat.

'Help me, Lord,' Brother Walt was praying, his voice thin and pleading. 'You know the trouble I'm in, helping this boy. Weakness, Lord, weakness. I never meant to get involved. It could mean a horrible death if I'm found out....'

Here there was a pause and, when he continued, Brother Walt seemed to be talking to himself rather than to his maker.

'A frightful risk. What chance has the boy got, after all? They'll never let him live. And yet – if he *were* to survive – perhaps . . . perhaps I could rid myself of this burden . . . a position in the household, perhaps, if he should ever, just conceivably, survive and take his inheritance. Just to imagine it!

A little money, yes? A little influence. Isn't it worth the chance? Anything's got to be better than this.'

And then he was back at prayer: 'I'll help the boy, Lord. It would put right a great wrong. We'll need your help, Lord, but I'll willingly sacrifice everything to see justice done.'

There was a further pause, followed by a new line of reasoning: 'Unless, oh Lord, you give me a sign that I am in error, that I ought not to be helping the boy at all. I am a weak and dim-sighted man, Lord. If I should tell the Baron what I know, instruct me so. If I should make a full confession. I wish to do what is right.'

Ranulph crept away, a decision forming in his brain. *Thank you old man*, he whispered to the air. *Thank you for your food and for your advice, but this is where we must part company.*

He made first for the river, where he stooped with cupped hands and took refreshing gulps from the fast-flowing current. Then he set off through the trees at a great pace, knowing he had several hours before the sun rose above the eastern horizon and the Baron's huntsmen would see their prey hurtling before them in full flight.

4 Ordeal by Water

At first he thought it was the soughing of wind through the high branches of trees – but, no, he had seen scarcely a single tree all day. This was bare, craggy country, battered by gales off a grey, malevolent sea. He sat on his haunches, precarious on a slope above the lapping waters, peering into the gloom of dusk. What enchanted place had he stumbled into, what spirits waited to ensnare him?

And then he could see them: a hooded procession moving through the half light, immediately below. Their leader held high a painted crucifix, and the chanting band followed the dying Christ into the gathering darkness away from the protection of the low cliff. He watched, with a feeling of wonder and alarm, their shuffling progress out towards the slapping sea. Could they not see that it meant to swallow them up?

'Stop!' he cried, but the sound was snatched away by a gust of the same buffeting wind which brought the chanting to his ears from down below. He saw the monks advance slowly, slowly into the frothing sea-wash and then – but he could not believe what he saw – walk upon the very water! They did not sink, but moved ever forward and away from him, still chanting, the crucifix now a blur in the gloaming. He felt a shivering as from a sickness to witness this weird, unnatural sight.

God spare me! he prayed wildly as he slithered down the slope and came to rest at the foot of the cliff. The sea sucked and spat at his feet, and now he could barely hear the voices of the monks or see more than what appeared to be a moving shadow, swaying in the middle distance, out on the chopping water.

And then he saw it, looming out of the sea like some creature from the deep: a narrow spit of land. Could this be the famed Holy Island which he had been travelling days to find? Might these unearthly monks lead him to the blessed relics of Lindisfarne?

He dropped to his knees and peered at the stony beach by the spot where they had begun their walk upon the waters. Now he understood their miracle: a causeway of rough rocks and lashed timbers ran out from the land towards the island. Sea spume dashed against it, eddying in little circles of froth about the posts driven into the underlying shingle. His heart pounding with terror, Ranulph took a step on to the raised track, gasping as the freezing water swept across his leather-cased feet and ran up his shins. Dare he follow the monks to their island home?

A few steps more and he had no choice. When he turned back, he saw only darkness, the cliff but an inky blur against the gathering gloom of night. At least, out towards the island, he had the ghostly figures of the monks to guide him. He kept his eyes on their bobbing heads, which now and then seemed to disappear, then emerged from the murk rather further to his right than he had expected. He had lost all sense of direction.

At first he lifted his feet from the swirling water, but this soon became impossible because the sea was up about his knees. *Dear God*, he prayed silently, his mouth gaping with fear. *Don't let me drown!* He had heard stories of men who were swallowed by huge sea creatures Was some great scaly beast waiting at this very moment to devour him? He stood still, quite unable to move. Minutes passed, and the water rose stealthily up his thighs. He shifted his position, cold and filled with a numbing dread. The light faded, so that he could no longer see the band of monks ahead of him.

Dear God, give me strength!

When at last he stepped forward there was no ground

beneath his feet. The causeway had gone! He pitched violently to one side and, instinctively putting out his hand to support himself, he plummetted into the ice-cold, swiftly-enveloping sea. He fell, and was aware of nothing but water in his mouth and in his eyes, a roaring sound in his ears and the idiot helplessness of his thrashing limbs. This was how death must come – blindly and relentlessly, with not a soul to help. His body rolled and sank. Then his foot kicked against something, and when his hands came down they grasped at what he realised was a length of wood – part of the causeway. He heaved himself across the timbers, pushed himself to his knees and rose heavily from the pestering waves, his lungs aching for air.

His eyes, stung with salt, might as well have been blind. Thick cloud had brought night in early, without the faintest glimmer of a star. He could see nothing of that island somewhere out to sea before him. It was obvious that the causeway must swing round towards land in an arc, but he had no way of knowing its direction. The water was already above his knees, lapping his tunic. How quickly would it rise to engulf him? He knew nothing of tides. All he knew was that the brothers must have crossed without danger and yet already the sea was trying to drag him down.

Whimpering, but unable to hear the shaming sound against a rising wind, he edged himself forward, his leading foot feeling carefully for the firmness of the causeway. When he found the edge of it he moved to the other side, but he quickly discovered that edge, too. He was crossing this turbulent, hostile sea on a pathway which would scarcely accommodate the width of a waggon.

Somewhere, way off, a seabird cried, lone and mournful. He bent low, hoping that his hands might find the trackway to speed his progress, but salt water rolled up his neck and across his face and he was terrified. A wave rocked him and he almost lost his balance.

He would rather, at this moment, have been in full flight across the open fields, with a pack of Baron Fulke's hounds at his heels. Better to die, he thought, in the landscape you knew, with the solid earth beneath your feet. And even the hounds, surely, could not tear at him as pitilessly as this cold and angry water which would bury him with never a mourner to answer the tolling bell.

Now he was aware of a new sea sound, a terrifying sound, a chocking and hissing sound as of something monstrous gathering itself to attack him. He froze where he was, wanting to cry out but knowing that the words would gibber in his throat. As he stood, lost and desolate in the darkness, he realised with confusion that the swirling water washed against him less deeply than before. Hesitantly, he edged forward again, and now the waves were only around his knees. He peered into the darkness and saw what made the noise which had so alarmed him: a few yards ahead of him the sea was lapping against a low shingle beach. Gasping with exhaustion and relief, he waded thankfully through the water which covered the end of the causeway and sat upon the island, trembling, his head between his knees.

A wide track ran inland from the causeway and, once he had recovered himself, he began to follow it. Now the singing could be heard again, and more distinctly than before. The night was so dark that he was aware only of the dark shapes of buildings against the lowering sky. He collided with the massive outer door of the priory, having imagined its blackness to be a gap in the wall.

He felt for the handle but, although it turned, the door would not open. Eventually his groping fingers found a bell-pull, and the loud clanging was followed within seconds by the sound of an opening hatch. Light from an oil lamp seemed to blaze through the darkness from a small grille in the wall of a guard-house to one side of the gate.

'In the name of God, who goes there?' came a quavering but determined voice.

Ranulph approached the opening: 'A traveller who needs shelter.'

'Your name, traveller?'

'William,' he invented instantly. For all he knew his own name had been spread around the land, with a tempting reward for his capture.

'And your destination?'

'I have a message to carry to Chester,' he replied, giving the name of one of the few towns he had ever heard of. 'I need shelter for the night.'

'And you're alone?'

Alone? Ranulph thought. *I've not so much as spoken to a soul for all of three days.*

'Not even a hound for company.'

A face came close to the grille and the lamp was thrust through it so that the interloper's features could be seen from inside. Then the lamp was withdrawn and, moments later, heavy bolts were drawn back on the other side of the door. It swung open.

'Christopher!' yelled the gate-keeper into the darkness. This was followed by a strange whinnying sound and then the running of feet towards them.

Ranulph felt his tunic tugged by wiry hands: 'Quickly!' cried the gate-keeper – an elderly monk with a wildness in his eyes, who slammed the door to with surprising vigour and rammed home the bolts as if an invading army were drawn up outside.

The footsteps drew closer, and a lad not much older than himself, but strangely overgrown and gangling, brought himself to a halt in front of them, sweating profusely. A long tongue lolled from his mouth and his eyes seemed to move independently of one another, quite unable to focus.

'Good boy, Christopher,' said the gate-keeper in kindly fashion, patting his shoulder. He handed him a lighted taper. 'We've a visitor. Will you care for him until the morning, please?'

'Viz-ta!' exclaimed Christopher with a gigantic smirk, cradling the taper against the wind with a huge, beefy hand. 'Viz-ta!'

The gate-keeper turned to Ranulph: 'He's a good boy and one of God's own children. Mind you treat him with Christian decency.'

'I swear,' he whispered, following the idiot boy across a courtyard, his feet kicking up gravel it was impossible to see in the darkness. All his eyes could make out, silhouetted against the evening sky, was the bulk of the monastery buildings. And then, as they turned a corner, there was a sudden stunning radiance – beyond the arcaded cloisters the old stones of the chapel were lit from within by a hundred flickering candles whose light spilled warmly through the open door and arched windows.

The loping Christopher came to an abrupt halt, an ecstatic grin transforming his face, an ear seemingly cocked towards the chapel. Puzzled, Ranulph strained to hear the slightest sound. Had his companion a sense which he himself lacked? At this moment a reedy voice wailed the beginning of a service, and the rich chanting of the brothers rose to the night sky.

'Compline,' Christopher smiled beatifically.

'How did you know?' asked Ranulph, but his guide set off again without answer.

'Compline,' he repeated over his shoulder.

Before they reached the cloisters they took a dimly-lit passageway to their left, and aromas of an agonising deliciousness wafted beneath his nostrils. It was so long since he had eaten that these smells from the bakehouse and kitchen drove him close to madness with a hunger he had almost forgotten.

'Food!' he gasped, but the eager Christopher lurched on and he had to follow. They came to a small cell, furnished only by a narrow bed, a low stool and a large icon on one of the cold stone walls. Christoper stooped with his taper and a small oil lamp flung heavy shadows throughout the room.

'Wait,' Christopher said, still smiling hugely, and instantly disappeared. Ranulph sat on the bed in the half-darkness, his limbs cold, his stomach tight with hunger, his feet aching from the miles he had walked and run and clambered. He was, at least, and for the moment, safe. There was a rough rug on the bed, and he drew it over his legs.

When his companion returned it was with bread, cold meat and a beaker of ale. He stood beaming down on Ranulph, who wolfed his food fiercely, then drained the beaker as if it were a thimble.

'Good?' poor Christopher asked, seizing the plate in his large, clumsy fingers.

'Is there more?'

'Ha-ha! Good?' was the amiable reply, and then he was left alone again. This time Christopher did not return Ranulph, feeling weariness take possession of him, lay full-length on the bed and within a minute was deeply asleep.

*

He awoke to a scraping sound on the other side of the wall. There was no window to his cell, so that he was unable to tell what time of day it was. He stumbled into the passageway outside, and then into a courtyard flooded with bright sunlight.

A lean young man in his early twenties was sharpening arrows against the wall.

'You're the guest who came in darkness,' he said, smiling. He held out his hand. 'I'm Henry.'

'William,' Ranulph replied, feeling the smoothness of the young man's hand against the calloused roughness of his own. The sun was yet early on its westward journey, but it had the heat of the incoming spring. 'On my way to Chester.'

'And may God preserve you.'

'Preserve me?' There was something Ranulph didn't understand. The arrows were the first surprise, in a place given over to the worship of God. Next he saw the crossbow-loops high above the church's great west door. And then, when he looked beyond the dark red stone walls of the monastic buildings, he saw what could only be a fortress on a rocky ridge to the south. 'I have something to fear?'

'I meant nothing particular by it,' Henry frowned, blowing powdered stone from the tip of an arrow. 'There are perils enough on the road, after all.'

'But why do you use arrows?' Ranulph persisted. 'Surely nobody comes here.'

Henry shook his head in wonderment: 'You come from far away?'

'Several days' journey.'

'I'm surprised that you know nothing of our troubles, nonetheless. You've not heard of the Scots? They come raiding all down this coast. We've had to fight them off more than once.'

'And you took part in the battle?' Ranulph asked, excited as he was fearful.

'No. That was before I arrived. I've been here less than a twelvemonth as a priory servant. I hope some day to become one of the brothers – if I prove myself fit for the calling.'

As he gathered his arrows together there came the sound of pounding feet and heavy panting, and the awkward bulk of Christopher lurched into the courtyard. He tried to speak, but an incomprehensible slavering mumble was all that escaped his heavy lips. He flailed an arm in Ranulph's direction.

'He says he lost you,' Henry interpreted, striding forward and wrapping his arms round the simpleton in an emphatic gesture of greeting. 'There, there Christopher. He's come to no harm, and you may lead him off to his breakfast.'

'I'm sorry,' Ranulph apologised weakly.

'Not at all,' laughed Henry. 'He's easily confused, poor lad, and he probably feared a heavy telling off if you'd been spirited away during the night. By the Scots perhaps?'

Christopher led them inside, past the cell where Ranulph had spent the night and into a small bakehouse where a red-faced old man was pushing loaves into an oven. There was another room beyond, and they sat on a bench by a worn wooden table, looking out of a narrow window across a yard towards the gatehouse.

'Come, Christopher!' commanded a high voice, presumably the old man's. 'The food is ready.'

He brought them plates smeared with a thin gruel, then returned for a tray loaded with newly-baked bread. Ranulph reached wildly for a small loaf, still warm to the touch, and pushed it into the gruel. He was one of those animals he had watched about his home village, foraging for food which they devoured with little regard for its taste – driven by hunger and the need to survive.

'Such eagerness, William!' Henry smiled. 'Haven't you eaten these last few days?'

'Very little.'

'Is it that you're short of money? Is nobody paying you for your journey to Chester?'

'I have no money.'

'Then in Jesu's name, boy, I shall give you some,' Henry cried, reaching into a pocket and pushing three pennies across the table towards him. 'Go on, I've little use for them here.'

'I can't.'

'Take them!' He leaned closer. 'How is it that you have no money, William?'

'Lost it,' he said weakly, thinking *May I have the wit to escape this questioning!* 'Crossing a river,' he added. 'It fell out.'

'And which river would that be, William?'

He shook his head, dumbly. He knew too little of the world to be able to invent plausibly.

'River!' Christopher grinned hugely, understanding. He brought his hands together and made a rocking movement with his body.

'That's right, Christopher, fishing in the river,' Henry said in a kindly tone. 'Which river?' he persisted.

'I don't know.'

'You have no money and you've no idea of your route. What kind of a journey is this, William? Is it altogether honest?'

Ranulph closed his eyes, desperate for an answer which would still these remorseless, perplexing questions. When he opened them he saw the great gate of the priory open and, with a violent scattering of stones, a horseman gallop inside. Christopher rose to his feet and began to make riding movements, formless sounds catching in his throat.

'Gently, Christopher,' Henry coaxed him, tugging at his elbow. 'It must be the King's purveyor, come again to arrange stores for the Scottish wars. Don't excite yourself.' He turned to Ranulph. 'And why so white and drawn, William? You've never seen a horse before?'

It wasn't the horse that frightened Ranulph, but the insignia on its rider's tunic: a stag's head transfixed by an arrow. Now this horseman, who had drawn close enough for his features to be recognised, called across the courtyard to the monk who had opened the gate.

'I come from Baron Fulke,' he cried. 'I seek a vile fugitive named Ranulph. If you should be harbouring such a felon I demand that you yield him up into my power!'

5 Raiders from the Sea

'Felon, you say.' It was the abbott who spoke. 'Pray sir, what is the nature of this felony?'

The new visitor found himself surrounded by a number of the brothers, who had assembled to witness the drama that he brought. His horse was being led to stable, its legs glistening with salt water, and Baron Fulke's angel of death stood red-faced and fierce, wondering why his appearance had so little effect on the calm figure who faced him. Generally men quivered before the thunder of his voice, the storm clouds of his gathered eyebrows. He served the baron well, and had long since learned the value of instilling fear at the onset of any human contact, but this abbott denied him so easy a victory. And was there a hint of mockery in the voice? Did he sense disdain?

'What business of yours is the nature of his felony?' he roared. 'Your concern is of other worlds than this: earthly justice is *my* concern. Do you have this Ranulph or no? An answer, sir, or I'll lop your holy head from its shoulders.'

The abbott smiled at the threat and, pressing his fingers together as if in prayer, gazed upwards, apparently seeking heavenly assurance.

'Ranulph, you say? And you come from Baron Fulke, you say?' He spoke slowly as if searching for understanding. There was a long pause, and then the abbott's eyes met his interrogator's. Oh, it *was* mockery! Ranulph could read it from where he hid behind Christopher who, in turn, hid behind a rough-cut but solid ashlar column; the gathered monks could read it; and, most important of all, the baron's man could read it.

The abbott continued to speak, but the smile had gone. 'I

seem to recall a little matter of tithes owed us by your master. Baron Fulke . . . Yes, I'm sure it was Baron Fulke. When was it now?' He closed his eyes and swung his head in an upward arc as if trying to dredge months and years from the air around him. He opened his eyes again, the smile returning: 'Five years, perhaps six, I'm not sure – but I daresay the baron will remember and we must have a record of it somewhere. Not a little amount, I seem to think. You have, perchance, brought us what is owed to accompany your threats? No?

'As for my head! Oh, dear . . .' He chuckled and rolled it back and forth several times between his hands. 'Poor old noddle, distanced from his good friend shoulders! Of little consequence to me, sir. Speed me heavenwards if you must. But, well, what *would* the bishop say?'

Fulke's man felt the ground slipping away from under him: a rift between the baron and the bishop would be bad news indeed, particularly for the man responsible for such a rift. He had underestimated this abbott, had sought to cudgel him when he should have played him like a fish. As it was, *he* was the one now hooked and being pulled shorewards.

'This Ranulph . . .' he began again, his tone more conciliatory, less bullying.

'Yes, this Ranulph. Perhaps we should talk over a meal and a little wine. You haven't eaten, I take it?' –- and the abbott took the baron's messenger gently by the arm and led him towards his quarters.

*

'So, Ranulph, what *is* the nature of your felony?'

He spun round to find that it was Henry who questioned him. There was no threat in the voice but, rather, a friendly regard for his new-found companion's predicament.

'Me?' Ranulph blustered. 'No, no, I'm not . . ..'

'Come,' smiled Henry, 'you turned quickly enough to his name, my vague traveller to Chester.'

'You won't give me away?'

The fear in Ranulph's voice startled Christopher, who still stood against the column, gazing in the direction of the recent confrontation. He stepped forward and, beaming, laid a hand on Ranulph's shoulder.

'Wiwwum,' he said affectionately.

'Well,' Henry continued, 'I'd as soon believe you as that brash lout who accuses you. Come on, persuade me of your honesty.'

And so, moving further into the shadows behind the column where he did, Ranulph began to whisper a clumsy and garbled account of his misfortunes, while Henry nodded his head sagely and Christopher gaped in befuddled incomprehension. Ranulph finished his story with the one question which he badly needed answered.

'Will the abbott give me up?'

Henry shrugged: 'He doesn't know that you're the lad the baron hunts. On the other hand, he must realise that you may be. He clearly doesn't much care for the baron, but he might be happy enough to do a deal and get the money which is owed to him. He's honest and God-fearing, true, but he doesn't know the circumstances which led you here, and he might believe that he's serving the cause of justice by giving you up. He . . .'

'Enough!' wailed Ranulph, perplexed. 'I must get away.'

'No chance just yet, I'm afraid. Judging by that fellow's horse, the water's too high at present. We'll have to hide you. I know just the place you can rest up for a while – and then, if you've a head for heights, you can escape that way, too.'

Ranulph, who knew nothing about tides, felt Henry take his arm and guide him through yet deeper shadows to a small door.

Christopher lumbered behind them. Once inside, Henry pulled the door shut, its heavy thud hollow and echoing. At first the darkness seemed total, the perfect darkness of the tomb, but as their eyes adjusted a thin grey light filtered in from above, and Ranulph was able to make out the bottom steps of a spiral stairway. This they began to climb, Henry leading and Christopher, muttering strange sounds that could not be understood, bringing up the rear.

Unused to such climbing, Ranulph steadied himself with his hand against the wall. The stones felt slimy, and there was the musty smell of damp earth and moss. But as they climbed higher and higher, and the light grew less dim, this smell was replaced by the fresh tangy air that came from the ocean, carrying with it salt and a thousand miles of emptiness.

And then they were out at the top of a tower, surrounded by mewing gulls and the roar of the sea below. Ranulph looked over the battlements, down to where the grey-green mass of water rose glassily and fell in a million white splinters on the rocks. His stomach churned. He felt sick and dizzy and stepped back, his legs weak.

Oh, where was his fern-fringed hide in the woods? Where was the wonderful woven enclosure of his drey? Perhaps Hell was the deep and burning pit that Brother Walt had described to him, but this high, cold and windswept tower was no less a horror for Ranulph.

'No!' his voice cried into the void, and he made as if to go downstairs again.

But Henry held him: 'Brace up, Ranulph. You'll come to no harm if you do as I tell you. We've strong rope which will secure you to a ledge where nobody will ever think of looking.'

'A ledge?'

'And a good length of rope for when you need to make your way down.'

He could not bear the thought. He stood, head lowered, shoulders hunched, eyes tightly shut, wishing himself anywhere but on this tower. Wrapped in his own darkness, he waited for Henry's arm to guide him, but he waited in vain. Henry had let Ranulph's arm fall, and now he kept silent.

Against the sea's constant grumble and the gulls' constant whine Ranulph could hear the rasping of Christopher's breathing, the gurgle of his spittle-filled mouth as, winded by his climb, he fought desperately for breath. Finally he opened his eyes, at first fixing his fearful gaze at his own feet, then slowly turning his head until he could see Henry. But Henry no longer seemed the slightest concerned with Ranulph's plight: rather, he was at the tower's margin, leaning out precariously from the battlements and totally absorbed by what he could see beyond.

'What is it?' Ranulph called, unable to move his feet for fear of plunging hundreds of feet to his death.

'I think the abbott has greater problems to concern him than your identity, my friend,' Henry muttered darkly.

'Tell me!'

'No, you come here. If you've no courage for such a small step you'll not survive what's in store for us all, that's God's truth.'

Ranulph, alarmed by Henry's tone, found himself blindly rushing to join him at the battlements. Out at sea he could see dark shapes upon the water.

'Scots!' Henry said.

Ranulph understood nothing of the sea, but the silent approach of this fleet, for all the world like upturned black beetles, their legs thrashing the water, spoke only of menace. They were still well distant, but the wind filling their sails added to the power of the oarsmen and they approached with a terrifying swiftness.

'They mean to attack?'

'What else, man? I must get down to warn the brothers. You'd best come, too. It'll be each for himself. They'll not be concerning themselves about you for a while, that's a certainty.'

With huge relief Ranulph scurried down the steps behind Henry, while Christopher, only just recovered from the ascent, trod heavily behind, perhaps believing that this was some form of malicious game the other two were playing on him.

Once back in the courtyard Henry raced to where a rope hung from a bell. Usually it called the brothers to their offices, but now he tugged at it vigorously, agitating wild sounds from it and all the while shouting 'Scots! Prepare yourselves! Scots!'

And then there was turmoil of a sort that Ranulph had previously seen only when he had kicked against an ant hill in the casual destructiveness of his early boyhood. Brothers raced here and there, some carrying treasures to be hidden or made secure, some gathering weapons and filling previously allocated defensive positions, some, apparently, simply running around in aimless panic shorn of effectiveness or purpose by their dread. Had he not so recently been in the grip of a similar dread he might have despised them, but now he actually took courage from their lack of it. The Scots were, after all, only men, and far less formidable than the green and hungry void which they travelled across and which could, at any second, open its giant maw and swallow them.

Nevertheless, he remained still and hidden in the shadows. He watched the abbott emerge, his face still a picture of calmness and self-possession, followed by Fulke's man, who seemed to rage and fulminate with even greater energy than previously. Standing in the courtyard, his legs apart, chest thrust forward, he waved his sword around his head and screamed abuse at the whole universe, animate and inanimate. This posturing, designed to strike fear into the hearts of the enemy, was both premature and fruitless: the only people able to witness it were the monks, who might be imaged to be on the same side even if they were hardly the allies he would have chosen. They, for their part, ignored him.

Ranulph found himself unable to suppress a smile, so absurd was the performance, but the smile was short-lived, for the air suddenly became alive with arrows. Like spiteful insects they hummed and buzzed, some tipped with burning pitch. Where their landing was stone they bounced and clattered angrily along the surface; where it was flesh they tore cruelly; and where it was wood or straw their flames sprang into newer, fuller life, licking outwards and spreading rapidly. And, as if these flames were not an adequate preview of the hell to come, they were accompanied by a demoniac screaming and howling which froze Ranulph's blood. Even the cruel roar of the sea seemed benign and melodious alongside this cacophony.

At this moment he was seized by strong arms, and when he struggled half-free he found his assailant to be none other than a terrified Christopher, clinging to him for comfort and protection. Ranulph, wrestling himself from the grip, clasped Christopher's hand and tried to drag him towards the monastery entrance and the causeway. But it was too late: the great doors were barred against the Scots, who could already be heard on the other side, splintering the thick wood with their massive axes, while others – dozens of them – swarmed up the outer walls with ropes and grappling irons, sinewy arms and blind, aggressive energy.

Still the arrows fell, still flames blossomed into fires, and it seemed certain that the monastery and its defenders must perish. Along the outer ramparts the monks fought with a feverish passion. Henry, his sharpened arrows useless now that their attackers were upon them, was transformed into a machine of destruction, wielding a huge staff and raining blow after blow upon the heads of the Scots as they climbed into range.

And then Ranulph felt Christopher tugging at his arm, and saw that he pointed, excitedly towards a door. He followed his ungainly, mumbling, sweating companion, who threw the door open and led him inside. It was cold and dark within, but as the door swung to behind them so the sudden silence refreshed their spirits: it was rather as if they had, by closing the door on it, trapped a raging monster -- whereas they had, in fact, trapped only themselves. Christopher had fallen to his knees and was struggling with a large flagstone whose edges were cut so as to allow two hands a grip. Prising it up, the muscles on his heavy arms taut almost to breaking, he revealed in the dim light a flight of steps which descended into a black chasm.

'Hole,' Christopher smiled lop-sidedly, each eye focusing on Ranulph in turn.

They went down and Christopher allowed the stone to fall into place behind them. Utter silence! The two groped their way downwards into the cellars, reading their passage by fingers and toes as the blind do, only with far less practice. In other circumstances these conditions would have plunged Ranulph into a despair similar to that which he had felt at the top of the tower, but now they offered refuge and comfort. Here at least they would be safe for a time. He sank down on the bottom step, not wishing to stray into the unknown beyond, and he felt Christopher settle beside him and begin a gentle sobbing.

As he sat, absently ruffling Christopher's hair as he might comfort a distressed animal, two thoughts occupied him. The first was that here, though they might be safe for the present, there was always a chance of discovery with no hope of escape. Indeed, even without discovery, there was no knowing when, if ever, it would be safe to emerge. The second thought (and far more chastening it was, too) was that they had no right to be in this cold sanctuary while Henry and the brothers who had given him refuge fought so desperately above. Had concern for self-preservation so robbed him of courage? If *their* spirits had been as frail as his, then this cellar must have coffined a far greater number than two!

'I must go up to help,' he said gently to Christopher. 'You stay here to guard the cellars.'

'No, no!'

Ranulph could picture the loose tongue rolling around his mouth as the words tumbled clumsily out.

'Have courage, good Christopher. I'll be back.'

The stone at the top of the steps was heavy, and Ranulph found the struggle harder than he had imagined. Nevertheless, he soon enough found himself regaining his breath and summoning his courage behind the door which stood between him and the battle beyond.

Pushing the door open he was immediately engulfed in choking smoke, through which he could see islands of scarlet flame. Men ran to and fro through this inferno, reminding him of the Doom picture painted with such gusto on the plaster wall of his village church. Moving forward into the fray he attempted to snatch up the sword of a fallen Scot, but the weight of the fierce weapon was such that he was in greater danger of inflicting injury on his own shoulder than upon any adversary. He allowed it to drop with a metallic clang and instead searched for something more manageable. This proved to be an iron ladle which one of the monks had held in his hand as he rushed from the kitchen at the onset of the attack. For all the fact that it was fashioned for soups and stews, the ladle sat happily in Ranulph's hands, and he swung it around his head in the way that, the smoke temporarily clearing, he now saw the Scots swinging their swords and axes.

God give me strength! his lips formed silently. Then, taking a deep breath, he rushed into a knot of flailing metal and limbs, where a group of monks gave unequal battle to three wild Scots, whose long red hair, greasy and tangled into fearful locks, contrasted strangely with the tonsured heads of their adversaries. Ranulph brought the ladle down with a resounding crash on to the back of the closest red head. With something between a scream and a gurgle the warrior sank to the ground, his legs and body folding and crumpling with such ungainliness that one of the remaining two Scots in the skirmish found his legs entangled and became easy prey for Ranulph's second enthusiastic blow. The monks, with an assortment of weapons, now struck more effectively at their third attacker, who collapsed into a thrashing and bloody heap until stilled by the massive cudgel of a fat brother.

Moving on, Ranulph struck with wild abandon at any enemy pate which came within range of his flailing ladle. It flickered through the air like a butterfly on a hot day, alighting here and there, but never settling for more than a second or two.

And then came sudden pain and darkness.

6 Dead and Alive

He was aware first of a dull pain which seemed to run through his entire head. Then of the motion, of an insistent rocking sensation as if someone were throwing him about like one of those dolls of coarse rag the village girls played with. That was all he knew for what might have been minutes or hours, until he felt a tightness in his stomach, a queasiness, and he felt that he was about to be violently sick. But all this time his eyes were tight shut, his arms for some reason held tight to his body, his brain scarcely working. His head swam and he felt the vomit rise into his throat and subside. Then he swooned right away.

When consciousness returned to him it was more sharply than before. He still felt the rocking and swaying, and his arms were as tightly strapped to his body. Now, though, he heard distinct sounds: a creaking, a rhythmic knocking, the suggestion of a human voice. His sense of smell returned, too: a mustiness, as of damp sacking. Surely it *was* sacking. He felt his head constrained, and twisted his neck to free himself. He was trapped. His gasping mouth sucked in cloth.

'Help!' he tried to shout, the sound hopelessly muffled. He opened his eyes and was enveloped in as great a darkness as when they were closed. Was this Hell he was in, the Hell he had seen pictured on the church wall, with ugly, malformed demons doing unspeakable things to one another? He kicked his legs and found them to be encased in yet more clinging material.

Dear God in Heaven, he prayed desperately.

Then the motion stopped, he heard a loud cry and there were hands upon him – but clumsy hands, fingers felt through heavy cloth. He was sufficiently awake to panic, imagining the point of a dagger thrust through whatever it was that held him and into his flesh. There was a tugging at his neck, and then the cloth came away and the light blinded him.

'Wiwwum!'

Ranulph, his body weaker than he had ever known it, trembled with a helpless, overpowering fit of bubbling laughter. He was reborn into a world of tall trees swaying overhead in a sky of glinting blue. He saw first a pair of raucous crows fashioning a rough nest among the branches of a towering oak and then, much closer to him, the moist, lolling lips of Christopher, broken open into a crack of utter joy.

'Wiwwum – awive!'

What was it constraining his limbs? Ranulph managed to raise his head a fraction and saw that he was trussed up in black cloth. And what was he lying upon? A cart, no less! He swivelled his head in the other direction and saw the horse that pulled it, a seemingly well-fed roan which nevertheless tugged at the grass by the roadside. Yes, it was a well-worn road, rather wider than a single cart, and it seemed to be running through low hills. Where were they taking him?

'My dear young man! Can this be?'

Now here was Henry at his side, also seeming to be quite overcome with delight. Was this, after all, some unexpected corner of Hell, where images of old friends appeared to gaze pitilessly upon the damned soul, in mockery of pleasures it had once known?

'Come, Christopher, untie him quickly. *Quickly!* Miracles require a helping hand, after all.'

Off came the cloth. Firm hands took his body and carried it from the cart. He closed his eyes and could smell the sweetness of the grass even before he was laid upon it. His shoulders were propped against cushions and the neck of a bottle was thrust between his lips.

'Drink,' Henry urged him. 'It's good Bordeaux wine. Fivepence a gallon!'

The thought came into Ranulph's head that it was expensive liquor which was running down his chin. He took deep draughts of it with his eyes still shut, and he dozed off for a time, a weak sun upon his face. He felt utterly at peace. When he awoke hefound Henry and Christopher standing over him. He was aware, too, of another figure a little further off.

'And so?' he asked simply.

'So I'll never believe a physician again,' Henry said. He cast a meaningful glance at the black rags on the cart.'Nor will I ever bury a man without a shudder to think of what might have been.'

'You weren't. . .' Ranulph struggled to bring the words out. His wide eyes spoke more eloquently than his tongue.

'By nightfall you'd have been six feet under, old fellow. That's your shroud you see on the cart. We'd made a sound job of the fastening.'

He lay back on the cushions, breathing deeply. The general pain he had felt in his head now became a distinct throbbing above his right temple, and when he lifted a hand to it he felt the flesh swollen and misshapen.

'What happened?'

'To you? A blow from a spear. You've lost a lot of blood, my lad, and there was no breath in you. We were sure you'd gone. Brother Anselm worked on you for an age with his medicines and then solemnly declared you a corpse. The proper prayers were said, believe me.'

Ranulph saw the position of the sun in the sky and stared at Henry in disbelief.

'But this is scarcely midday,' he said. 'How are we away from the priory already?'

Henry laughed: 'You've lost a day of your life, William — if so I am to continue to call you. You prefer it to the more dangerous Ranulph, I presume? Yes, I can see you do. It was yesterday morning that we fought the Scots. You spent the day in Brother Anselm's hands and the night on the mortuary slab.'

Ranulph was about to protest that his death seemed to have been accepted rather lightly, but then he saw Christopher, squatting with his arms tight around his knees, his eyes staring at him with undisguised happiness, and the words stopped in his mouth.

'As for the Scots,' Henry continued, 'we were very lucky. They usually begin their raids in the spring, and with February not yet spent we simply weren't ready for them. Fortunately for us the King's purveyor had decided to make one of his rare visits with all his retinue, and they were half way across the causeway before they realised what was happening. Otherwise, I can't help thinking, they'd have turned tail and made for home as quickly as they could.'

He laughed.

'The sight of so many waggons crossing the causeway unnerved our attackers, who thought it was some kind of an army come against them. They fled for their boats leaving two corpses behind them. We thought we were fortunate to suffer only a single death.'

'Who was that?'

'Why, *you*, you young idiot! You really aren't supposed to be alive, you know.'

'And the baron's man?'

'A brave enough fellow. We should have fared worse without him.'

'I meant . . .'

'Oh, he guessed nothing. I'm afraid that I led him to believe you were one of the priory servants. Not with an outright lie, you understand.'

Now the figure Ranulph had noticed a little way off came forward. He was a tall, thin man with a whispy beard, wearing a grey cloak with a hood on top. Attached to the leather belt round his waist was a fat pouch, which he patted in a meaningful way.

'An answer to prayer,' he addressed Henry in a wheedling voice, clearly having listened to everything that had been said.

'How come, old man?'

'Why, I petitioned for the life of this young fellow with a more painful concentration than I've spared for any unfortunate in many a month – and now it seems to me that he's breathing the same air as the rest of us. That must be worth a donation.'

Henry laughed: 'We all of us prayed for him, I assure you.'

'Ah, but there are those the Good Lord listens to, are there not? And did I not continue long after you had mentally resigned him to his grave? Besides, would you not sooner have a friar pray for your soul than any man in Christendom?'

'Frankly, no. We're from the priory at Lindisfarne, my friend. We've no need of outside help, thank you very much.'

'A small donation?'

'None at all, you rogue.'

'For your soul's sake, master?'

'Be off,' Henry growled, 'or I'll set my mastiff on you.'

He inclined his head in the direction of William who, understanding sufficient of what was passing, lumbered closer in what must have seemed a threatening manner. Strange sounds rose in his throat and the startled friar backed speedily away.

'You'll pay for this,' he called.

After some little while, when Ranulph was feeling stronger, he was helped to the cart where Henry had improvised a seat. The journey would not be long, he was assured. His friend had business at a small town a few hours' ride away: the plan was to spend the night there and to return to Holy Island the following day.

'We would have buried you there,' Henry explained in a matter-of-fact voice. 'It's a pleasant spot among trees.'

It was a hard journey. The track had the iron ruts of winter scored into it, and they set their wheels in them when they could. Often enough, however, they had to pull over onto he rough land beside the road to allow the passage of waggons coming in the other direction, and at the best of times the shaking was a torment to Ranulph in his weakened state. The more he considered his hopeless situation the more miserable he felt. He was, after all, but a little way from home, and the baron's huntsmen must be scouring all the countryside about. There was a handsome price on his head.

'Tell me,' he said, a sudden thought arriving in his head. 'Are there precious relics in the priory on Holy Island?'

'Why yes, a few,' replied Henry, pulling hard on the reins to keep the horse steady down a steepish incline. 'But not as many as in former times.'

'How so?'

'Because there were savage attacks on the monks long before the Scots ever came. Hundreds of years ago the Danes ravaged our English shores here in the north. In the time of great King Alfred the brothers fled the site and took the sacred relics of St Cuthbert with them to Durham.'

'And what have you now?'

'Oh, a few items which the devout think it well worth travelling to see. We've a splinter from the very Cross of Christ, brought long since from the Holy Land at greatest risk. And there's a lock of hair from the head of John the Baptist, displayed on a platter by the cruel Salome.'

'Ah.'

Henry smiled as he settled the horse into a comfortable

walking pace. 'That's not enough for you, eh? What did you hope to see -- a goblet of wine from the last supper? They have such a thing at Walsingham, I've heard say.'

'Do you possess, by chance, a phial of Christ's blood?'

'No, by the Rood we do not!' Henry looked over his shoulder, a puzzled expression on his face. 'Why do you ask these questions?'

'Tales I've heard, that's all,' Ranulph replied, closing his eyes and feigning sleep.

The cart rumbled on. After some time they passed the friar, who scowled at them and made a sign whose meaning could only be guessed at. He was muttering unintelligibly as they thankfully left him behind. The road twisted through empty countryside, now skirting a bog, now climbing zigzag fashion into hills and snaking carefully down again.

About an hour later they came to a strange site of ruination where, on either side of them, broken-down wooden buildings stuck their bare rafters into the air like maimed beggars. Sunken tracks showed where roads must once have criss-crossed the small settlement. Extensive drystone boundary walls still remained, guarding nothing. Ranulph, hoping to be soon away from so weird a spot, was amazed to see Christopher leap from the cart and, with a loud, wailing cry, rush along one of the thoroughfares and stumble into the pathetic shell of what must once have been a small house. He stood in the centre of it, tugging at his hair and moaning.

'Unthinking fool that I am!' Henry exclaimed, bringing the horse to a halt and tossing the reins to Ranulph. 'Don't fret, Christopher, don't fret!'

Ranulph, tugging at the leather straps to keep the beast from wandering, watched Christopher sink to his knees, Henry all the time stroking his head and murmuring in his ear. The sobbing gradually subsided, but the two of them remained inside the derelict shell of the building for several minutes. When they eventually returned Henry gave Ranulph a glance which instructed him to ask no sudden questions.

'Hwome,' Christopher said.

'Yes Christopher, home,' Henry agreed gently. 'But now you have a new home, with us.'

'Hwome,' the sorrowing lad agreed. 'New hwome.' He stared vacantly into space as the cart started up again, and soon lay down full length and fell into a deep sleep.

'Poor creature,' Henry said quietly. 'He lived there until but three years ago. I had forgotten that we should pass this way. He may lack understanding about many things, but did you see how he rushed straight to the spot where he was born?'

'Where are his people?'

'Dead, every one. The plague took them all. You've witnessed the Pestilence?'

Ranulph nodded: 'Many were stricken, but our lord the baron ordered them to be removed from the village. Any strangers who came to us with the sickness were instantly put to death and their bodies burned. Eventually it went away.'

'It is a mystery how God works – to take every last inhabitant of a community except for this poor witless soul.' He nodded towards Christopher in his sleep. 'Does this not test human reason?'

After another hour on the road they saw a church tower in the distance and, soon afterwards, the huddle of buildings around it. This was their destination, and Henry, perhaps unconsciously, urged the horse on faster now that the promise of rest and refreshment was so tangible. Christopher, waking from his slumber, seemed to have forgotten everything that had passed at his former home, striding forward to sit by Henry on the front board.

'Church!' he exclaimed contentedly, happy with the familiar.

'And an inn,' replied Henry with a laugh. 'There's a little daylight left yet, but I feel almost ready to retire. No doubt supper will revive us. It's a shame not to be sociable, after all. How goes our young corpse?'

'Exhausted,' Ranulph admitted.

'Then we shall see that you get plenty of rest tonight. No dancing and gaming for you, I insist.'

'And *you*, Henry?'

'Nothing beyond sociability, I vow. I've been known to indulge in my time, God knows, but I have higher ideals these days – and hopes of becoming one of the brothers.'

They passed a half-acre of land in which a ploughman trudged grimly behind a single oxen, but there were other fields nearby which had been given back to the wilderness. Weeds sprouted in the bottom of old, forgotten furrows. Ranulph guessed that the plague had visited this area, too.

'These folk,' Henry said, 'must be grateful for wrinkled peas come harvest time.'

It was scarcely a proper town that they now came upon, although there were a few humble merchants' stalls set out alongside the road which passed the church. The place had a forlorn air, and the few people they saw seemed to glower at them in distrust before averting their eyes. Just beyond the church was the inn, with a large sign outside depicting a fox carrying a bloodied chicken in its mouth.

'Sanctuary,' Henry smiled, a note of irony in his voice.

Inside, the atmosphere was livelier than Ranulph had imagined. There were upwards of twenty people in a large room which had benches along all its walls, hefty wooden tables at its centre and a large fireplace in which logs sputtered as if they had newly caught. Two women sat alone, stitching; a pair of young men bent over a game of chess, with a few more standing behind them, watching the play; and a sprawling family of tinkers (at least four generations, judging by the white beard and wrinkled visage of the oldest and the stumbling gait of the youngest) clustered in a corner, taking turns to drink from an earthenware bowl of soup.

'Two rooms, landlord,' Henry ordered cheerfully of the aproned giant who stood guard over the congregation, his ruddy face topped by a mat of thick black hair. 'A quiet one for my friend here who's somewhat weak of constitution just now. We other two will share.'

They were taken up a wide flight of stairs. Ranulph's quarters were cramped, tucked away under the eaves at the rear of the building, but he was grateful for Henry's consideration and looked at his simple bed with great longing. His friends were accommodated down the passage in a room which had a small curtained window overlooking the main room of the inn.

'We'll rest now,' Henry decided, 'and go downstairs for supper when our spirits are equal to it. Give yourself to sleep, William – I'll call you later.'

Ranulph returned to his room, sank on his bed and slid into unconsciousness within seconds.

*

It was the noise of music and laughter which woke him. He stumbled along the passage to his friends' room, still rubbing the sleep from his eyes, and discovered that they had risen without him. Tugging the curtain aside, he was aware of a bustling scene below, though he witnessed it only through a grimy veil of swirling smoke. A ruddy light from the great fire spattered on the walls, and iron cressets hung from the roof beams as lanterns, their baskets packed with glowing coals. The stench was pungent in his nostrils, but the liveliness snatched him into its current as a twig that falls into a river is caught up by the foam-flecked waters and swept inexorably downstream. He yanked the curtain across the opening and hurried downstairs.

A minstrel troupe held centre-stage, a white-haired grandfather bowing a fiddle, two younger men with recorders and a third with a drum, and a young girl in her teens who was banging a tambourine and singing in a rasping voice which had all the roughness of a carrion crow in a treetop.

Fair Bessie lay upon a bank
A-harking to the sweet birds sing,
And spied a gentleman of rank
Bent low to cool him at the spring.

Lovers met in May-o
Always shall be gay-o.

Beyond the entertainers, in a shadowed recess, Christopher sat open-mouthed, gazing into space, while Henry beat time with one fist on a ricketty three-legged table, the other wrapped round the handle of a tankard. Seeing Ranulph, he leapt to his feet and beckoned energetically.

'Awake at last!' he called, with a huge grin.

'No thanks to you,' Ranulph replied testily, falling on to a bench. 'You said you'd call me.'

'It would have been a cruelty. You must have slept a good three hours. Are you hungry?'

'Like a wolf.'

'Then we shall feed you. The fare's good, Christopher, eh?'

'Good,' Christopher agreed, nodding slowly. 'Soup good. Bread good.'

'And the richest of rabbit pies,' Henry added, his eyes brighter than Ranulph had ever seen them. 'Wait here.'

The evening must be half gone, Ranulph thought, looking about him. Certainly sufficient hours had passed for the friar to have arrived on foot: he sat in a corner with two noisy companions who were playing dice. The long room was full to overflowing, the landlord and his two manservants raising trays above head-height as they threaded their way among the throng. The musicians continued to play, and the girl threw her voice so energetically that every word cut through the smoke and the chatter.

'Come Bessie,' cried this noble wight,
'A man needs more than cooling water;
And I have such an appetite!'
And in his lordly arms he caught her.

Lovers met in May-o
Always shall be gay-o.

It was a delicious pie the landlord fetched, and the more he ate of it the more drowsy he felt. Christopher, sitting close by, put a clumsy arm around his shoulder, but it was a long time before Henry returned, and then his eyes appeared brighter than ever. He had a glass of ale in his hand, and Ranulph noticed that he spoke in a rather louder voice than usual.

'What a delightful place this is,' he enthused. 'Don't you feel that you're among good companions, William?'

'I don't trust that friar,' Ranulph replied.

'Nonsense! He's a friar, that's all. It's in his nature to pester. He won't bother us again.'

Ranulph, surprised by the change in his friend's behaviour, studied his face a little more closely.

'Ah, I can tell what you're thinking,' Henry exclaimed. 'You believe I've been drinking too much, eh? But not at all,

William. I know my capacity. It's only that it's a sociable thing to do when you're in company, and we've a Christian duty to be on good terms with our fellow man. Eh?'

She took him to a feeding place
And bade him kindly take his pleasure:
'Oh, gluttony's a sad disgrace,
But we'll repent it at our leisure.'

The singer fascinated Ranulph. All the women he knew seemed to be one of two types – those who dressed in fine clothes and were always seen from a beguiling distance, and the slow-witted, overworked, underfed wives of the village peasants, whose daughters were much of a piece, too. But this girl, though she was obviously not of the gentry class and probably possessed no more money than she had earned in this evening's work, flaunted a wild and brazen independence, like a prowling feral cat ready to seize whatever took its fancy. There was a saucy knowingness about her. And what a rasp of a voice!

Lovers met in May-o
Always shall be gay-o.

Henry joined in the singing lustily, and Christopher, unable to remember even so simple a refrain, uttered loud shouting sounds which more or less kept to the beat. Ranulph had his eyes fixed on the girl, wondering what it was that fascinated him about the way the muscles in her neck moved when she sang; about the swirl of her simple dun-coloured skirt above bare, dark-skinned feet; and about the insolence of her expression, her eyes glancing sideways as if barely acknowledging the audience which stamped and clapped and bawled.

When the song was over, the musicians took their instruments to a spot near the fire where a table had been laid with drinks. She passed close by him, and he leaned forward and clapped his hands together softly as a mark of praise. Pausing, she turned towards him, put her face close to his, flared her nostrils, narrowed her eyes and stuck out her tongue.

'Not quite a conquest,' Henry laughed, punching him playfully on the arm. 'Too much of a handful for you, I'd say.'

'Vixen!' Ranulph muttered, reddening.

The entertainment finished, they sat drinking for some long time, Ranulph sipping at the strong ale in his tankard, but Henry repeatedly replenishing his supply. His mood had passed from the loudly jocular to the sluggishly whimsical. Christopher drank very little, but wide yawns betrayed his tiredness and drew answering facial contortions from Ranulph.

'Time for you to retire,' Henry decided, rising unsteadily to his feet and taking Christopher by the hand. 'I shall play the proper role of guardian, even if I do intend to spend a little more time in this good company myself.'

Ranulph followed them up the stairs, but when he made to take leave of his friends and find his own room Christopher began to howl.

'Wiwwum here!' he demanded. 'Me, Wiwwum.'

After an attempt to console him, Henry gave way: 'If you don't mind taking my bed, William, I shall be quite happy with yours. Christopher's too exhausted to keep you awake tonight.'

Ranulph nodded, sat down on the nearest bed and found himself almost asleep before he had stretched himself full length.

'I shall perhaps go down for one more cup,' was the last thing he heard Henry say.

*

Horses' hoofs woke him. They hammered and clattered in the yard outside, and then stopped. Three horses, he guessed with his heightened sense of such things, one lighter than the others. What time was it? He tugged the curtain aside and there was only blackness in the room below, not even a glow from the dying embers of the fire. Then someone lit a taper, which suddenly flared brightly, and he saw the head and shoulders of the landlord and heard the bolt drawn back from the sturdy outer door.

'Softly!' he heard. 'There are folk sleeping here.'

There were sounds of an urgent conversation and then another light appeared. Two tall shadows came in from outside. He could also make out the thin figure of the friar, who had perhaps been sleeping in front of the fire. He was holding a candle in one hand and pointing up the stairs with the other.

At once Ranulph was fully awake. He knew what these men had come for, and he struggled into a sitting position on the bed. Escape was impossible. Their heavy footsteps were already on the stairs. Even as he braced himself for their entry, however, they hurried passed his room and on down the passageway. He could hear them opening another door, and immediately afterwards there were the sounds of a tussle.

Of course! Henry was sleeping where he should have been. Ranulph stood behind the door, immobile. In a moment they would discover their error, enter his room and carry him away – to his death. He heard them approaching, more slowly than before. They stopped outside, and Henry's voice, unusually slurred, asked stupidly: 'What *was* it the cockerel said to the dancing dog?'

'You take his legs,' a harsher voice said, 'and I'll have the shoulders. He's drunk as a lord.'

'Easier for throwing over the horse,' came the reply.

Ranulph froze to the spot as Henry was carried away, down

the stairs and out into the yard. What should he do? Surely, Henry was in no danger. They would release him as soon as they realised what had happened. But how long would that take?

He peered out into the yard. Henry's body was slumped over a horse's back as if there were no life in it at all. One of the men gave a shout and they galloped away into the enveloping darkness.

'Wake up, Christopher,' he urged. He shook his friend's shoulder with increasing desperation but the idiot lad slept on, the breath caught in his throat and expelled huskily in a monstrous snore. '*Please*, Christopher,' he pleaded to the unconscious form, 'or I'm a dead man within the hour!'

7 Dry Bones

His nose picked up the stench of dog fox, and he followed it in the smothering darkness, knowing that it would take them across the river which they heard splashing vigorously close at hand. Christopher clung to his jacket, whimpering with fright, but Ranulph maintained a steady pace, putting the inn and the little town behind them and striking out for the concealment of the countryside. He had no need of light.

'We're safe, Christopher,' he whispered, as much for his own consolation as for that of his friend. 'Don't worry.'

They crossed the torrent on a fallen elm, its rough bark providing ample grip for his fingers. Poor Christopher, however, made heavy going of it, straddling the trunk and falling forward as if to wrap his arms around it for security. Ranulph had to coax him across, tugging gently all the while, trying not to imagine how perilous it would be hauling the heavy lad from the swirling water below should he topple and fall.

Soon the river was left behind. He had seen where it ran as they journeyed to the inn, picking up its route miles away by the willows and alders that grew by its banks. Then it had been casual observation, gathered without thought, but now it was vital knowlege. He had to strike out for the south, away from the lands where the baron held sway.

The faintest glimmer of light pressed against the darkness of the clouded sky and he grunted with satisfaction. His sense of direction had not deserted him. They skirted a wood and climbed a steep path to open country where small blotches of grey turned themselves into sheep, which started clumsily to their feet as the pair approached and careered blindly down the slope.

Now Ranulph paused. Somewhere close there would be a farm, which they must avoid. He sniffed, seeking the scent of bedded animals. The first smell to reach him, however, was wood smoke. There was little breeze, and he led them instinctively away from the farmhouse and its early morning fire, his nostrils ever aquiver. When a dog barked he swiftly placed a hand over Christopher's mouth to stifle the frightened yelp he knew would follow. For the moment his own fear was under control. He was in his own element.

By the time the sun was up in the sky they had put the inn several miles behind them. Concealment was difficult, because this was a countryside almost entirely bare of trees. Ranulph kept them below the ridges of the hills, where their silhouettes would easily be seen, but he was nervous of descending to the valleys, where the occasional hamlet lay surrounded by its squares of drystone walling. Beyond, there was a road, and occasional drifts of dust showed where travellers moved.

'Hungry,' Christopher said, looking down at his stomach in a perplexed manner, as if it had been sending him messages which he only now properly understood. He was, after all, used to regular meals, and this was well past the time when he would normally have taken his breakfast.

'Want food.' He stopped still and made eating motions with his hands. 'Hungry.'

'Soon,' Ranulph assured him. 'We must keep walking.'

But now he had a rebellion to contend with. Christopher, having realised how ravenous he was, could think of nothing but the emptiness inside his guts. He shook his head and refused to budge. There was an angriness in his eyes which he could express only by sitting on the ground, crossing his arms over his chest and going very red in the face.

'This is foolish, Christopher,' Ranulph protested. 'I haven't any food to give you. Look!' He opened his jacket and shook his clothing to show that he was hiding nothing. The fragment of crimson brooch fell out, and he swiftly retrieved it and thrust it deep into a pocket. 'We can't stay here.'

'Food.'

Down below there was a small farmhouse by a narrow stream. He had been eyeing it anxiously for some minutes, praying that they would not be seen, but now he decided that he would have to take a risk he had hoped somehow to avoid.

'Come on,' he said, admitting defeat. 'We'll ask for food down there.'

'Hungry,' was all Christopher said, lumbering behind him towards the little grey stone building.

Since he had no wish to be regarded as a thief, Ranulph made his presence known by talking loudly to Christopher as they came across the last field. Nobody emerged, so he called out in a piercing voice: 'Here come strangers!' There was no response.

Approaching nervously, he put his face to a window. The room was empty.

'Hallo!' he cried again.

He lifted the door latch and stepped inside. The place was cold, as if uninhabited. He continued to call out as he moved from the kitchen into a living area almost bare of furniture and then up a narrow ladder staircase to the bedroom above.

Nothing stirred. There were two straw pallets on the floor with rough blankets thrown across them. On one wall there was a simple wooden crucifix, and a low table close to the beds held a bowl and a plate, on which there was something dry and crumbled. As he stepped closer there was a movement under one of the blankets, and something hard hit the wooden boards. He stared at it for some moments before he recognised it as a human hand, all the flesh long since gone.

He shrank back in horror. Now he made out the top of a

skull peering above the cloth. And the other blanket? Scarcely breathing, he sank to his haunches and gently tugged at the material until it, too, revealed its hideous secret.

'Hungry!' Christopher called woefully from below.

How long ago had this couple succumbed to the Pestilence? He should have noticed (as now he realised that he *had* noticed) that the fields outside were overgrown. There had been no work done here in many a month. He was on his way down the steps when he was aware of something else he had seen but barely registered.

'Want food,' demanded Christopher, beginning to snivel.

'In a minute,' he replied agitatedly, returning to the bedroom and, willing himself to be bold, inching forward on tiptoe. No, he was not mistaken: one of the skeletons held a leather pouch in its talon-like fingers. Ranulph knelt beside it and, his own hand shaking, tried to prise the little purse from that bony grip. The fingers resisted him, surprisingly strong and tenacious, so that he had to tug hard. The long, smooth arm rose and dropped to the floor with a crash.

Christopher had gone quiet. Ranulph found him in the kitchen, one hand clutching a sack, the other stuffing grain into his mouth.

'Look, Christopher, money!' he cried triumphantly, tipping the contents of the pouch into his palm. Three of the coins glinted gold. He had no idea what they were worth, but knew they must be a lifetime's savings. 'To buy food.'

'Mmmmrrrnnnn,' his companion replied, and then all but choked on his rough and ready meal.

There was nowhere to buy food, that was the bitter truth, but he was unable to reconcile himself to Christopher's raw fare. He wondered how long it would be before he began to snivel himself.

'People!' boomed Christopher, blowing husks all over the

kitchen. Ranulph thought he must have misheard until he saw the hand with the sack raised towards the window. Then he grasped Christopher by the arm and pulled him out of sight. A horse was pulling a large waggon up the track from the road, and several people were preparing to jump from it.

'Shhhh!' Ranulph warned him. 'Quiet, Christopher.'

His instinct was to climb the steps to the first floor, but he feared his companion's reaction to discovering the two skeletons tucked in for their last sleep. The new arrivals appeared to be familiar with the place and to know that it was unoccupied. Chattering happily all the while, they took water containers from the waggon and sauntered to a well in the yard. As they drew closer to the house, Ranulph realised with a start that he knew these people: they were the minstrels from the inn. The girl who had put out her tongue at him passed just under the window.

'Shall we eat?' she called in that strangely hoarse voice.

'It's a fact, Janie,' came the reply from one of the three young men, 'that you scarcely think about anything else.'

'Scarcely,' she replied with a saucy little laugh.

It was a torment to watch them unwrap legs of chicken and slices of ham and, sitting together on a low bank, make a great feast of them no more than a few yards from where he stood. Ranulph, at length, could bear it no longer. He took two of the smaller coins from the pouch, swung open the door and marched across to the group as confidently as he could manage.

'May I buy some food?' he asked directly.

They studied him carefully.

'The question,' said the old man in a reasonable manner, 'is whether we have enough to spare. We are not provisioners.'

'We haven't enough,' said the girl emphatically, cocking her head at Ranulph as if in challenge. 'We have to get to York with what little we have in the waggon.'

'We ought to ask how much you're prepared to pay,' threw in one of the young men.

'And whether,' added another, studying the coins suddenly thrust out to them, 'we can possibly provide what you need. Shall we say fourpence for a best roast hen, a shilling and a penny for a pheasant? How many would you like of each?'

'Give us the money,' said Janie, 'and we'll bring them to you next time we're passing.'

It angered him that they were amusing themselves at his expense when he was so painfully hungry, but he felt shame, too, in front of the girl, because he did not know the worth of the coins in his hand and was likely to prove a simpleton in her eyes.

'If you've no wish to help, I'm sorry to have wasted your time,' he replied bitterly.

'No, no,' smiled the third young man. 'You're too quick. We haven't yet decided.'

At this moment Christopher emerged from the house, dropping his sack in the doorway.

'Still hungry,' he said.

The effect of this dramatic entrance was immediate. Within seconds space had been made for the two starvelings, who found food thrust upon them in quantities vaster than they could possibly cope with.

'Poor lamb,' Janie said, stroking Christopher's hair and looking at him with warm pity.

Now the introductions were made. The old fiddle player was Thomas. The drummer was his son, Roger, and they came from the Lincoln area. The recorder players, Robert and Nicholas, were brothers from Wales. Janie had been born in Coventry, but had last seen the place a dozen years ago.

'And you, Master William?' Thomas asked.

'Oh, I come from a little further north,' he replied hesitantly, terrified of being found out. 'I'm amazed at how far you've all travelled.'

'It's the age of the traveller,' Thomas said. 'God help those who lack the strength to escape bad masters. We see a thousand free spirits every day on the roads of England.'

'And desperately poor most of them are, too,' Roger broke in. 'This Pestilence has broken the backs of the people, even when it's freed them from their feudal overlords.'

'There are many free?' Ranulph asked, knowing only his home village and the absolute power of Baron Fulke.

'The serfs are rebellious everywhere,' Nicholas told him. 'Now there's a shortage of workmen to till the fields they can name their price. They're beginning to learn how badly they've been treated.'

'But,' added Thomas, wagging a finger, 'they don't know how to be free, that's their problem. What do they know of the world outside their own villages? How can they prosper without the ability to read and write? I feel bad times coming.'

Janie had kept her silence during this social and political talk, and now she leapt to her feet and clapped her hands.

'But *we* enjoy our freedom,' she laughed, instantly lightening the mood, 'and I demand the freedom to ride to York!'

With loud hurrahs they followed her to the waggon and began to climb on board. Old Thomas insisted that Ranulph and Christopher come, too, and it was impossible to explain that safety demanded a wilder route. Besides, Ranulph felt himself beguiled by this happy company of musicians. They were soon swaying along the dusty road, with Robert and Nicholas playing merry tunes on their recorders.

'You don't play an instrument?' Ranulph asked Janie, merely for something to say to her.

Her only response was to show that wicked little tongue again.

They had been journeying for several hours, and were on a wide and busy stretch of road, when they saw a large congestion of people and vehicles up ahead of them. Everything had come to a stop.

'Some lawlessness, I dare say,' Roger guessed.

'But a good crowd for a performance,' chuckled Janie.

Ranulph, sitting as close to her as he dared, felt suddenly cold. He had a presentiment of danger, and called out to the first person to approach them from the other direction, a fat man leading a donkey: 'What trouble is it?'

'No trouble for the innocent,' the traveller replied cheerfully, and would have gone on his way.

'But what . . . ?'

'Armed men, seeking a fugitive. A lad wanted for some crime in the north country. I wouldn't be in his shoes!'

They were drawing close now. Ranulph could see men with swords moving among the crowd, singling out individuals for questioning, pushing them brutally to one side. He knew who these men were.

'Please,' he begged in a quavering voice, grasping old Thomas by the arm. 'Hide me.'

'Hide *you*, Master William?'

'In God's name, or I'm dead!'

'It's you they're seeking?'

'I'll pay you . . .'

He felt for the pouch, but before he could pull it out he was caught off balance by a pair of thrusting hands so that he tumbled into the back of the waggon. For a second he saw Janie's triumphant face grinning down at him, and then he was covered by sacking and a great many other things he could only guess at.

8 On the Road

Something plunged through the matted darkness, struck his arm and embedded itself in the woodwork of the waggon. He felt a sharp pain and heard old Thomas call out in protest: 'Careful man, we've musical instruments in there!'

The flooring shook as the sharp point was tugged clear.

'We have our orders,' came a sneering voice. 'They don't make mention of musical instruments. It's a criminal we're after.'

Christopher began to wail and clamour: 'Wiwwum! Wiwwum!' he bawled.

'What's his offence,' asked Nicholas, 'that such extreme measures should be taken to find him?'

'He's an enemy of Baron Fulke.'

'And your Baron Fulke,' queried Robert, 'has been wronged by this villain?'

'Wiwwum!' The waggon rocked and there came the sound of a struggle, with Roger desperately attempting to calm the idiot lad.

'He has violated a young woman who is to marry the Baron's son. We have orders to return the miscreant's body to the castle.'

'You'd kill him?'

The reply was a hearty laugh: 'Gladly! Do you know a man who'll stop us?'

'Wiwwum!'

'Get this oaf away from here or I'll run him through!'

Another thrust from the sharp spike was evidently about to follow, for Ranulph felt a sudden weight fall upon him and heard Janie's cry of protest very close to his ear.

'No, please! We vow that we're carrying no violator here.' That hoarse singer's voice softened, and she continued coaxingly: 'You wouldn't wish to impoverish a group of honest minstrels. We need our instruments to live.'

'Orders, my lovely.'

'Come,' she replied simply.'A word in your ear, soldier.'

Ranulph experienced the scene which followed as much through feel as through what he heard. The Baron's man approached the waggon and leant heavily across it, his arm pressing down on the sacking. Janie gave a guttural little laugh and whispered something in his ear. Breathing heavily, he planted a lusty kiss upon her lips.

'Oh!' she exclaimed, as if surprised, and slipped further into the sacking so that Ranulph actually felt the press of her calf upon his arm. It was firm and warm. 'Enough, sir, lest you prove a violator yourself!'

Muttering to himself, the Baron's man pushed himself upright again.

'We'll perhaps meet again,' he called as he moved off.

The waggon began to roll forward, and one of the Welsh brothers played merrily on his recorder as if trouble was many miles away. After a while Roger found words for the tune, and then Janie joined in, too, not moving from where she lay. Ranulph, on an impulse he did not understand, reached out a hand and grasped her by the ankle.

'In heaven's name!' she screamed.

He was about to apologise for his unmannerly behaviour when he realised what it was that had frightened her. The arm he had raised to grasp her leg was running with blood.

'Rags, quickly!' Janie called to her father. 'He's injured.'

They stopped the waggon, found cloths and water and, with many a furtive glance about them, began to clean his arm. Christopher lumbered close and stroked his head with clumsy, loving fingers. The water stung his wound.

'It's not deep,' Nicholas said, tying a bandage around it.

'Can we be seen?'

'No, they've turned back towards the north,' Thomas told him. 'How do you feel, William?'

'Fine,' he admitted, rather regretting that he had no real need of pampering. 'It's nothing.'

'And you are the lad they were seeking?'

'Yes, but I'm no criminal. The charges against me are false.'

'We believe you,' the old man said simply, flicking the reins to start the horse. 'We shan't talk about it.'

Ranulph sat up beside Janie in the waggon, feeling dishevelled and coarse. It was some time before he dared to glance in her direction, and then he found that she was staring at him with an expression he had not expected at all. It suggested interest.

'A wanted man,' she laughed quietly.

By now they had caught up with the large throng of people detained by the Baron's men and only now beginning to think about continuing their journey. It was a fine day, with a faint warmth in the air suggesting that spring was perhaps not so very far away, and some sat on the grass by the road to rest and take refreshment while others, whose living was made from parting other people from their cash, seized the opportunity to sell, to beg or to entertain. The minstrels were quickly about their business and Janie, her feet moving to the rhythm, thrust a leather bag into his hands.

'You can collect,' she said in a voice which forbade refusal.

He moved among the crowds, light-headed with relief at his survival. A few small coins were tossed into the bag, and he found himself humming the tune to himself as he went. He had first heard it at the inn, but already the words were becoming familiar to him: *Lovers met in May-o . . .* Was his plight perhaps not so very desperate after all?

At this moment he was struck violently from behind, so that

he was thrown forward and crashed heavily to the ground, the breath knocked from his body and the coins scattered from the bag to roll around his head as if in mockery of his brief feeling of contentment.

*

Baaaaaaaaaaaa bleated Hosea's Wife, and made as if to charge at him all over again.

'No, no, you stupid creature!' exclaimed Brother Walt, lunging forward and managing to grasp the short length of rope around the animal's neck.

Ranulph began to wonder if his brains had been bruised along with his body when he opened his eyes and saw, not only the old hermit, but the smiling face of Henry.

'Not dead?' was all he managed to say.

Henry's smile grew broader: 'Thanks to Brother Walt here, no. We had a lucky meeting in the darkness after I was overpowered at the inn. But perhaps I should really proffer my thanks to the goat.'

Christopher now appeared from the crowd and helped Ranulph to his feet. He seemed not in the least surprised to see Henry. Time had no meaning for him. He began to collect the coins which had fallen from the leather bag.

'It was an answer to prayer,' explained Brother Walt. 'I had long conversations with the Lord about you . . .'

'Hoping,' Ranulph remembered with a spurt of anger, 'that he might advise you to betray me to Baron Fulke.'

'. . . and His instructions,' the old man continued without a pause, 'were that I should leave my cell and travel the world in search of you. I left immediately, although the sun had long since set.'

'And along the road,' Henry broke in, 'he met two horsemen

in a great hurry to take a captive to Baron Fulke. Unhappily for them Hosea's Wife broke loose and lost her temper with the horses. They shied and threw their riders to the ground.'

'What of the two men?'

'One was knocked senseless. The other must have thought he was being attacked by something out of Hell. He remounted and fled.'

'And you weren't hurt, Henry?'

'Alas, young William, I was rather too far gone in drink to feel anything. To think that I boasted what a changed man I was! My failing almost brought about my death.'

Their playing over, the minstrels were making ready to leave. Thomas called to Ranulph: 'You're coming with us, Master William?'

He paused, uncertain, and Henry intervened.

'You can't follow this road,' he insisted. 'It's far too dangerous. We'll strike off across country until we're further from the Baron's influence. Are you with us, Brother Walt?'

'Wherever the Lord leads me I shall go,' the frail old man replied piously in his reedy voice. 'So much better than that chilly cave, without a doubt. How wonderful prayer is!'

'Me, Wiwwum!' declared Christopher, clutching at Ranulph's jacket for fear that he might be left behind.

Ranulph exchanged reluctant farewells with the minstrels and set off with his companions towards the south. They were an incongruous group – a fugitive peasant lad, a would-be cleric, an idiot boy, a reluctant hermit and a goat.

By midday the sun was high and bright and, although Ranulph's arm was sore and Henry's head evidently still felt as if it were stuffed with old rags, their spirits were lifting. The rough track led now through dark woodland lanterned with the first white blossom of the blackthorn, now through open fields where villeins worked to bring life back to their precious strips of land while the sun laboured to bring colour back to their winter-whitened skins.

As they journeyed, these villeins would look up from their labours, sometimes following their passing with a dull stare, sometimes waving a friendly greeting. This worried Ranulph, who had hoped for a less conspicuous means of travel. Who could people imagine they were, and where headed?

The answer came simply from the lips of a broad-shouldered fellow digging a ditch: 'Be you the new preachers we hear of?'

Their silence was taken by this inquisitive peasant as an affirmative, and leaning forward until the stink of this breath could be discerned, and touching the side of his nose in the universal sign of knowingness, he said in a low voice: 'When Adam delved, eh?'. With a suppressed chuckle he returned to his work.

This allusion meant nothing to Ranulph and, in truth, even Henry knew little of the new preaching, though the very mention of Master John Wycliffe's name had caused the Holy Island brothers to shudder.

'He means the Lollards,' he explained. 'They are preachers who desire a revolution in the Church. If that is what we seem, perhaps we should be grateful for the disguise.'

An opportunity to play the Lollard role came sooner than he can have expected. Early afternoon brought them to a small village, where a few pence provided them with a flagon of good ale, a loaf of coarse bread and some fish so heavily salted that they looked like strips of wet leather. They took this meal seated on a green before a poor wayside inn, and were so intent on their eating and drinking that it was not until they rose to go that they saw what an audience had gathered. Keeping to doorways and to the shadows of their hovels, two dozen or so women, children and old men watched them as if afraid to approach too closely.

Ranulph feared that they might be attacked and robbed, but his fears subsided when one of the women spoke. Her voice was loud and forceful, and she was clearly a leader in this small community.

'Do you bring us words from the scriptures then, Master, that we may hear and repent?'

The words had been spoken to Brother Walt, whose ancient, vaguely holy appearance suggested that he should have been the prophet among them, but it was Henry who took the situation in hand and began to speak to them of Heaven in a clear ringing voice that reverberated through his own head like all the bells of Hell ringing at once. Oh, whatever the repentance of his audience, his was surely the greater: never would he drink to excess again!

'Amen,' chorused the congregation when he came to the end of his sermon, and the woman who had asked for a message called out to Henry: 'God has punished us for our sins through the Pestilence.' There were murmurs of support when she said this, but Ranulph noticed, too, that a group of men on the periphery of the crowd only scowled and muttered among themselves.

'We shall leave,' Henry whispered to him. 'These are dangerous times when the old truths are not everywhere believed.'

Thus they continued travelling for several days, sometimes passing through busy fields and busier communities, sometimes through country so ravaged by past plague that the fields had become a grassy wilderness, the villages a gathering of ruin. In these places even the birds lacked song, sheep chewed at the dead land and the only habitation was the shepherd's hovel pressed against its sheltering hedge well distant from the ruined homes whose rotting timbers, crumbling daub and scattered thatch must still hold the malignant vapours of the pestilence.

The four travellers also avoided these places, gladly clambering through thick hedges and wading chill waters in order to skirt them. Close to one of these villages they had encountered an old mad woman, a toothless, skeletal crone who hurled abuse and frightened Christopher until Hosea's Wife chased her from them and left her cowering pathetically behind the hurdles of a deserted sheep pen. Before continuing their journey Henry left her some of the bread and cheese that he carried in his pouch. It was little, and he could not be sure that she would reach it before dogs or rats or birds snatched it away, but the gesture set him right with his conscience and he travelled the more easily afterwards.

By night they slept in woodland, Ranulph's skills providing them with woven shelters snug and concealing, loose baskets lined with moss. From these they crawled refreshed into the morning light ready to journey again.

And then, early one morning, they reached a low hill where the road became a dusty rut leading upward towards a perfect blue sky. Their legs wearied as they climbed, but at the top their hearts leapt. A few miles off lay a large town, traversed by a swiftly-flowing river. Its tumble of roofs was held in by stern walls, and close to one of them rose the bulk of a huge, unfinished minster.

'York,' breathed Henry, a guarded expression on his face. 'Civilisation.'

'Good ale and well cooked food,' chuckled Brother Walt, his eyes bright with anticipation. 'How good the Lord is!'

'Food!' chimed Christopher, reminding Ranulph that they had not yet eaten breakfast.

Henry, however, seemed disinclined to rush down the slope towards the town.

'Let's be careful,' he warned. 'If we're to find your sacred relic, William, we must visit these places, but Baron Fulke's agents won't be sleeping. This is foreign territory for them, so they won't be riding about armed to the teeth and stopping innocent folk by the roadside. But that's worse in a way, because they'll be hidden – waiting to strike when we least expect it.'

'God will provide,' Brother Walt stated comfortably.

'Perhaps,' Henry said, leading them down to where the path joined a narrow road and then, a few hundred yards on, one of the major routes into the great town. 'It would be a good idea to give Him some help though, don't you think? Not a word out of place, Brother Walt.'

'As if I would! You surely know me as a man of the greatest tact.'

Once they were on the main route into town, progress was slow. It was the busiest street Ranulph had ever seen. The massive gate they approached was surrounded by colourful market stalls so that it seemed as if they would never be able to force their way through.

'Remember,' Henry said, 'that we're itinerant preachers. At least, Brother Walt and I had better be the preachers. You two are our servants.'

'Lollards?' Ranulph asked.

'Perhaps not, on second thoughts. A little too controversial. We'll try to be vague about it.'

In the event they passed through the gate without difficulty, and soon found themselves in front of the minster. Scaffolding rose along the south wall where a transept was being built, and a dozen chisels rang against durable stone. From inside they could hear the voices of monks at their service.

As they reached the west door there was a flurry of activity, and they were fussily ushered away by a pompous church official who muttered something about the Archbishop. That great figure, the Primate of England, then suddenly appeared, in glorious purple robes, and stood for a few moments framed by the arch, squinting up at the sun.

Alas, those moments were critical. For all his boast of extreme tact, Brother Walt chose this occasion to let go of Hosea's Wife's halter, and the happily released goat leapt friskily forward to butt the mighty prelate mightily in the rear.

9 Jailbirds

'Truly the goat should be here and not us,' protested Walt for the hundredth time, and for the hundredth time the gaoler ignored him.

'Save your breath, Brother Walt,' Henry suggested wearily. 'The goat made good its escape, and had we been as quick-witted and fleet-footed we might have avoided this misery, too. As it is, we'll have to sit it out until the mighty rump of the church eases and anger subsides.'

Ranulph grinned at this despite the desperate danger of their position. Here they were, unwilling residents of a cramped, cold and damp lock-up, dependent for their future freedom on their ability to act out unfamiliar roles. Many questions had been asked, and more would no doubt follow: for how long could their hastily invented explanations hang together?

Lollards? That would have been no defence against church and state, but rather an incitement. Instead they had become wandering entertainers.

'Is that so?' the sheriff had demanded. 'In which ways do you entertain?' There had been withering contempt in the voice that asked the question. 'You fail,' he added, 'to entertain *me*. And my lord the archbishop is very far from having been entertained.' A grin had flickered across his face at this last observation – not much, but enough to give some faint hope to the quartet which stood before him. The face resumed its stern, inquisitorial expression. 'Vagrants, I should say.'

'No, sir,' Henry had protested. 'Actors looking for a play.'

'Temporarily unemployed,' added Walt.

'Resting,' threw in Ranulph.

'Actors! Unemployed!' The sheriff had guffawed his appreciation of this, and the gathering of listeners, a motley collection of soldiers and officials, had shared his joke. Three heads hung low, red-faced and humiliated, but the fourth, Christopher's, stared straight ahead, a little frightened and very confused. His mouth gaped, his eyes stared.

The sheriff fixed his gaze on him and asked cruelly of the others: 'Moonface here, what does he do? Hang above the stage and shine?' The audience had been almost beside itself at this. 'Or perhaps you stand him near the front to catch coins in his mouth.' More laughter, even an appreciative clap or two.

Yes, if there was an entertainer in the assembly, it was the sheriff.

'I suppose he might act a tree with passable conviction. Or,' (and here he lifted a lighted torch from its holder on the wall of the chamber and waved it in front of Christopher's face) 'even a burning bush. What would Moses make of you, eh?'

Christopher's eyes stretched even wider with fear, and he began to whimper. And then the sheriff seemed to tire of his mocking.

'Oh, get them out of my sight! They can act their plays between four walls. Perhaps their next performance will be more polished.'

So now they sat in chill discomfort, and Walt added one more plea for release, as if a hundred were not enough.

'Just tell us, brother gaoler, how long we must endure this unhappy place?'

'Not long, if you don't shut up,' he growled from the far side of the small barred window. 'The bones of the last occupant hang bleaching on Gallows Hill. Be sure that yours don't follow.'

Walt gulped dejectedly.

'But —'

'Shut up!' unisoned Ranulph and Henry, almost as provoked as the gaoler.

'He only has the key,' Henry added. 'Others turn it in the lock.'

But they shared Walt's frustration at the uncertainty of their future. For how long did the sheriff intend them to be locked up? Would their release be conditional – and, if so, upon what?

'Hungry,' Christopher muttered quietly and miserably. 'Hungry.'

The cell was lit by one small horizontal slit high in the wall. Gradually the pallid light dimmed, as afternoon gave way to evening and evening to night. The four sat in what had become a black pit, the only thing visible being the narrow rectangle of stars that hung suspended above their heads. A gloomy silence wrapped them, and presently only Ranulph remained awake and staring up at the stars, each one of which he recognised.

'So far away,' he thought to himself. 'So very far away.'

*

Release came as a shock. It was a little after first light the following morning. One minute they sat in the stygian gloom of the cell, the next they stood blinking in the sunlight. It was not only sudden, but unexplained. Indeed, the gaoler's task had been accomplished with the use of one single word.

'Out!'

And yet, as they stood gathering their wits, their relief was not untinged by a certain wariness. They looked around them. The street, a narrow evil-smelling alley, was empty of anyone but themselves. And yet was it? Did something move in the shadows? They moved uneasily towards the spot where the street opened into something more airy and substantial. There again! A brief flickering movement . . .

Ranulph was aware of it, but said nothing. Mere fancy, surely. Henry felt it rather than saw it, but said nothing. A trick of the imagination. Brother Walt sensed unwanted company, but said nothing. Too old. His wits were growing addled. It took Christopher to speak out.

'Hungry,' he said, continuing his mournful litany. 'Hungry. Man with food there? Man with food?'

'What man?' all three asked together, but Christopher's finger pointed to a dark vacancy between two houses.

'Nothing,' they reasoned.

Somebody, they thought. *A city is full of somebodys. Why should somebody concern us?*

The street widened to a market place where the earliest stall-holders were beginning to arrange their displays. Ranulph felt in his purse. It still held coins. They breakfasted as they walked, chewing hungrily on strips of salted pork and some tough root vegetables, dried and withered beyond recognition. They hurried along, uncertain of their destination, certain only that they needed to put as much distances as possible betwen themselves and the sheriff's lock-up.

More and more people were emerging onto the streets, and Ranulph paused for a moment in wonder. Clearly this was only the beginning, but never had his village known these excitements. Men in furs and gorgeous tunics strode by; scholars carrying heavy books spoke to one another of things he could not hope to understand; a group of beggars marked out an area of roadway and settled down upon it, two maimed children at the front to arouse sympathy in those who passed; and a man with a box of dice began to scatter them on the ground and invite the good citizens to chance their luck.

He saw that a small crowd had gathered where a man held a chained bear and, prodding with a sharpened stick, goaded it into a grotesque caricature of a dance. The bear's huge bulk lumbered clumsily in a wide circle around its persecutor, its pelt giving off the rich wild smell that Ranulph associated with the animals of the forest. He remembered nights at the edge of a clearing, watching families of wolves less than the throw of a stone away. He remembered leaping into the branches of a tree to avoid the vicious attack of a boar. This animal, by contrast, had been robbed of all dignity, and by a man whose skinny frame it could so easily have crushed had they met on a forest path. It sickened him.

Rejoining the others, he walked along in silence. The crowds had begun to upset him. True, he had never known such vitality, such colour; but he had never been pushed and jostled in this way, either, had never felt this crush of bodies around him. Whichever route they took there were people in front of them, to the left, to the right, behind – and they were being followed! He knew it, knew that the darting shadow had become one of these faces. But how could he know which it was?

His three companions no longer seemed concerned. They had relaxed into the life of a city, as a leaf bobs along the surface of a river. Even Christopher was so held by the variety of events around him that confusion had turned to unalloyed pleasure. It was almost his undoing.

A group of jugglers threw bright batons in the air and snatched them back with ease, amazing the audience with ever more complex patterns of movement. A troupe of acrobats twisted their bodies into impossible shapes and then unwound themselves in order to assume even more improbable, more grotesque, positions. They seemed to re-assemble themselves as if each joint were an individual element to be moved at will. Christopher gasped and tried to imitate, hunching his ungainly body, craning his neck and splaying out his fingers. The gathered crowd cheered him good-humouredly, but the acrobats, resentful of his stealing their show, cuffed him round the ear and sent him back to his companions who, unwilling to retaliate in case they drew unwanted attention to themselves, simply hurried him away.

'I feel uneasy, Henry,' Ranulph confided in his friend's ear as they continued to push their way through the streets of the city. 'I'd like to be rid of this place.'

'Not too much haste, my friend. There's comfort in a crowd. It can be draped around you like a heavy cloak in a storm.'

'But a cloak can hide things in its folds. I feel followed.'

'Perhaps our imaginations are dancing away with our wits.'

'I'm sure of it, Henry. I know it.' The plain speaking came as both a relief and a fresh pulse of fear. 'And if it's an agent of the Baron you're safer without me.'

Henry, who had turned his head to observe a falconer with young birds of prey to sell, their jesses tied to a stout horizontal pole, only felt the sudden movement. When he pressed forward again he found to his considerable unease that his young friend had disappeared and that where Ranulph had walked now stood an evil-smelling vendor hung with hammered tin talismans. He lifted one by its leather thong and, smiling a good-natured but toothless smile, warbled sweetly: 'Luck, sir! Every wish locked in a charm. Never palsied, sir, never blind!'

Anxious to find Ranulph, he tried to push the vendor aside, but the man was not so easily dissuaded. Henry felt a knife poke at his ribs, its sharpened point pressing at the skin.

'Not so fast, sir. One charm to prevent the letting of blood.' The vendor's warble had developed a threatening edge. 'One charm to rid you of dangerous friends.'

'Damn you and your charms!'

But the knife opened the skin, and Henry gasped with the sudden pain and with the realisation that one lurch, one barge, one jostle from the surrounding crowd could press the blade home.

'Who are you?' he hissed.

'Just a seller of charms, sir.' He held a few before his eyes: a snake with exposed fangs, a hand clutching a cross, a St Christopher with the Christ-child on his back. 'A third, perhaps, for the safety of your slow-witted friend.'

'How much?'

'Oh, your purse, sir. That will suffice.'

Robbed! To be robbed in a street full of people. It was preposterous. Could no-one see what was happening? The man had an unwashed, peppery stink. Henry's eyes searched desperately, but not a soul that passed showed the slightest interest in his plight. The knife goaded him again and he parted with his purse, feeling absurd and humiliated. The vendor slipped a metal token into his pocket and in a second was lost in the crowd.

To be rid of dangerous friends! The phrase seemed to echo in the busy streets. Had the vendor heard Ranulph's parting words and played on them, or . . . The alternative trickled through his brain like icy water.

'Wiwwum,' Christopher wailed when he saw Henry approaching alone. 'Wiwwum gone.'

'Don't worry, we'll find him,' Henry replied, more bravely than he felt.

He fished in his pocket and fetched out the talisman. It was a strange thing, thin metal that had been beaten into the shape of a stag's head with an arrow through it.

*

Ranulph had done the right thing, and now he regretted it bitterly. If he was the quarry, he must draw the huntsmen from his friends, but now he felt horribly alone and more vulnerable than ever.

Doubling back, he found himself in the shadow of the newly-risen minster. Above him wooden scaffolding reached up to where a group of masons worked, silhouetted like insects against the sky. A shower of fine stone chippings fell around him, and he heard laughter fall from the sky with them. There was no crowd here, only groups of workmen going about their trade. A group of glaziers worked at a bench beneath a rough wooden roof, to protect them as much from the masons as from the weather.

He stood near and watched, feeling safer for their presence and fascinated by their craft. He watched an apprentice take a grozing iron from a brazier that held glowing coals and give it to the glazier who ran it across the surface of a sheet of glass that lay on the bench before him. The hot iron was followed by a cold yellowish liquid poured from a jug. The glass fizzled and then, with a sharp crack, fell in two. The craftsman lifted it, holding both pieces to the light, before working at the edge of one piece with an iron implement until it more nearly formed the shape that he needed.

Another glazier, noticing Ranulph's rapt attention, called over to him: 'Like to try, eh, lad?'

He nodded, fascinated, but the man who had proffered the apparent invitation shook his head: 'Only members of the guild may know our secrets. But we'll share our magic potion with you if you like.'

He mimed a drinking movement and held the jug of liquid towards Ranulph. The other glaziers and their apprentices looked up from their work to watch. Why did they stare so eagerly? He took the jug, held it to his lips and, tipping his head back, took a mouthful of the liquid that cut glass. Immediately he straightened and spat it out, grimacing violently, while the audience guffawed with such wildness as to blow the minster down with the force of the gale.

'What, in God's name?'

'Why, lad, cold wine and piss. Now run back to your companions over there and stop gawping at us.'

The cruel prankster inclined his head, and Ranulph half expected to find Henry, Walt and Christopher behind him. No, they were four, not three. Silent. Facing him in a row. Ten yards behind him and patiently waiting.

'Who are you?' he cried, terror seizing him by the throat.

In reality he had no need to ask, or to look closely at the piece of white cloth which one of the men waved before his eyes. On it was drawn, very crudely, the head of a stag transfixed by an arrow.

Slowly they moved forward. Yes, these were faces he had seen before around his home village, hunting in the forest with Baron Fulke. Each held a sword, and as they moved forward they fanned out in order to cut off any means of escape.

Behind him the glaziers stood with folded arms. This was better sport than translating the Bible into coloured light.

'Please help me!'

He pleaded with them, tears in his eyes, but they only shrugged and grinned. This was not their fight.

'They'll kill me!'

But the glaziers simply did not care.

10 Assassins

What followed was determined by desperation and instinct. Ranulph stepped back a few paces. To his right, and close enough to hurt his leg with its heat, was the brazier with the irons resting on smouldering coals. He snatched up one of these irons and advanced rapidly on one of his attackers, forcing him backwards as the red hot tip thrust at his face.

Without pausing, Ranulph let drop the iron and sprinted towards the wooden scaffolding that rose beside the minster. He leapt at one of the poles and, using all his old forest skills, scrambled rapidly aloft. In no time he was on the first platform, some twenty feet above the ground. It swayed.

The Baron's men followed, but they were too solidly built and too heavily weaponed to repeat Ranulph's lithe trick. Instead, they made for a ladder which would take them to the platform. Ranulph, realising that it could be his undoing, skipped along to where it came to rest against the platform. He pushed at it but, heavy with the weight of the first two pursuers, it was no easy thing to shift.

'He's ours!' one of the men cried triumphantly.

Holding on to a vertical pole of the scaffolding, Ranulph placed both his feet against the top rung of the ladder and pushed until the veins stood out in his neck. He felt it move. The first of the two men, who was now nearing the top, grabbed furiously at Ranulph's foot, but he was too late. The ladder swung outwards, and its backward arc carried him screaming towards the ground below. His death was clouded in dust and commemorated by a roar from his companion, who had managed to jump to safety and a broken ankle.

'Blast the lad!' this crippled victim groaned, sinking to the cobbles close to his lifeless comrade at arms.

There remained two, and Ranulph, pinned to the side of the minster, felt no great confidence in his ability to evade them. There were other ladders, other ways of reaching him. The answer was to climb higher. He clambered past more ladders, more stages, past laughing masons (spectators as entertained and impartial as the glaziers at ground level) and up to where birds flew among beams as yet uncovered by a roof.

Stopping to peer over the edge, he felt his fear of heights surging back. Here was the sea-washed tower again, only this sea was human – a tide of faces, among whom he would have made out, if only the distance had not been too great, the features of Henry, Christopher and Walt.

'See how high he rises,' marvelled one of the crowd.

'He'll need wings to climb higher,' said another.

'Ah, those he has are soon to be clipped. They're nearly upon him, poor creature.'

They were, indeed, but yards away, approaching him along the wooden staging, their swords ready. Behind Ranulph a beam spanned the void between the unfinished west wall of the transept and the other, in a similar state, on the eastern side. Beneath was a frightening drop, but it was his only chance. He straddled the beam and began to shuffle forwards, an awkward, painful movement, but one which took him beyond the swords of his adversaries.

*Teach me your courage, Master Squirre*l, he implored silently, recalling days in the forest when he had scaled huge oaks and hidden himself in precarious dreys.

He sat, his feet dangling in limitless space either side of the beam, his hands clasping it tight. The distance to the other side seemed impossible, but return was no option either. His only relief was that the two swordsmen had hesitated in following him. Their faces were red with exertion and anger.

'You go back,' the leading man shouted to his companion.

'I'll drive him down to you.'

He advanced on Ranulph's back, flashing his sword as menacingly as he dared while needing to keep his balance on the narrow beam. The other one was already climbing back down the scaffolding, planning to trap him at ground level.

'Let go, lad,' the swordsman bellowed. 'It'll be a cleaner death for you to fall and crack your skull open.'

'What have I done to you?' Ranulph pleaded, not turning his head towards his pursuer, but manoeuvering himself as swiftly as he could towards the scaffolding on the far side. At every moment he expected the slash of the blade against his unprotected back. 'I'm innocent of any crime.'

'You're good money to me,' came the rough reply, 'dead or alive.'

Ranulph reached the scaffolding and gratefully pulled himself into its wooden web. When he turned, however, he saw that the blade he feared was but a yard away from him. As he began his descent there was a rush of air and the sharp edge of the sword smashed a wedge out of the woodwork only inches from his fingers.

He swung lower, the sweat running into his eyes, and saw that the second man was already more than half way towards the ground. There was no way of escape.

Swish! He looked up, flinched – and let go of the scaffolding with his left hand a fraction of a second before the sword would have taken it off at the wrist. The whole structure shuddered with the impact.

'Next time, boy!' his assailant bawled with relish, tugging the sword from the deep split it had created. He was tall, and he moved more quickly through the trellis-work. His eyes were fierce. He was close enough for Ranulph to see the stubble on his chin. He was breathing heavily.

'Now!'

The blade rushed down once more. Ranulph instinctively let go of the scaffolding with both hands, rocking his body backwards away from the arc of the swing, desperately trying to keep his precarious balance, swaying on the slender spar of wood which alone supported him. The vicious sword cut across the face of his tunic, slicing two buttons clean off it, and buried itself deep into a beam.

What happened next was too quick for thought. He toppled forward, grasping at a vertical support to save himself, and found himself up against the arm which had wielded the sword. His attacker, tugging at the weapon to free it, hung down from the scaffolding by his other arm, his head out in space. Ranulph, leaping to a higher perch, aimed a kick at the man's wrist with such force that the fingers sprang open and the heavy body plunged away from him, away from the terrible cry it left behind it, splintering cross-beams as it plummeted down and down to the ground far below.

He thought of seizing the sword for himself, but knew that he had no chance of using it effectively. It was heavy, and the skills had to be learned. The fourth assailant, at this moment leaning on his own sword and patiently waiting, no doubt knew exactly how to wield it.

The crowd had fallen silent. Painful death was a common enough occurrence, God knew, but this mess of blood and guts was enough to turn the stomach of the hardest. All faces were turned up towards the trembling lad who slowly picked his way down the scaffolding, closer and closer to his executioner.

What he hoped to do, Ranulph could not have said. He was uncomfortable at that great height, sick with fear and the horror of the two deaths, but he knew he was safe until he put himself within reach of that sword. When he was about eight feet from the ground he stopped, propping himself in the wooden rigging as comfortably as he could.

'Come down,' the man said in a reasonable voice. 'You're mine.'

'You'll kill me.'

The swordsman chewed on something in a leisurely fashion, and a full minute passed before he replied.

'Not necessarily. Alive will do, the baron said.'

'I know that you'll kill me.'

'Ha!'

They stared at one another for a long time. Nothing could be heard but the shuffling of feet, sharp intakes of breath. Minutes passed. Deadlock. The slow chewing continued remorselessly. Ranulph's hands ached from gripping the woodwork.

The silence was at last broken by a frantic hollering. The onlookers had kept well back from the posse of northern ruffians, but now a large and ungainly figure plunged out of the crowd, gesticulating wildly.

'Wiwwum! Wiwwum!'

'Come back, Christopher!' Ranulph heard Henry's voice echo around the heavy stones of the minster.

The baron's man turned in an instant, his sword raised before him, and he swung the point towards Christopher's grossly agitated adam's apple.

'Back!' he cried.

'Want wiwwum!'

'Back, you loon, or you're a dead man!'

Ranulph, despite the near certainty of instant death, found himself shinning down the last few feet of scaffolding to rush to the aid of his friend.

'No, don't!' he cried.

It was too late. Whatever the Baron's man intended to do, his head turned towards Ranulph, his sword waving in front of Christopher's howling face, any voluntary action on his part was prevented by an abrupt explosion of hoof and fur as

Hosea's Wife hurled itself from its hiding place among the builders' rubble, crashed into his unarmed rear and sent him sprawling, his sword skittering across the flagstones like a tossed pebble hopping across the surface of a calm sea.

*

They pounded through the narrow cobbled streets as if chased by the hounds of Hell. Ranulph had a hand firmly clasped by one of Christopher's. The idiot lad blew hard, his eyes wide with terror. Henry, unshackled, was out in front, his heels kicked high behind him. Walt, whimpering, chased behind with a kind of skipping motion, alternately tugging at and being hauled along by the short lead attached to Hosea's Wife's collar.

'Enough!' Henry cried at last, leaning against a wall, his chest heaving hugely as he gasped for breath. 'They won't catch us now.'

'Not yet,' Ranulph replied, refusing ever to have an optimistic thought again.

They were well away from the centre now, in an area of poor housing and low-class inns. They entered one of these doubtful hostelries and sank down on the wooden benches, their legs shaking. Henry, having ordered ale, suddenly patted his tunic in horror.

'But, of course,' he moaned. 'I've been robbed! Can you pay, Walt?'

'A poor hermit?' came the feeble reply, accompanied by a shrug of his thin shoulders.

Ranulph sank his hand into a pocket: 'Will this be enough, Henry?'

'What's that, then?' Henry took the leather pouch and let the coins fall into his palm. He almost dropped them to the floor in surprise. 'By the holy rood! You came by these honestly, William?'

'What do you accuse me of?'

'Don't be offended with me, but this is a large sum of money. Enough to see us many miles on our way. How did you come by it?'

Ranulph put out his hand: 'If it's not worthy to be used . . .'

'No, no, I didn't say that.'

'I've never taken a penny from a living soul,' Ranulph said, pleased with his wit.

'Then we'll say nothing more about it,' Henry decided, keen to seize the opportunity of using the money with a clear conscience. He gave a single coin to the serving maid, and Ranulph was amazed to see him receiving a palmful of others in return.

They settled down to a council of war – or, rather, of survival. Henry revealed that the sheriff's men had been called to the fracas in the minster and had been waiting in the crowd for a chance to overpower the baron's bounty hunter. Violent interlopers of that kind were not welcome in a well-ordered city. Nevertheless, it was hastily agreed that they should be on the move by the following morning. The authorities must regard them, at the very least, as noisome trouble-makers.

'I hate cities,' Henry said vehemently.

'Evil places,' Walt threw in, but without much conviction. 'Loose women. Drink. Robbers.'

This reminded Henry of his morning's experience. He told them of the sinister character with his peppery smell, and he took the talisman from his pocket and put it among their pint pots on the table.

'I can't think why he gave it to me,' he said. 'He already had my purse. William – why so white?'

Ranulph's face was, indeed, drained of colour.

'A stag's head transfixed by an arrow. That's the Baron's sign.'

'A coincidence, perhaps.'

'No. I know it too well. Count the tines of the antlers, see the angle of the arrow. That man was yet another of my pursuers. I can't escape them. Ever!'

'Don't distress yourself, William.'

'But I know they'll never give up.'

'Unless we find that holy relic. We *shall* find it.'

'The blood of Our Lord. I don't believe it's possible, do you?'

'It must be possible. What do you think, Walt?'

'Eh? Oh yes, certainly,' said the old man lamely. 'I'm sure we can find it. Have faith.'

He seemed to have so little himself that they all lapsed into a dejected silence. Ranulph drank deep of the ale and at least felt thankful to be alive when, so recently, death had seemed inevitable. As for Christopher, he had probably failed to realise how close to death he was himself. He had, nonetheless, had a fright followed by an exhausting run, and the result of all this excitement was perhaps inevitable.

'Hungry,' he said.

At this moment someone came up behind him and a pair of arms fastened about his neck.

*

'How's my lambkin?' asked Janie in that cracked little voice of hers.

'Janie!' Christopher beamed, loving the attention.

'And you, William?' she asked, so that for some reason his ears burned. She had never seemed to have any regard for him before. 'You fugitive from justice.'

The minstrels had brought their instruments, but seemed in no hurry to play. They commandeered the next table and whistled the wench up for food. Henry fished coins from the pouch and followed suit. There was suddenly a party atmosphere about the place.

'Where to next?' queried old Thomas, spiking a lump of cheese with his knife. 'You're still moving?'

'To the south,' Henry said guardedly. 'And you?'

'Lincoln. We shall do well there for business and lodgings. Then I'm thinking I may rest these old legs for a spell. Wandering's not kind to the old, you know.'

'On the contrary,' chipped in Walt. 'I've never had so much fun in all my life.'

'It's new to you, I believe. Wait until you've visited every town a good half a dozen times, then you'll feel some weariness, my friend. Then the open road won't seem quite so inviting.'

The food was hot and filling. Ranulph was all for dozing off, but the two Welsh brothers leapt to their feet, recorders in hand, and began to play a merry tune. The space was too small for singing and the beating of a drum, and Thomas evidently felt in no mood to play his fiddle. Nevertheless, Janie accompanied the players with a bag in her hand, collecting coins from those who felt the sound aided their digestion.

'She's wasted with us,' Thomas said, gazing at her in admiration. 'She's more than a singer. She can dance and mime. She can juggle. And she has character. What a little polecat she is!'

Ranulph felt pleased to hear her spoken of in this way, but he couldn't begin to understand why. He watched her moving among the guests, throwing her head back to laugh, wagging a finger at someone who had evidently made a ribald remark.

'Did you hear,' Roger the drummer asked, 'that there was

shedding of blood at the minster this morning? A lad pursued by men with swords, I heard say.'

'It's true,' Henry agreed.

'And two men killed. Can that be so?'

'It was so.'

'And the lad. Did he escape?'

'Escape?' laughed Walt, putting a hand on Ranulph's shoulder. 'Why, here he is, safe and sound!'

Ranulph and Henry gave the poor fellow such meaningful glares that he turned away and began patting his goat, muttering little endearments to her as if he had said absolutely nothing at all.

'It was *you*, William?'

Now that the secret was out, they put fingers to lips and endeavoured to keep voices low.

'If you'd rather not speak of it,' Thomas said.

'We fear ambush,' explained Henry. 'Believe me, William has no guilt that he needs to hide.'

They spoke softly, beginning to explain, and when Janie, Robert and Nicholas returned to the table they were obliged to tell it again, each time revealing more of Ranulph's story. Their conspiratorial mutterings could not but arouse some suspicion, and heads frequently turned in their direction.

'I've heard of wonderful relics,' Nicholas said, 'but never the blood of Christ.'

'Oh, I have,' said Roger, 'but I think it was across the water in France. Have you asked the holy men?'

'Those that *call* themselves holy,' Janie laughed, pulling a face. 'I don't meet many as fit the description.'

Henry nodded: 'We ask where it is sensible to ask. We must be careful of arousing suspicion.'

They discussed where to stay the night in York; how to avoid the authorities; which gate to leave by in the morning.

'And how will you travel?' Thomas enquired. 'Shall you be disguised?'

'Difficult,' Henry said, 'with so distinctive a company.' He glanced at the goat. 'We were passing as Lollards, but came to think this unwise. Now we are entertainers.'

'Entertainers!' chaffed Janie. 'What are your talents?'

'We have none,' Ranulph replied sullenly. 'We need some identity, that's all.'

'How stupid!'

Her face wore that disdainful look which he had known at their first meetings, and it made him feel uncomfortable. Now, however, she dropped it for an impish smile, and she brought her face close to his.

'If you call yourself entertainers you ought to learn to entertain, isn't that so?'

'And who would teach us?'

She laughed, that hoarse catch in the throat again.

'Why, *me*, of course!' she cried.

11 Entertainers

Ranulph had changed. He was a different person from the ignorant, vulnerable lad who had fled his home village those few weeks before. He recognised this wonderful and rather shocking truth about himself on the day he dealt with the pardoner.

It was the twenty-fifth of March, the first day of a new year – 'the year of our Lord one thousand, three hundred and eighty one,' Henry had intoned – and they had paused by a bustling fair set up outside a large town some five days ride from Lincoln. There were flags flying on the town's highest towers, and from their vantage point they could see processions of multi-coloured banners wending a snake-like course through the narrow streets.

'The mystery plays,' murmured old Thomas. 'In other parts they're performed at Corpus Christi, but it's a New Year festival here. It's something to watch.'

'After we've parted a few of these good folk from their money,' grinned Janie, looking around at the noisy crowds in their festive mood.

They had been training hard, the novice entertainers. As he gathered seven round apples in his arms, holding them precariously against his chest, Ranulph remembered how clumsy and self-conscious they had been at first. Even now they were unprepared for a fully coordinated show, but they had a few skills perfected and could earn money from them. He himself was a competent enough juggler; Henry had developed a cunning conjuring trick which involved other people's money; and Walt had achieved the impossible and taught Hosea's Wife some rudimentary discipline which ought to come in useful one day. For the time being he had taken to parading her before audiences on a long leash which continually tripped him up (this always brought loud guffaws), all the while reciting a ridiculous, but appropriate, rhyme. As for Christopher, he was the easiest of all to train, perfecting a few exaggerated gestures and not caring one bit whether the audience laughed or hurled abuse.

'Come high summer,' Janie had stated confidently, 'we'll have an act to be proud of.'

He heard her now as, torso inclined backwards to support his cargo of apples, he staggered towards the busiest part of the fair.

Fair Bessie lay upon a bank.
A-harking to the sweet birds sing . . .

Old Thomas was positively skipping to the tune he played on his fiddle, no matter how tired his legs might be. Roger beat lustily on his drum, while Robert and Nicholas wandered along the fringes of the crowd with their nimble recorders. Janie's gravelly voice, her liquid hips and insolent eyes, held the audience with the power of a stoat mesmerising a rabbit.

Lovers met in May-o
Always shall be gay-o . . .

Ranulph took up a position close to Janie and beckoned Christopher to act as his assistant. He had an apple in each hand, ready to begin, but he paused from cautious habit to glance at the faces of the onlookers pressed close to him. He had felt more safe on the road than in the confines of a town, but not an hour had passed without a flutter of the heart – a sudden movement seen out of the corner of the eye, a cloud of dust heralding another, unknown traveller in the distance. He knew that the danger had not passed but was slyly hidden, lying in wait.

'Higher, lad!'

'Catch it in yer gob!'

He had begun to toss the apples into the air and, as ever, there were raucous catcalls from the spectators. Most of them got more enjoyment from his frequent disasters than from any appreciation of his fragile skill. With one apple still in the air and the other just landed in his palm, he reached out and took a third from Christopher. Up it went. Three, now four. Now five. He couldn't hear the shouts any more; he was concentrating too hard. Six!

Did he dare attempt the seventh? He knew he must, for it sat in Christopher's hand on view to all. And yet . . . He kept the six in the air for a little longer.

'Swindle!'

'The boy can't count!'

'Saving the other one for dinner?'

He heard the taunts and knew what this meant. He was wavering; his mind had slipped. He grabbed the last apple from Christopher and flung it skywards. Too hard, he knew. It was inevitable, what would happen, but he persevered desperately for a moment longer. Another up, and another.

Then they began to come down. One hit his shoulder, another bounced off his nose. The jeering was deafening.

'Harvest time!'

'Wassail, lad!'

'Best get inside boy, it be raining!'

But he knew what to do. Crestfallen? No, he was not, to all outward appearances, in the least downcast. He smiled bravely, picked up the trusty leather bag and strode forward to claim his earnings for every bit as if he had used twenty apples and kept them aloft for a fortnight. He was, after all, an entertainer, and this was one of the first lessons he had learned. Have a little cheek!

'Bravo, boy!'

'Good try!'

'Give it a year and you'll master it!'

Yes, people loved a trier. He'd given them good sport, taken their minds off their sufferings for a few happy moments. He thought he was well worthy of the small coins that were dropped into his bag.

It was then that he was accosted by the pardoner. He was a man of about thirty with a sallow complexion, his head topped by a small embroidered cap. He carried a large wooden cross in one hand and a sizeable wallet in the other.

'A successful performance, my friend,' he smiled ingratiatingly.

'Small pickings,' Ranulph replied.

He marvelled at what he had learned in so short a time. In his home village he had never seen a pardoner, never even heard of one. The Baron controlled his territory so carefully that only rich prelates ever found their way to his castle. Travellers, vagabonds, the footloose of any kind, were cruelly treated and were lucky to escape with their lives.

'But they could be put to good use,' suggested the pardoner, still smiling broadly.

The baron's domain, he had come to realise, was a narrow one, cut off from the changing, vibrant world outside. His peasants were forced to suffer, even to die, at his pleasure, whereas elsewhere the poor were on the move, looking for new masters and payment in hard cash. His castle, which had seemed a grand, if forbidding, place, was as nothing compared with the architectural glories Ranulph had seen on his journeyings. If new ideas ever reached the castle they remained very well hidden, whereas beyond those walls everything was in turmoil. He had been amazed by the outlandish fashions, alarmed by the spirit of restlessness he experienced everywhere about him, threatening insurrection and bloodshed.

'What should I buy?'

'A pardon from some vile sin, perhaps, easing your way through Purgatory. No? A holy relic, then. I have one to suit every purse.'

What he had not discovered for himself, Henry had taught him. It was his friend who had told him of the many servants of the Church, some of whom could be trusted, most of whom could not. Henry believed in pardons and in relics, but warned him not to deal with common pardoners who traded in deceit to make themselves wealthy.

'Have you by chance,' he now enquired, 'a phial of the blood of our Lord Jesus Christ?'

The pardoner laughed.

'Dare I carry anything so precious? Certainly, my lad, you couldn't afford it if I had. But may I interest you in one of the nails from His cross? I believe even you could afford this small, slightly damaged relic.'

'But is Christ's blood anywhere to be found?' Ranulph persisted. 'Anywhere in the kingdom?'

'Possibly.'

'Then where?'

He shrugged: 'You're travelling to Lincoln? Ask there, boy. It has a great cathedral and many other holy places. But this nail . . .'

Before the awakening of spring and his headlong flight, Ranulph reflected, he would either have run from this man in terror or been shamefully duped by him. But he had had his own awakening since then.

'What else do you carry?' he asked in seeming innocence.

'Oh, a bag full of treasures. Look, a chipping from the stone which was rolled across Our Saviour's tomb. That's cheap, too. This one's rather out of your range, I'm afraid – a tub of the ointment Mary of Magdalene used to anoint Our Lord's feet.'

'I'd like that!'

'Very expensive. But the nail . . .'

Ranulph seized him by the arm: 'I have more money hidden away. I'm sure there'll be enough.'

He led the pardoner through the crowd. Henry, noticing the company he was keeping, stepped forward to intervene, but Ranulph waved him away so confidently that his friend gave way without a word. He passed Walt, who sat next to Hosea's Wife, almost absent-mindedly holding its lead while the hungry creature tugged at fresh stalks of grass. Yes, it should work. He was an entertainer now, wasn't he? They were all entertainers.

At the edge of the field there was a small pond, its surface weed-covered, its margins tussocked with grass and slippery underfoot. Ranulph beckoned the pardoner to the edge and pointed into the depths.

'I lowered my purse in here for safe-keeping,' he confided, 'and tied the string to a small stake. The problem is that I'm not sure exactly where.'

'You've no idea?'

'It must be close to this spot. Perhaps if the two of us look for it . . .'

While the pardoner obligingly stooped to the task, Ranulph turned towards the newly-trained goat, thrust two fingers into his mouth and gave a piercing whistle.

*

The blare of trumpets almost took the senses away; the air billowed with dust and stank of stale sweat; and the crooked streets were practically at a standstill, the thronging multitudes jostling violently to enjoy the spectacle of the creaking, swaying carts with their superstructures of outlandish tableaux making their laboured progress towards the square where the plays were to be performed. It was no place for the weak in body or spirit.

Ranulph had found himself a broken barrel which was yet strong enough to take his weight, and he peered over the heaving shoulders and bobbing heads, awestruck by the procession's scope and colour. Each of the local guilds had taken a Biblical scene to recreate, and there had been no stinting of expense or imagination. A band marched before each cart and men in extravagant costumes brought up the rear, but the glory was in the vivid scenes which passed high above the crowds.

The fishmongers had built a huge blue whale some thirty feet long: it had wicked white teeth, and there was a poor Jonah inside it bawling his head off and crying out to be rescued. The bakers had staged a magnificent Last Supper, with breads moulded in the shape of every kind of food imaginable, a terrible charcoal-faced Judas shaking his fist angrily at the crowd. The carpenters had fashioned Joseph's workshop, with a child Jesus wielding a hammer and chisel, and the goldsmiths displayed an Adoration of the Magi which elevated the sparkling products of their trade far above the humble and rather rickety manger in which a real baby genuinely kicked and screamed.

As the last of the carts trundled slowly by, the crowd began to shuffle in the same direction, lapping against it and folding it in like an incoming tide. Ranulph had long since lost contact with his friends, but they had already agreed their meeting place for supper that evening and he was intent only on witnessing the knock-about drama for which these wonders were an exhilarating static prologue. He was almost carried along by the foaming wave of spectators.

Outside the church a large stage had been erected, and here the Biblical story began to unfold. Each guild was responsible for a single episode, and the spirit of the play swung wildly from the comical to the tragic, from the devotional to the bawdy. The onlookers joined in from time to time (indeed, were often encouraged) and the actors had to shout to make themselves heard. Ranulph, who had no experience of theatre, was surprised to find that it was possible to laugh uproariously at one moment and be moved almost to tears the next.

The surgeons were performing the tale of John the Baptist, their particular skills being required for the climax of the piece, the saint's beheading. Salome was a man dressed in a long robe and a wig, who spoke in a falsetto voice and argued her case like a seller at a cheap-jack stall, albeit in rough verse:

Do any here not reck my right
To slit his throat this very night?
Do any here feel too much dread
To split a body and a head?
But he is mine and, by St Thomas,
I'll make old Herod keep his promise.
If he should flee, then understand
I'd chase the fellow through the land!

Despite being caught up by the performance, Ranulph could not help being unnerved by this parallel with his own predicament, and when the knife began to be sharpened with great relish (Salome ran his/her finger along it and howled), he turned away, feeling faint with horror.

It was then that he saw the girl. He thought, for a moment, that it was Janie: she was of the same height and dressed in a similar way. Was she smiling at him? No, it must be that she knew someone in the crowd close by. He looked away.

The knife had done its fell deed, St John and his persecutors had been spirited away, and now a few sheep were herded on to the stage. One of the actors from the surgeons' play pushed past with a friend, complaining: 'Fourpence for all that work! *And* I provided the blood, fresh from my aunt's pig. Shan't do it again.'

'I know someone,' his companion said, encouraging him, 'who got fourpence for simply crowing like a cockerel.'

'It's shameful.'

She was still smiling at him, the girl. She inclined her head, as if in invitation. Now she beckoned with a finger. Should he follow? No, it must be a mistake.

The play was still in full swing, in any case. It was early evening now, and the sun was on its way down, but there was plenty of business yet to be enjoyed on the stage. He watched the Nativity, and tried to join in when the audience was encouraged to sing, although he didn't know the song. This was followed, rather rapidly, by a powerful Crucifixion scene, with much moaning and lamenting. Was there to be more? Yes, his neighbour told him, the greatest spectacle of all was yet to come! He watched, goggle-eyed, as large vats were wheeled on to the stage and their contents torched until they threw flames into the darkening sky. This was the Harrowing of Hell, with noisy parts for both God and the Devil.

For deeds of base depravity
All human souls belong to me....

No, Satan! Turn and get thee hence –
Christ's blood has earned full recompense.

Through the drifting smoke he saw the girl, her eyes still fixed on his. She beckoned again. What did she want? He began to push through the crowd towards her, but as he drew closer she slipped away, all the time looking over her shoulder. He continued to follow, not knowing what propelled him, half his mind still on the colourful spectacle of the plays.

Once away from the stage area, it was much easier to move about, although the streets were busy and the whole town seemed agitated by the spirit of carnival. Wherever he looked there were food stalls and entertainers, and half the population appeared to be the worse for drink. He stepped out of the path of a staggering reveller and saw the girl waiting at the mouth of a narrow alley. As he hurried towards her, however, she screwed up her face in an impish grin and ran away out of sight.

'Come back!' he cried, and his voice echoed from the walls.

The cobbled path led downhill and soon became but one of a criss-crossing network of minor thoroughfares in what was obviously the poorest part of the town. Many of the houses had crumbling walls which had not seen a repair in many years. Shutters hung loose from rusty hinges. Dirty snot-nosed children wandered listlessly in the gathering gloom, their parents carousing in the run-down taverns that littered the area like the scabs on the back of the mangy dogs which everywhere sniffed hungrily for scraps.

He saw her again outside a crooked timber-framed house. Again she beckoned, and this time she waited until he was almost upon her. Then, with a chuckle loud enough for him to hear, she disappeared under an arch of badly weathered brick.

'Please wait!'

He approached the arch. It led to a small courtyard at the front of the house. A door stood open, still swinging gently from human touch. She could be nowhere else. He stepped inside a dark room, lit only by a single slit of a window and furnished with nothing but two upright chairs and a bare table. The door swung to behind him. There was another door in one wall, but he hesitated to go any further into the hidden depths of the house. What right had he? Perhaps, despite the evidence of his eyes, he had been mistaken all along.

Behind him there came the rasp and thud of a bolt being shot into place. Overcome with a sudden apprehension, he turned and pulled at the latch. The door would not open. His return had been cut off.

'Who's there?' he called.

Silence.

Standing alone in the half-darkness, his pulse racing, his breathing shallow, he became aware of a strange and pungent odour. It was stale, unclean, with an unpleasant peppery quality.

12 Trapped

Now he sprang towards the inner door, hammering violently upon it when it would not open, less from hope of its yielding than from sheer rage at the girl's duplicity and his own stupidity. Eventually, dropping his bruised fists to his sides, he slumped against the wall and allowed anger to subside into despair. Hopeless! So pathetically hopeless! He had allowed the oldest of tricks to entrap him. They had snared him with more ease than a rabbit.

He remained still for several minutes, wrapped in his own misery. No sounds betrayed what was happening beyond the door. Was the girl inside the house? Was she alone? He examined his surroundings more carefully. It was the most ordinary of rooms but safe as a dungeon, the doors strongly built and more than a match for his shoulder. The window was so narrow as to allow vision only to single eye. He swivelled his head and had a glancing view of a mean, shut-off space between two buildings. Nettles smothered the ground, and a stooped tree hung across the small patch of darkening sky visible between the constraining roofs.

Was there no way out? He snatched up one of the chairs and hurled it against a wall. A lump of plaster fell away, exposing the woven lathes that formed the wall's inner core. He grabbed at the fallen chair and struck again and again until the legs had become splintered stumps. The wall remained intact.

The room seemed to darken by the minute. He fell upon the remaining chair and covered his face with his arms. Was this how the stag felt, pursued by the Baron's huntsmen until it cowered, trembling, in some dark recess of the forest, waiting for death? Was this how the fox felt, hearing the baying of the marauding hounds?

He himself now heard sounds inside the house. A door opened and closed. There were footsteps. He thought he caught the low murmuring of voices.

But no, that was not the fox's way, to lie in wait of the inevitable! He remembered those he had watched from the concealment of his drey. They would never sit passively in a trap waiting for the snapping fangs, the hunter's knife. Master Fox had sharp teeth of his own but, more important than that, he had his renowned cunning. There was never more a time for cunning than now.

Ranulph leapt from his chair, put his face close to the door and let out a fierce howl.

The sounds within stopped for a moment, and then there was a renewed murmuring, more urgent than before.

Now his throat produced a low growling followed by several eerily high pitched yelps. More of a wolf than a fox, he thought, and so much the better for that. He knew the full range of wolf-sounds, had practised them to perfection to bring the pack close to him on nights when the moon was full and the forest glades were bright. He picked up two of the shattered chair legs and scraped them at the door with a sound for all the world like the tearing of a pair of desperate claws.

'What the devil?' he heard a man's voice say. 'What sort of a creature is this we've got?'

'It was the one you pointed out to me, father, I swear it. It had a human form.'

'This isn't good. It has the touch of evil.'

'I'm frightened, father. I've heard of devils which can take a human shape. They say they prey upon the innocent.'

'Hush, Avelina. It can't get out, be assured. Old Sourskin paid me good money for trapping a boy, but I'm wondering what purse this demands.'

Ranulph growled again, and then began a curious undulating

whine, a thin, insinuating sound that meandered through the air and must surely cause the skin of any listener to crawl. He could picture them behind the door, father and daughter clinging together in terror, and he renewed his wild attack with the chair legs.

'What's this folly?' came a sudden voice, loud and strident, with an edge as sharp as worked flint. 'You've got the lad in there?'

'Don't ask what we've got. Only listen!'

Ranulph snarled and scratched. He was so close to the door that he could hear the girl whimpering. The peppery smell pricked at his nostrils again, stronger, repulsive.

'Open up, Master Leofric.'

'I don't dare to, sir. See the state of my daughter.'

'You've been paid, damn you. The bargain was struck, the rest is of no concern to you. Let me see the boy and I'll bid you farewell until it's time to collect him.'

He had to raise his voice because Ranulph's howling rang through the house. It held in its folds all the forests of the frozen north.

'You mean you won't be taking this thing away with you?'

'Soon enough, but not just now. Open up, I say!'

'But it's not human. What have we got here, for the blessed Mary's sake?'

There was a heavy banging on the door.

'Enough, boy!' commanded Sourskin. 'I'm not fooled by your play-acting, though it's improved since the performance you gave for the sheriff at York, I'll give you that.'

A snarl. A long, low, threatening growl.

'I don't like it,' the man called Leofric said.

'You weren't paid to like it. Unbolt the door. I'll exorcise this boy's demon by ripping his tongue out.'

'I think we should reconsider the price.'

'Oh, you do, eh? But the bargain was struck. You have your purse. Move away from that door and give me the boy.'

'This is no boy, hear you! It's a devil. Who knows but it's Old Horny himself, and my daughter's at his mercy if ever I open that door.'

'Then I'll have to move you myself, rot your wretched lily liver!'

There followed the sound of scuffling, a smashing of earthenware, the breaking of furniture, and at last, amid much grunting and panting, the wicked sound of steel on steel. The girl screamed. The blades struck with a ringing sound three, four times. Something hit against the door. There was a groan and a low cursing.

For a moment there was nothing in the silence but a pitiful sobbing. Then there came a shuffling close to the door. Ranulph heard heavy breathing, slow movements made with the greatest effort. The bolt rattled and was painstakingly withdrawn. It was very dark in the room now. He heard the raising of the latch and was ready for the opening of the door.

As soon as he saw the first crack of light around its edge he thrust his shoulder against the woodwork. He felt it give, and he forced it away from him, stumbling over a pair of legs, kicking against an outstretched arm and bolting towards a narrow corridor which seemed the only way out.

He was aware of a figure by the door, groping for a sword, of another on its back and seemingly lifeless, and of the girl, huddled in a corner with a shawl over her head, shaking. Then he was along the corridor, through a door and out into the freedom of the street.

*

Janie's cheeks were flushed and there were tears in her eyes, but Ranulph hardly noticed such things as he breathlessly told his story to the gathered company at the inn.

'And I howled like a wolf!' he grinned, finding a swagger he had certainly never felt while a prisoner in the small, dark room. 'They shivered with fright, thinking I was some kind of demon!'

The others hung on his every word, open-mouthed, as if hearing one of the romances told by old men in cottage gatherings. Only Henry and Walt knew the full implication of these events, however, and they sat silent while the others laughed at the audacity of his trickery. Indeed, Henry's expression seemed somehow strained and uncomfortable, but this was something else he barely noticed in the excitement.

'So I staggered outside,' he concluded, 'leaving at least one corpse behind me, maybe a couple.'

Supper came round, and they fell to their eating with the lip-smacking noisiness that hunger brings to working men. They dipped bread into thick soup, wiped the bowls with the crusts and called for more.

Walt at last tugged at his arm: 'If Old Sourskin survived,' he said, 'which pray God he did not, we've yet to see the last of him. Did you get a good look at his features?'

'It was impossible. I simply ran.'

'Better to have grabbed the sword and dispatched him there and then!'

'That would show a lack of charity, brother,' broke in Old Thomas, who could not know a quarter of it. He seemed to imagine that Ranulph had been waylaid by nothing worse than a gang of pick-pockets. 'Come, we can't accuse the boy of not becoming the very devil he managed to mimic so effectively!'

The company applauded the minstrel's little joke, but Ranulph returned to the theme of the man's identity.

'No, I'd not recognise his looks again, but the stench!

Something hotter than Hades came off his body, I'll swear to you. I'd certainly know that stink at some distance.'

Henry started at the words. In a world where everybody carried their own rich smell, where most of them wore clothes stiff with stale sweat, dried urine and worse, and where washing was thought an eccentric and fastidious thing, to comment on a man's stink was indeed unusual. And yet he, too, remembered a particularly vile odour, a stench that stung the nostrils with its sharpness, the smell of overspiced rotting meat. Yes, Henry thought *he* could put a face to Old Sourskin.

Ranulph saw the shadow of this thought pass across Henry's face, but something about his friend's demeanour made him wary of saying anything. What was the matter with Henry? Then he looked across the room to where Janie sat alone, her cheeks glazed with tears. Had he missed some adventure in the tavern while he was involved in one of his own? He stood up and started towards the girl, but old Thomas pulled him gently back.

'Best not to,' he said. 'She needs time to herself.'

'Something's happened?'

Thomas threw a swift glance at Henry before replying: 'The problems of growing up,' he said mysteriously. 'Nothing very serious, although it seems so at the time. You'll know such things soon enough, my boy.'

What would he know? The question continued to trouble him, even after the musicians had picked up their instruments and begun to play. Janie continued to sit alone, with no thought of singing for the crowds who thronged into the inn. Occasionally she turned her head, but her eyes passed him by and fixed themselves, very briefly, on Henry's unsmiling face.

'Is there something I should know, Henry?' he asked at last, exasperated.

'No, nothing at all.'

Walt grinned and prodded a finger at Henry's chest: 'A heart of steel,' he said. 'Not worthy of a maiden's love.'

'Don't talk such nonsense!' Henry blurted out, and he stood up and stalked away towards the fire, where he stood warming himself for a long time while Robert and Nicholas played dancing tunes on their recorders, Roger beat time with his drum and old Thomas skipped and jigged with his fiddle tucked under his chin.

Late in the evening, with Christopher already in bed and Walt gone, yawning, to say his goodnights to Hosea's Wife, Henry called to Ranulph and began speaking earnestly to him in a low voice: 'This pursuit is becoming hard to bear. A man can't sleep at nights.'

'There's no reason,' Ranulph said, 'why you should suffer, too. Leave me here!'

'What nonsense you speak. This Sourskin's no fool. He's followed us from York, and presumably beyond, and I don't intend to give him the satisfaction of finding you friendless.'

'Then what can we do? I'm sick to the heart of being hunted."

'Perhaps,' Henry said, 'it's our turn to do the hunting. Sourskin's hardly a difficult quarry for anyone with a nose. I think I also know his face. I believe we should remove this particular weapon from the baron's armoury, and hope that he hasn't too many others at his disposal.'

'Brave words, Henry,' Ranulph smiled weakly, 'but we're hardly knights in armour, you and I. How do we overcome him?'

'That I can't tell you. All I know is that it's better to be the pursuer than the pursued. Could you find your way back to that house where he trapped you? If we went there tonight, under cover of darkness?'

'I could try.'

They shook hands on it and, throwing warm cloaks about

them, slipped from the tavern into the moonlit street. It was, in truth, too late for honest folk to be abroad, and the streets were deserted. Was it nerves that gave Ranulph the feeling that they were being followed?

The geography of the town began to confuse him. He found the church easily enough, but without the girl for a marker the dark maze of the narrow alleys began to appear impenetrable.

'But you found your way back to us,' Henry protested impatiently as Ranulph paused at yet another corner.

'Because I asked,' he replied simply. 'I've no idea where we're going now. Let's go back and start at the church again.'

They turned – and at once collided with a slender figure which tried unavailingly to shrink into the shadows.

'Janie!' two voices chorused in surprise.

'I'm sorry,' Henry said quickly. 'You can't come with us. It's not safe.'

She gave a brazen laugh: 'I'm probably as tough as the pair of you put together.'

'By all that's holy, girl,' Henry persisted, 'can't you see that your place isn't here? Obedience is seemly in a woman.'

'Ha! That's what your good books tell you, is it, Brother Henry?'

'Don't mock, Janie,' he said. 'I didn't mean to hurt you, but there's no point in following me now.'

'Follow you? Why should I have the least interest in doing that? It's William I've come for, don't you know!'

She slipped an arm through Ranulph's and tugged him on his way. Henry shrugged and fell in beside them, muttering darkly about modern girls not being as they ought, and what would his Holy Mother in Heaven make of such behaviour? Ranulph, although he enjoyed having this vivacious girl pressed up close to him as they walked, sensed that he was really only being used as a prop in a drama whose first act had entirely passed him by. What had Henry done to upset Janie? Why, if she was so hurt and angry, was she determined to come along with them?

They plunged once more into the labyrinth of streets and alleyways. Here and there behind a window a rush-light would be burning like some dim star. At one point someone called on them to halt, but as they could not see who it was they took a sharp turning into the darkness and carried silently on their way. The houses seemed to grow ever closer to them and to arch ever more completely above them, until their imaginings suggested that the town was a living organism that closed itself around their helpless bodies and must finally crush the very life from them.

'What does the place look like?' Janie asked.

'Old,' he said. 'Broken down. With an arch beside it.'

'But most of them are like that!'

It was true. Shrouded in darkness, the houses were like rows of funereal sentinels silhouetted against the narrow strip of moonlit sky that was visible between their jettied upper floors and their jutting roofs.

'It's a good question,' Henry put in with a sigh. 'Without knowing the house, the search is futile.'

At this moment, however, Ranulph knew, without quite knowing why, that he had found it. He stopped. A pricking in the nostrils, a tightening of the throat: he was as sure of his instinct as the animals he had known in the forest were certain of theirs.

'This is it. Through this arch. Look: behind that door. That's where I followed the girl.'

A thin shaft of moonlight penetrated a small space in the clustered buildings and drew a silvery line upon the door in question. They drew closer. It was closed tight.

'Hush!' counselled Henry, putting his ear to it. A look of

concern stole across his face. 'Someone's within,' he whispered, 'weeping.'

They all heard it now, a monotonous keening sound, and a rhythmical movement, as of somebody tirelessly rocking to and fro, to and fro.

'The girl,' Ranulph said needlessly. 'Avelina.'

'We'll terrify her,' Henry murmured compassionately. 'How can we?'

But Janie pushed him aside and called softly through the door even as she pushed it open: 'It's me, Janie, a friend. I've come to help you. Don't be frightened.'

They let her go before them, and when at last they followed through the darkened house they found her cradling the girl's head in her arms and crooning softly a mournful song they did not know but which seemed to answer the weeper's sorrow. The sobbing Avelina continued to sway back and forth, hardly flinching when Ranulph and Henry entered the room and crouched beside her.

'Your father,' Henry said after some minutes, 'is dead?'

She nodded.

'And the other man? He's dead, too?'

Ranulph's nose had picked up that foul peppery smell, but it was nothing but a faint, lingering odour now. She shook her head. Old Sourskin had gone.

'In the name of the Father . . .' Henry began to recite.

They sat in the darkness for a long time. The girl's sobbing at last ceased and she slept a little, her head in Janie's lap. When she woke, she began to tell them something of what had passed. She was a simple soul, ignorant, superstitious, unworldly, now fatherless and totally unprotected.

'Come, Avelina,' Henry said, putting out his hand and lifting her to her feet. 'You have friends now. You must come with us.'

He put his arm around her and shepherded her outside. When she stumbled, he drew her closer to him, muttering soft words of comfort.

'Hold tightly, Avelina.'

A fugitive moonbeam lit up the narrow street and Ranulph was surprised to catch a most venomous gleam in Janie's eye.

13 A Public Hanging

They slept late their first morning in Lincoln, and were woken by the sawing of wood and the ringing of hammers. Roger the drummer had friends who lived north of the river under the shadow of the great Norman castle, and the travellers had been given the free use of a large and airy wooden outhouse in which to rest their weary limbs.

Ranulph, not used to lying a-bed, leapt from his mattress of loose straw and pulled away the heavy sacking which curtained a window. On the castle hill men were busy erecting a large wooden structure of a kind he had never seen before. There were sounds further off, too – from the cathedral where, he had seen the previous evening, builders were erecting a spire on one of the three towers.

'The finest cathedral in the land,' old Thomas had told him proudly, pleased to be back in his home city after years on the road. 'Back in my great grandfather's day an earthquake turned it into rubble, but the great St Hugh rebuilt it. Now pilgrims without number flock to his shrine in the Angel Choir.'

'Is it a place of relics?' he had asked urgently, and Henry had broken into the conversation to assure him that it was.

'Tomorrow,' he had promised, 'I shall make enquiries for you. I have contacts among the churchmen here.'

Now, with the warm air of a fine early spring morning on his face, Ranulph wanted nothing but to be outside among the people who were already thronging the streets beneath the castle walls.

'I'll fetch bread and milk,' he offered, stooping to grasp the handle of a small churn.

Henry stirred and rubbed his eyes: 'You'll want money.'

'No, I've enough,' he replied, patting the leather pouch in his pocket and swinging open the heavy door. He stood in the sunlight, blinking, and felt a hand clutch his arm.

'I'll come with you,' Janie said, as bright and alert as he was. She gave a chuckle: 'We'll let these sleeping dogs lie.'

They took a path which soon joined one of the city's main thoroughfares, the castle up high on one side and the cathedral on the other. He felt strangely proud to be walking arm in arm with this salty, mischievous girl, though he knew full well that her choice would have been to be strolling the streets with Henry. Alas, Henry had, as politely as he knew, spurned her ardent advances. That had been the explanation of those tears in her eyes in the inn at the last town, and of Henry's strained expression. She had made her feelings too much known, and the poor, startled would-be monk had shied like a frightened horse. Ranulph had been faintly uneasy to discover these unspoken passions, perhaps because, for the first time in his life, he had become aware of similar stirrings within himself.

'By St Hugh, I'm hungry!' he exclaimed, chiefly in order to break the spell of his musings.

'But let's not hurry back,' Janie urged him. 'There's too much to see. Those lazybones can wait for their breakfast.'

They walked all round the large cathedral, admiring the brightly coloured circular window at the transept's northern end, pausing by the many-sided chapter house where, Thomas had told them, the first King Edward had held several parliaments. They peered at the displays on ramshackle market stalls which stood close by the walls, selling food, clothes, simple children's toys. They bought warm loaves and filled their churn with thick, creamy milk, its foam speckled with the corpses of large flies which had been tempted by the rich odour and had found their feet held fast. Always, though, they were aware of the furious activity across the way on the castle hill, where the foot of a wooden gantry not unlike a huge carpenter's square was being lowered into a deep hole.

'What is it?' he asked.

'A good chance for money-making, I'd say,' she replied mysteriously, leading the way forward.

Groups of people stood watching the workmen at their labour, and it seemed to him that they paid more attention than seemed justified by such a simple operation. The gantry was at length fixed in an upright position and held firm by tongues of wood hammered around its base by heavy mallets.

'Who's it for?' Janie asked a woman who stood close to them, each of her hands grasping the hand of a tiny child.

'Why, Hickey the candlemaker. You don't know?'

'We're strangers here.'

'And lucky to be so with such devils about.'

She moved away, not keen to talk, and Janie turned to a young man who stood picking his teeth with a knife.

'What has this Richard done?' she asked.

The youth raised the knife and made a thrusting motion through the air, a cruel grin showing gaps in his yellow teeth.

'His own mother,' he said. 'Shall I tell you how?'

Janie shook her head and pulled Ranulph away, pausing only to address a girl of about her own age who stood watching the workmen, her arms folded across her chest, her head on one side – for all the world as if expertly assessing the progress of a tray of buns in an oven.

'At what time will they bring him out?'

'A little after noon, I reckon. The bell will ring.'

The realisation of what was to happen seeped only slowly into Ranulph's brain.

'What's going on?' he asked, not really wishing to know.

Janie shook her head, pitying his ignorance: 'A hanging, of course. You haven't seen one before?'

'Never.'

'Large crowds,' she said, 'and a lot of excitement. Very good for business.'

*

By the time they returned to the outhouse Henry and Walt had gone, but the others were ravenous and tore at the bread as if they had seen no food for a month.

'What kept you?' Robert asked, fishing a cluster of dead flies from the milk with bunched fingers and tipping the churn to his lips.

Christopher, a crust in one hand, sat down close to Ranulph, making little noises of contentment. Avelina, still terribly shy, would have eaten nothing whatsoever had old Thomas not thrust some bread upon her.

'We've been finding rich pickings,' Janie said. 'There's a hanging by the castle this afternoon.'

'Ah!' Nicholas agreed, 'A hanging's good.'

Roger nodded: 'And a fine chance for our new entertainers to prove their skills. They'll be on their own soon, and they'll stand or fall by what they've learned.'

Janie's brow puckered.

'Why on their own? Do we go different routes?'

Old Thomas held up an arm with a submissive gesture.

'Not a gentle way of telling,' he conceded, giving Roger a rueful look. 'But we've been talking about our travelling, the four of us here – and not for the first time, Janie, as you know. Speaking for myself, I've had enough of the road, fruitful though the life has been. I'm weary of it, and this is my home town. I'm minded to stay.'

'And me, too,' Roger said swiftly. 'I rediscovered some old friends last night. We climbed the hills together as children. We swam in the river and chased rabbits.'

Janie snorted: 'You imagine you could catch even a lame rabbit today, do you? And you think the authorities will approve of you splashing around under the bridge, shouting and splashing like a ten-year-old? Those days are gone.'

'But I like the place,' Roger said sullenly, 'and that's all there is to it.'

'And you?' Janie demanded, turning to the Welsh brothers with an expression of defiance.

'I long for summer in our hills, look you,' Robert said. 'We haven't enjoyed them for many a season.'

'You wouldn't believe the beauty of those hills,' Nicholas supported him. 'And we've family to see.'

'Family you were glad enough to leave behind you,' she mocked. 'Have they matured in your absence like old wine?'

'That we shall see,' Robert replied simply.

The hostile silence that followed was broken by the arrival of Henry, who looked from face to face with some puzzlement before shaking his head at Ranulph and frowning.

'Believe me,' he said, 'but I've tried. I've been to the cathedral and spoken to at least a dozen deeply learned people in different parts of the city. They have relics here by the score, but nothing like what we're after. It's always the same story: "Try Lindisfarne, try London, try a certain abbey in France". The truth is, nobody knows.'

'Walt went with you?'

'Not him. He speaks proudly of his own contacts, without divulging what kind of men they may be. Feckless friars, I shouldn't wonder. His luck won't be any better than mine, I assure you.'

Ranulph felt despair settle upon his shoulders like some awful bird of prey. Why had he allowed himself to hope? They were destined to travel on and on in search of the impossible, all the while stalked by a loathsome creature with a mission to kill. And soon, when the musicians deserted them, they would lose the protection of numbers, too.

Old Thomas began to play softly on his fiddle, ignoring the hot glare which Janie cast upon him. She crouched in front of Henry.

'Tell me,' she challenged him. 'Are you ready for your first public performance?'

'Tolerably, I suppose. Why do you ask?'

'Because you'll never have a better opportunity to test the skills I've taught you. There's a hanging in Lincoln today.'

'Dear God!' Henry crossed himself. 'An execution?'

'A man who murdered his own mother. The crowds will be enormous.'

'It hardly seems . . .' Henry began. He was a serious young man. He wished to be a monk. It was gross to clown in front of a scaffold. That was what he felt, but he closed his mouth before he could express the thought. He had come on this journey to help Ranulph, and he would not allow himself to be squeamish.

'And after this we're on our own,' Janie said, 'because the musicians are betraying us.'

'Steady on, girl,' Thomas rebuked her. 'We're all wanderers brought together by chance. We're bound by no duties to one another that I know of, save those dictated by common humanity.'

'I call it betrayal,' she insisted. 'We'll have no music for our act.'

There was another silence, broken at last by Nicholas.

'Would you like to learn the recorder, William?' he asked. 'I've a spare one I'd gladly give you.'

'Is it difficult?'

'I could get you started. You'd have to teach yourself the rest.'

'I'd like to,' he said.

He reached out for the proffered instrument and rolled it between his fingers. He placed it between his lips and blew. Nothing happened. Nicholas stooped over him, placing a thumb and two fingers across holes in the barrel, and this time a thin note pierced the air. Everybody laughed.

'Eureka!'

They had been aware of no movement outside, but now the door was flung wide open and Brother Walt stood on the threshhold, his tongue lolling, his eyes gleaming, his forehead glistening with sweat and one hand concealing something under his tunic.

'Eureka!' he repeated, and brought out into the light of day a small bottle with a dull liquid inside it. Enjoying their surprise, he drew closer to Ranulph and tipped the bottle so that a small bead formed at its mouth.

It hung for a second, then dropped and became a spreading stain on the floor, deep crimson.

*

It was an atmosphere such as he had never encountered before. The customary noise and bustle of the crowds was touched by a mounting nervous tension, the unspeakable thing which was going to happen giving their merry-making a fevered intensity. When they laughed, the sound was shorter and harder than usual, abrupt. Their shouting was louder, as if they sought to smother their fear with a wild, unnatural commotion.

These conditions were meat and drink for hucksters, con-men, entertainers. Anything that would distract attention from the empty gibbet, that bare stage to which all heads were magnetically turned, was seized upon with relish. Never mind that the spectators were parted from their hard-earned money, the transaction relieved their over-heated brains from dwelling upon a scene which both excited and appalled.

Ranulph made the final adjustments to his costume, suddenly anxious to be performing. When Walt had produced the precious blood, the life-saving blood, his first reaction had been to forget all thoughts of acting and to travel north immediately. It was the expression in Janie's eye that checked him. Was he about to betray her as the musicians had done? That was the question she had silently asked him, and he had given in at once. There would be time to explain: first they must show that they had been deserving of her hard training.

He watched her expertise in forcing an entry to the milling crowd, reciting loudly to advertise an entertainment, amusing them even as she controlled them:

> *My lords and ladies, listen here,*
> *We'll fiddle and frolic and fetch good cheer.*
> *Only give your goodwill and gather about,*
> *You'll make merry and mirthful without e'er a doubt!*

Roger followed close behind, beating steadily on his drum, and within seconds an invisible arena had opened up within the crowd, an area for performance which she swiftly marked out with brightly-painted wooden squares. Robert and Nicholas skipped into this arena, playing jauntily, and then came Old Thomas, scraping a popular tune on his fiddle. Soon enough it would be time for the apprentice performers to appear: for the moment the music had everyone in thrall. The spectators clapped in time with the drumming, and the livelier souls among them danced on the spot and fluttered their scarves and handkerchiefs.

A rough hand clasped Ranulph's shoulder. It was Christopher, with a a huge beam on his face.

'Dance, Wiwwum!' he said. 'We dance!'

'In a moment, Christopher. Wait for the signal.'

The idiot lad loved taking part in the show, and had quickly learned a succession of actions that might have been considered beyond the powers of his memory. In truth, they had all enjoyed their coaching, even if they would never quite admit it to one another. Only Walt had complained about today's performance, which had evidently taken him completely by surprise. He feigned a sudden and unconvincing illness which Ranulph could not understand. After all, his was the least demanding role – a little nonsense at the end with the goat. Why should he try to escape it? The others forced him to submit.

'Look sharp, Walt,' Henry said to him now. 'We'll be on soon. Time you fetched Hosea's Wife.'

'In a while,' the old man replied, strangely ill at ease. 'No point in hurrying.'

Henry was first on, marking his appearance with a remarkably agile somersault which had the crowd yelling in appreciation. Then he stood before them and produced a bright red ball from out of nowhere. They roared their surprise. He stooped to his boot and brought out a green one. They leapt up and down with innocent pleasure. When he discovered a blue ball in his mouth they could barely contain themselves, their own mouths gaping open in broad smiles which revealed bare gums and carious teeth.

Bowing, he quickly advanced on a stout woman in his audience. Giving her no time to protest, he reached towards her ear and extracted from it a little fan which he fluttered in the air and presented to her with enormous chivalry. The amazement in the crowd was comical to behold. Between their cheering and their stamping they turned to each other in bewilderment, asking how it was possible for a mere mortal to do such things.

Ranulph, taking his eye off Henry for a moment, caught sight of Avelina moving around the spectators with a collecting bag. How shy she was! She never looked people in the eye, but seemed to shuffle around the circle of onlookers in a trance of disabling embarrassment, the bag held out stiffly in front of her.

Why did the sight of her awkwardness touch him so deeply? He knew the answer to that. It was because she reminded him of the peasants in his home village. No, it wasn't only that. She reminded him, too, of *himself* among the rural peasantry. She had been brought up in a town, but it made no difference. People of their sort had no prospects of any advancement in life. You rubbed by as best you could, your diet simple when you had enough to eat, your work hard and little rewarded, your master as likely as not vicious, demanding and uncaring. That was always how it had been for him, not knowing his birthright, and that was how it was for the common millions. You quickly knew not to hope. You knew to keep your place and not cause trouble.

Compare Avelina with the feisty Janie! *There* was a girl who would look anyone in the eye! He watched her jigging to Thomas's fiddle while Henry brought his turn to an end, and he wondered how she had escaped the mire of life which sucked most people in. Certainly her years on the road must have strengthened the pinions of an airborne spirit already determined to fly free.

Then he thought of his own travels, and of how he had learned to lift his cast-down eyes to a level with people who would once have scared him to death. He had discovered a richness of life which his peasant's existence had never even hinted at – new people, new places, new ideas. He journeyed in constant fear of a swift and brutal death, yet felt almost dizzyingly free.

'Pssst! William, you're on!'

Henry alerted him just in time, giving the audience the bonus of a last somersault as a way of covering what would have been a slight, but unprofessional, break in the proceedings.

It was a lucky accident. The applause which greeted it served to waft Ranulph to centre-stage with a feeling of elation rather than the first-time nerves he had secretly been dreading. He executed a neat forwards roll and, in the same movement, scooped up the coloured balls that Henry had discarded. As he began to juggle with them, he gave a sharp nod to Christopher who bounded forward, his arms swinging like the sails of a manic windmill. How the audience howled! He swooped towards Ranulph and one of the balls, falling, caught him full on the head. He fell on his back as if knocked unconscious, his eyes closed, his tongue moving wetly between beaming lips as he lapped up the applause.

Now Ranulph touched one of his feet with his own, and Christopher sat up and took out a handkerchief to mop his brow. It was a huge handkerchief, and seven large dice rolled out of it. More laughter. He collected them together and gave three of them to Ranulph, who began another juggling performance. Each time that he seemed smugly satisfied by his skill, Christopher would nudge him and hand him another. The amazing thing to Ranulph was that something they had rehearsed over and over again in private should actually work in front of a crowd. It more than worked: they loved it, and applauded them to the skies.

The musicians skipped to the centre of the makeshift arena then, and Janie gave the audience another song in her lilting, rasping voice. Henry, Ranulph saw, was gesturing urgently to Walt, who approached in a very hesitant way with the goat on a leash some way behind.

When Janie reached her last verse, which was the cue for the one-time hermit to begin his capers, he still lagged some way off.

'What's the matter with him?' Henry demanded angrily.

'Perhaps he's truly unwell.'

Henry's reply was uncharacteristically severe: 'I'll make him feel pretty sick if he doesn't play his part properly!'

Just in time, Walt broke into a comical little trot, twisting and turning with the leash as if Hosea's Wife was quite impossible to control. Ranulph was aware that something wasn't quite right, but when the old fellow managed to get himself entangled in the rope so that he fell flat on his face he put the niggling feeling out of his mind. The rehearsed act was working well enough: the raucous bellowing of the spectators was proof enough of that.

A bell rang, loudly and solemnly. As the sound died away a second chime reverberated around the castle walls and then, after the same interval, a third. It was a slow, mournful sound, and the mood of the crowd changed in a moment. The man called Hickey was about to be brought out to the scaffold.

The performers had just time enough to complete their show, with a routine that must put a few extra pennies in the bag if only it worked. The idea was to manoeuvre themselves into a line, with Walt at the rear, and for the goat to give her master a good thwack across the backside so that they all toppled to the ground one by one. Ranulph was directly in front of Walt and, after waiting some seconds for an attack that never came, looked over his shoulder in some trepidation.

Hosea's Wife was on her way, but she hobbled. Yes, of course: that was what he had been half conscious of before. She was not well. She seemed to take an age to reach them, and the butt she managed was so weak that Ranulph had to counterfeit its strength by throwing himself against Christopher as if he were a goat himself.

As he lay on the grass, the applause of the crowd in his ears, he watched the poor creature sink to the ground beside him, trembling from the effort. A badly tied bandage, heavily blood-stained, slid from one leg. It revealed a neat cut of a kind that Ranulph had seen before — a cut made by a doctor, lacerating a vein with his surgeon's knife in order to bleed one of his patients.

*

'It was a cruel trick!' he complained for the twentieth time, unable to shake off the mixture of despair and foolishness that had overcome him as he stretched on the ground by the goat and realised what Brother Walt had done.

'With the best intention,' the old man whined. 'Only the best intention.'

They had all retired for the night, and lay on soft straw matting in the darkness of the outhouse.

'Forgiveness, William,' Henry counselled. 'Walt meant well by what he did.'

'Encouraging false hopes that my life might be spared?' he demanded. For the moment, at least, he found it impossible to forgive. 'And what would the Baron have made of a phial of goat's blood? He'd have run me through on the spot!'

'How would he have known?' Walt asked, eager to defend himself. A thought came to him. 'Is there a test for Christ's blood, Henry?'

There was no immediate answer, and the question hovered in the darkness above them.

'If there's no noticeable difference,' Roger's voice rose from a corner, 'why not use what you have?'

'No,' Henry reacted instantly. 'That would be a blasphemy. I could not be a party to counterfeiting our Saviour's blood.'

It had been a bad day for Henry. The hanging had unnerved him. True, life was cheap enough; death was everywhere around them. Nevertheless, he hadn't the stomach for executions. He had hurried away as soon as their performance was over, determined not to even set his eyes upon the condemned man.

Ranulph had seen Hickey the candlemaker. Why concern himself about a man who had committed a crime as vile as that? He had watched the gaolers lead him from the tower by the castle, his hands bound behind him, a clean white shirt tucked into trousers that had rubbed around the dirty floors of a cell for several days. The crowd had at first fallen silent, then growled and brayed.

What drove Ranulph away was the expression on Hickey's face. It was abject defeat. Hopelessness. Submission to fate. The pathetic, cringing humility of the common man. It brought back those thoughts again, about his own peasant sense of worthlessness and his attempts to rise above it. Of course Hickey deserved to hang, but Ranulph saw the crowd exulting in his misery and he fled.

'I know a holy man who'd verify it as Christ's blood,' Nicholas threw in helpfully. 'For a small fee.'

'An abomination!' Henry fumed. 'We'll find the real thing or nothing at all.'

'Or have William stuck through with a sharp knife?' Janie enquired pertly, though she knew full well that Henry was not to be budged.

They all knew his story now. His anger with Walt had loosened his tongue, and one revelation had led to another. They knew about his life in the village, about the evil ploy of Baron Fulke to deprive him of his inheritance, about the long, murderous pursuit the length of England.

'God will provide,' Henry said stoutly.

'Amen,' came Walt's reedy voice.

Ranulph could not believe that God would provide. He was a good Christian, of course, whatever that meant. It meant, as far as he was concerned, that you believed in Mother Church and her teachings, even if you had no clear idea what those teachings were. You believed that there was an Almighty God. You believed in Heaven and Hell. Those things were apparently true without the need to think about them. When he *did* try to think about them he soon became lost. He marvelled at Henry's ability to discuss religious matters, his knowledge of Latin, his blind assurance that God would provide.

He imagined, lying in darkness, that he could smell smoke. Was Hell not as likely a resting place as Heaven for the likes of him?

'We shall pray for your deliverance, William,' Old Thomas said. 'I shall look forward to visiting you in your northern castle.'

'And will you marry your Lady Elizabeth?' Janie's cracked voice broke in. 'Such a fine creature, I'm sure.'

'I've told you, she's betrothed to the baron's son.'

What he had told noone was that he still carried with him the piece of broken brooch that Elizabeth had given him in the moment that he was torn away from her. Occasionally, during these long weeks of travel, his fingers had accidentally come upon it tucked inside his tunic. Always the discovery took him by surprise. She seemed a creature from a fairy story, beautiful but utterly distant. It was a strange thing to hear her talked about now.

'A mere technicality,' Janie laughed.

Was that smoke imaginary? He sat up, his nostrils twitching.

'But first,' Robert said, 'we have to help you find Old Sourskin. You're sure he's still following you?'

'It's inevitable,' Henry said emphatically.

'Unless,' Walt threw in, 'he was mortally wounded by Avelina's father. We don't know what happened to him. We may be safe after all.'

At this moment Ranulph leapt to his feet and rushed in the darkness towards the door.

'Fire!' he yelled.

Amazing to think that the smoke had been only a suspicion a few seconds ago, because now it rose all around him and he could hear the greedy crackle of flames. He pushed at the door, then barged at it with his shoulder.

'Can't breathe,' he heard Janie gasp.

'Hurry!' Thomas cried.

Ranulph kicked and heaved and pummelled, then turned to face them, a tremor in his voice: 'It's no good,' he said. 'Someone's shot the bolt – we're trapped inside!'

14 Fiery Furnace

There were two windows in the outhouse, but when they ripped the sacking away from them the smoke billowed inside, sharp and acrid in their throats. The fire seemed to have caught the building on all sides.

'Stand back!' shouted Roger, and he took a running jump at the window nearest the door and hauled himself into it. He stood framed in it for a moment and then dropped back inside.

Impossible: anyone going through there would be roasted.

It was a scene of utter panic, with fists hammering on slatted walls, voices raised in prayer to the Virgin Mary, the tearing sound of the advancing flames growing more furious by the second. In all this confusion, however, Thomas had the presence of mind to collect the players' instruments together and hurl them through the second window into the safety of the yard beyond.

'Here, Roger!' he called. 'There may be a way!'

His son now took a run at the second window, clutching desperately at the frame and almost toppling into the swirling smoke beyond.

The fire was already devouring one wall, throwing a bright light against the grey drifts of smoke. Ranulph saw Christopher, his eyes rolling with fear, fingers in his mouth, running round and round in little circles, whimpering. Avelina stood impassively, stoically, watching the advancing flames as if it was her destiny to perish in them and she could do nothing whatsoever about it. Not really thinking what he was doing, he plunged his outdoor cloak into the butt they used for drinking water and threw it over her head and shoulders.

'This way, Avelina!' he commanded her, leading her to the window from which Roger now jumped back into the building.

'The smoke is dense,' he said, 'but I don't think the flames have spread here yet. Hurry!'

He took one of Avelina's arms and Ranulph the other, and they lifted her and practically hurled her out of the window.

'Are you safe, Avelina?' Ranulph bawled.

The furnace was seething around them, but he heard her faint 'yes' even as he turned towards Janie, who seemed close to collapse. They dispatched her in a similar fashion and next bellowed for Walt, who weighed nothing at all.

'Hosea's Wife!' the old fellow bleated as he picked himself up from the ground. 'Where are you?'

Christopher was the next to go. He was almost numb with fright, and too heavy for Ranulph and Roger to manage by themselves. Robert and Nicholas helped support him and they pushed him out like a huge sack of turnips.

'Wiwwum!' he cried.

'In a moment, Christopher,' Ranulph shouted back at him. 'Get away from the smoke.'

Old Thomas closed his eyes while they manhandled him to the opening, his lips murmuring what sounded like a prayer. There was no doubt in Henry's case. He stood with his hands clasped together reciting Hail Marys, and Robert had to shake him and then kick him up the backside before he would consent to leave.

'If it is God's will,' he intoned as the Welsh brothers rocked him off his feet, ran at the window and dropped him into the maelstrom of churning smoke.

Breathing was difficult now. Nicholas had soaked rags in water, and they clutched them to their faces, but their lungs were already swimming with the poisonous stuff and they scarcely had the energy to move. Since Roger and Ranulph still stood by the window, they instinctively reached for Robert and then Nicholas, lifting them up with the greatest of effort so that

Ranulph felt that his back would break in two and his chest ignite.

'Now you!' Roger said, and he bent his knee so that Ranulph could use the thigh as a stepping stone.

'But how will you —?'

'Get out!'

He clambered up and, in his panic to escape, struck his head against the window surround. He fell to the earth outside and was aware of smoke and creeping flames and yet more smoke, smoke which invaded every pore of his being, before his eyes closed and he lost consciousness.

*

He came to propped against the nearest building. The air was still heavy, but teams of fire-fighters had been at work, and the blackened remains of the outhouse smoked wispily under a night sky of flecked cloud.

'Thank God, William,' Henry exclaimed fervently, seizing his hand and pressing it. 'I thought for a moment you were gone.'

All around them there was the sombre activity of people reclaiming what they could from the wreckage. Old Thomas sat silently stringing his fiddle, bright tears in his eyes. Janie stared into space, shaking: he thought never to have seen her in so wretched a state. Christopher, by contrast, seemed almost to have forgotten his ordeal, strolling about the yard looking closely at anything that caught his eye.

'Wiwwum!' he cried now, running forward and crouching by his friend. He put his cheek against Ranulph's.

Walt cradled the goat in his arms, murmuring sweet nothings in her ear. The blackened end of the animal's tether revealed how she had managed to escape burning.

'Roger,' Ranulph suddenly remembered. 'Where's Roger?'

'Inside the house,' Henry said very gently.

'How is he?'

Henry winced: 'The smoke was dense. I think perhaps he lost his way in there, and lacking the strength . . .'

There was no need to say anything more. Ranulph felt sick at heart. Although nothing had been said, he was sure that the fire was no accident. He should have run away from his friends long ago, They didn't deserve to share his dangers. Why should they? He felt as if he were a murderer.

'You see where the fire caused most damage,' Henry said, seeming to read his mind. 'Bales of straw were placed against the building and set alight, but one small stretch of wall was spared. It was as if that window was intended to be our only way out. Why should that be?'

Ranulph tried to imagine his enemy lurking outside, setting fire to the building and watching the window.

'Because,' he said after some consideration, 'he knew we would have to come out one by one. Does that make sense?'

'It does! But you, surely, were the target – and here you are. I don't understand it.'

'And everyone's here?'

'I think so, yes.' Henry looked around him, mentally making marks on a list. 'Walt, Christopher, Janie . . . Avelina!'

'She's gone?'

'I don't remember seeing her. Walt, have you seen Avelina?'

Nobody had seen her, but the first fire-fighter on the scene told of witnessing something that did seem rather curious in retrospect: he'd been too busy at the time to think about it. The first person to be rescued had hurried away from the smoke only to be seized by two men and swiftly carried away. He had thought they were friends giving a helping hand.

'But, of course!' Ranulph cried. 'She was wearing my cloak – they thought it was me!'

'Dear God,' breathed Henry. 'What will have become of the girl?'

'We must find her,' Ranulph said desperately, but when he tried to climb to his feet his legs gave way and he fell flat on his back. 'Please, Henry.'

'In the morning,' Henry said. 'We've no chance of finding her in the hours of darkness, not in a city like Lincoln. We'll get some sleep and set off as soon as we wake. If they realised their mistake soon enough she should be safe.'

And if they didn't? If they didn't?

Ranulph fell asleep with the terrible thought that he might have two deaths on his conscience.

*

They decided to split up in the morning, the better to cover the city as quickly as possible, although not before Walt had made a suggestion which immediately brought a tumult of abuse about his head.

'It's possible,' he mused, 'that Avelina might prefer to remain in the city, since she's accustomed to urban life. In which case, we could ourselves depart the sooner . . .'

'And leave her here, to the mercy of such people?' Henry exploded. 'What a vile proposal!'

'She suffered with us,' Ranulph said hotly, 'and deserves our protection.'

'Would you leave your stupid goat in such circumstances?' Janie demanded, bristling.

'No, no, no, no,' trilled the old man. 'Don't misunderstand me. Merely a thought to provoke a spirit of comradeship. Just what I intended. Let us venture forth.'

They bade an affectionate farewell to Old Thomas, who had a most sombre task of his own to see to. The Welsh brothers, vowing to delay their return to the land of their fathers until such time as Avelina should be discovered, set off to search the eastern part of the city. Henry took Walt in tow ('to prevent him absconding') and headed west. Ranulph, Christopher and Janie were to cross the river by the ancient bridge and patrol the tenements there.

'But no heroics,' Henry insisted, arranging a meeting place and time. 'If we find her, we must plan a rescue operation together. These are dangerous people.'

The sun was high in the sky and shone warmly on the walls the Romans had built to protect their city of Lindum. Normally Ranulph would have enjoyed walking here, admiring the prospect of the castle, watching birds skimming low over the river. Today, however, even the presence of Janie by his side failed to lift his spirits. Although he remained in a state of exhaustion after last night's fire, his gloom had quite another cause -- the knowledge of the danger he had brought to his friends.

'When we have found Avelina you must leave us,' he told Janie.

'I'm to be exiled?' she asked with a grin.

'It isn't safe to be with me. Henry says we make for Coventry next. Isn't that where you come from?'

'Once upon a time. Nobody there will know me now.'

'Your parents?'

'No, I think I was born without any.' She laughed, that broken little laugh. 'I've no reason to stop in Coventry.'

'It would be better for you.'

She pursed her lips: 'You'd rather I did that? You don't like my company?'

He blushed and said nothing. In truth, he was afraid of saying something stronger than he would wish to say. He did like her company, in a way that made him uneasy.

'All life is dangerous,' she stated, bringing the subject to an abrupt close.

The buildings by the river were huddled together as if to keep the chill and damp at bay. Those closest to it had deep cellars for storing goods brought to the city by boat, and Ranulph thought how easy it would be to lower someone into those depths and bring the heavy doors down tight. They would never find her if she was in a place like that.

A little further on they came to a warren of narrow streets, with jettied houses almost brushing each other at first floor level. They slowed their pace, peering down every alley, looking in every window. Christopher, as was his wont, stared fixedly at anything which took his fancy, so that they had to drag him away in order not to attract suspicion.

'Do you think,' she asked him, 'that Henry has been a little warmer to me of late?'

'I don't know. I haven't noticed.'

'He was angry with me before, you know.'

Ranulph felt that he could do without this conversation: 'Was he?'

'I didn't like making him angry. He's so sweet.'

Christopher spared him further agonies by pointing to a house they were passing and crying in a loud voice 'Avleena! Avleena!'

'What is it, Christopher?' Ranulph asked, trying to hush him. 'There's nothing there.'

'Avleena!'

It was a derelict building in a terrace of ramshackle dwellings. The wall plaster was cracked. The roof was thatched and in bad need of repair. Up high, where Christopher pointed, there was a slatted window, and a length of cloth fluttered from it in the breeze.

'What's he thinking of?' Ranulph wondered, fixing his gaze upon it. It was a broad band, green and purple.

Janie gasped: 'He's right! That's Avelina's girdle.'

'You're sure? You know the colour?'

'Of course.' There was a hint of derision in this reply, as if to say that men never noticed such things. 'But how he recognised it at such a distance I'll never understand. Well done, Christopher!'

The gauche lad skipped from one foot to the other in his pleasure at receiving such fulsome praise. But he quietened down. He could tell from the tone of their voices that it was a time for secrecy and caution.

'We should go back for Henry and the others,' Ranulph mouthed softly.

'And leave Avelina here a moment longer?' Janie challenged, the hoarseness of her voice emphasised by her whispering. 'Anything might happen while we're gone.'

'You're prepared to risk going in there?'

She nodded, and her courage reinforced his own. There was an open porch at the foot of the house, with steps leading up inside. They stationed Christopher there, despite his protests.

'We'll only be a moment,' Ranulph comforted the mewling lad. 'If we had to leave in a hurry you'd fall down the stairs.'

'Janie will give you a big hug afterwards,' the girl told him – and this promise calmed him in a trice.

Climbing the steps, Ranulph was immediately aware of a familiar smell, a sour smell. He could scarcely go on for the feeling of terror which turned his legs to jelly, his feet to ice, but the closeness of Janie behind him forced him upwards though the stench grew worse.

They came to a landing with three rooms off it, each with a closed, ill-fitting door. All was quiet. They continued stealthily higher to another landing, with a matching set of doors.

'Is it here?' Janie asked in his ear.

'No. A flight further yet, I think.'

They climbed more slowly now, fearful of what they might find as the steps spiralled to the upper landing. The house was narrower here, and there was but a single room above them. The door was similar to those below, but there was a heavy iron bar across it. Ranulph put his ear against the wood, straining to hear. He caught Janie's enquiring glance and shook his head. Nothing.

Did he dare? He put his knuckles against the door and gave three sharp raps.

Silence.

He rapped again, and this time there was a movement on the other side. A low voice spoke: 'Who is it?'

'Avelina, is that you? It's William and Janie.'

'Oh, yes it's me,' came Avelina's woeful voice. 'Please let me out of here.'

The bar lifted away from two stout hooks set into the wall, but the door was locked and the key had been taken away.

'Stand back, Avelina,' Ranulph warned her. 'I'm going to try to smash it down.'

He turned a shoulder towards the door and threw himself at it. He was aware of both a sharp pain and a tiny splintering sound. The woodwork was, as he had hoped, old and weak. He attacked it with his shoulder again and then raised a boot to kick at it as hard as he could. A hole appeared, with Avelina's eyes peering through it.

'Nearly,' he said. 'Back a little!'

This time he ran at it and launched himself into the air with both feet in front of him. The wood broke with a great crack, and he came to earth half inside the room and half on the landing. Avelina stooped to help him up and, to his utter amazement, planted a kiss full on his lips.

'Wiwwum!'

Christopher's cry from down below was followed by the

most almighty din, as if two wild beasts had met in combat. Ranulph was through the gap in the door and half-way down the first flight of steps before either of the girls appeared to be aware of what was happening. *He* knew. He knew that a certain foul-smelling man with a knife had found poor, unprotected Christopher at the entrance to the house, and he dashed down-stairs to the sound of his innocent friend's scarcely human bellowings mingled with the ragings of the other, the pursuer, the killer. He felt in these terrible moments no fear for himself, only the helplessness of one who knows he must arrive too late.

'I'm coming!'

There was noone at the foot of the steps. The furious commotion continued outside, and he rushed through the porch expecting to find a trail of blood with a large, ungainly body slumped at the end of it.

'Wiwwum!'

His appearance only served to distract Christopher's attention, otherwise he would surely have strangled the unfortunate creature who had dared to attack him. Ranulph, his nose picking up the familiar stale stench, took in with amazement the discarded belt with its knife, ripped powerfully from the body of its owner; the shirt torn to shreds; the puce-coloured face of the man whose neck was clamped in the vice of a powerful forearm.

Even as he approached, however, Christopher slackened his grip and Sourskin wriggled free, gasping desperately for air. He was gone along the street and down an alley before Ranulph could reach him.

'Bad man, Wiwwum!'

Christopher, breathing deeply, tried to communicate his indignation through a succession of sounds which were as eloquent as they were indecipherable. He re-enacted the highlights of his violent encounter, waving his fists and bringing back an arm in a hurling motion. When he saw Janie emerging from the house with Avelina, however, he at once fell silent, his lips breaking into a vast smile.

Shambling forward, he claimed the hug that was his due reward.

*

'I want no more of towns and cities,' Ranulph complained to Henry when they all met up again. 'The dangers are too well hidden. Let's forget Coventry.'

'But it's one of England's four great cities,' Henry replied. 'York, Coventry, Bristol, London – we'll have looked for your relic in three of them.'

'And been at constant risk of being murdered in all three.'

'A flying visit, I promise. We'll stop at no towns in between.'

'Only at village inns,' Ranulph countered sardonically, 'where cut-throats lie in wait down dark corridors, or kidnappers arrive at the dead of night.'

'No,' Henry said with a bright smile, 'not even country inns. I've a surprise for you.'

He led the way past the cathedral to a part of the city where the buildings were more scattered. A little way beyond were huge fields, divided into strips for farming. Here there were a few barns, with ducks and chickens pecking for food in the dirt, and as they turned a corner Henry held out a hand as if to introduce them to his little secret. All Ranulph saw was a sturdy brown horse with a white mane, hitched to a large waggon.

'There he is,' Henry said simply.

'There's who?'

'Don't know his name, but he's ours. I spent the last of my money on him, so he'd better be as sturdy as he looks.'

They all clustered round the horse, which seemed the most placid of creatures, enjoying a good pat on the neck and quite unperturbed by the flies which buzzed around his head.

'There's a good bit of Welsh blood in that one,' Nicholas said, admiringly. 'A bit bigger than those we get on the hills, Robert, but the same hardy stock, eh?'

'I'd say his grandfather grazed on our slopes,' Robert agreed. 'Best call him Taffy, don't you think?'

'Taffy,' Janie repeated. 'I like that. Will you be Taffy, Taffy?'

He was Taffy. Henry explained that the cart was big enough to carry the whole party and their possessions, and that they could sleep in or under it as the mood took them. No more country inns. They were independent.

'All we need,' he said, 'is enough money from our entertainments to feed ourselves and the horse.'

'Phouah!' complained Walt grumpily, his nose put out of joint. 'Can't it content itself with grass like Hosea's Wife? You'll spoil the great ugly beast.'

They said their farewells to the Welsh brothers and clambered aboard. Henry volunteered to take the reins first, although he had no more experience than the rest of them, and Christopher clamoured to be up alongside him, where he proceeded to wave madly at every passer-by. Ranulph, Janie, Avelina and Walt made themselves comfortable in the back, while the goat trotted along behind, tethered to the waggon.

It was a beautiful warm afternoon, and once they had left the city behind Ranulph reached for his recorder and put it to his lips. Nicholas had already taught him the basic skills and, though he often enough produced a piercing shriek rather than a pure note, he was already learning which fingers to use in order to play the tunes he knew. He was surprised to find that Janie, although she was inclined to close her eyes and pull a face when he went horribly wrong, was full of encouragement.

When he managed the chorus of *Lovers met in May-o* she at once joined in, singing gently at the slow pace dictated by his beginner's playing.

Did Avelina know the song, too? He thought he saw her lips move along with Janie's, but when he winked at her she blushed and turned away.

'It *will* soon be May-o,' Janie exclaimed as they trundled along a track between tall hedges, 'and I can't think of a better thing to be doing!'

Christopher clearly felt the same, for he jiggled about on his seat clapping his hands and crooning unintelligible anthems until Henry, laughing, said he would either be sick or overturn the waggon or both and ought to have a rest in the back.

'Whoa, Taffy!' he cried, but Christopher hadn't understood that the operation was better carried out while in a stationary position, and he toppled into the back and all but crushed the life out of poor Walt. (The ensuing language was not, Henry thought, fitting for a former hermit.) Ranulph took his place on the driving-board and was soon restless to hold the reins.

'If you promise not to take us off at a gallop,' Henry consented severely, standing rather precariously to change positions with him.

But he had no need of those excitements. Sitting up behind the horse, watching that thick neck and heavy head nod and rise, nod and rise, he thought that he had never been more contented in his life. The sun warmed his face, the wheels crunched comfortably on the roadway and he was with the best friends he had ever known.

Of course, he knew that he was allowing himself a moment's holiday from fear. Had one of his friends not been killed but a few hours since? Had another not been carried off to a prison room and used as bait to trap him? Was a man not stalking him even now, with a mission to take him dead or alive?

So be it. For this short spell, at least, he would be happy. He grinned at Henry and flicked the reins, ever so gently.

'Careful,' Henry said, but he was happy, too.

The landscape for a while became flat and empty, but as the sun began to go down they came towards what looked like an extensive forest. They stopped a little way short of it and took shelter under an outlying pair of oak trees. Henry unharnessed Taffy, tethered him to one of the trees and gave him fodder. Walt tended to Hosea's Wife. Janie and Avelina went for a stroll to stretch their legs and Christopher helped Ranulph arrange the bedding. The girls and Walt were to sleep in the waggon, the other three beneath it.

'Safer than the treacherous inns?' Henry smiled as they prepared for sleep.

'And the air far sweeter,' Ranulph said, his eyes already beginning to close.

It was his soundest sleep for many weeks, and when he awoke under an April sky of the lightest blue, with blackbirds and thrushes warbling in the trees, he felt that he had been washed clean of all his troubles.

They were all in a lightsome mood. You could tell it from the way Janie stretched herself before the glimmering sun. You could see it in the bounce that energised Walt's old legs. You could even glimpse it in Avelina's eyes which, rather than bashfully looking away, gazed at everything and everyone around her with a kind of disbelieving gratitude.

It was something of shock, therefore, when Henry uttered a loud exclamation and strode to the side of the waggon. They gathered round him, staring at a large piece of white cloth which had been affixed to the woodwork with a dagger.

He stretched it out. Daubed across it in an ochre dye was a crude representation of a stag's head transfixed by an arrow.

15 Fellow Travellers

Their eyes scanned the forest edge, expecting a movement between the trees, a tell-tale rustling from the undergrowth. Nothing. Ranulph angrily tore the cloth from the waggon, starting back in alarm as the dagger came with it and fell with a thud to the dust of the track.

The freshness of the morning was instantly gone. No sun could penetrate the clouds that gathered in their minds. Ranulph felt his eyes filling with tears of fear and frustration, and he threw the material from him as if recoiling from a leper.

Henry sought to comfort him, laying a hand on his shoulder, while Walt stooped to gather the dagger and blew the dust from it. The oak leaves shook delicately, catching the sunlight on their upper surfaces and tossing it around as if it were a handful of newly minted coins.

'Courage,' Henry said queasily.

'Frightened!' Christopher blurted.

They made hurried preparations to leave, saying nothing, looking about them all the while. As they urged the horse forward, the waggon creaking noisily with every rut it crossed, they rehearsed the desperate safety plan they had devised some days before: that the party should at all times keep together; that they should trust nobody; that they should always have daggers to hand, however poorly they might be able to use them; that they should travel only in the hours of daylight, finding a secure spot to spend the night.

One again Ranulph protested that they were foolishly endangering their five innocent lives for his sake, and yet again they chorused their determination to see the business through.

All their journey the road flanked the great forest, and when, at times, it closed in on the other side, too, seeming to engulf them, they flicked the reins more urgently, anxious to escape its menacing confines.

It was a busy road, and other travellers often slowed or increased their own pace in order to accompany them for part of the way. On the first day a fat merchant on a large white horse enthralled them for hours with tales of far-off ports, of castles which almost touched the sky and of strange beasts which no Englishman could ever expect to see in his own country. One of these creatures, he insisted, stood as tall as a mature elm tree and had eyes in the palms of its hands.

'And its feet?' demanded Janie, with a mischievous grin. 'To see where it's been?'

'No. In its hands, I assure you. How far have you travelled that you should doubt me?'

'Oh, I've met creatures strange enough here at home,' she countered lightly, and might have carried her teasing too far had Henry not given her a sharp pinch on the thigh. He envied Janie her easy disbelief of tall tales and superstitions. Although he clung to the sound doctrines of Mother Church, he found it distressingly difficult to discredit another man's beliefs.

On the second day they caught up with a summoner, who stretched his legs to keep abreast of them as they journeyed between two hamlets. He seemed affable enough, but Brother Walt evidently feared that their many sins would be discovered and that they would be reported to the Archdeacon. Who knew what might follow: heavy fines, imprisonment, even excommunication . . .

'We pray regularly,' Walt assured him earnestly. 'We stop the waggon six times a day for services, don't we friends? And we give alms to all the poor we meet.'

At this the summoner produced his purse and began to talk meaningfully of the fines he had levied in recent weeks for immorality, witchcraft and the refusal to pay tithes.

'There's many a scoundrel,' he told them, shaking his head, 'will excuse himself payment to the Church because the Pestilence has taken his workers or his family or his beasts. We know how to deal with such people.'

'Always paid our tithes, haven't we?' Walt urged his companions, with a nervous little laugh. 'And a little extra besides for the Kingdom of Heaven on earth.'

'And the land is full of reckless men and loose women it's a pleasure to drag before the ecclesiastical court.'

'Only clean and righteous living here,' chimed in Walt.

'And blasphemers . . .'

'God rot them all!' declaimed the old man fervently.

'And usurers . . .'

'Our money is given freely or not at all.' Here Walt fished in his tunic and brought out a coin which he dropped in the summoner's purse. 'Praise the Lord!'

'I've enjoyed your company,' the summoner concluded, at once slackening his stride and quickly falling behind them.

On the third day they fell in with a herbalist, an elderly fellow with a spindly frame, a goatee beard and a slurred and murmuring speech that perhaps owed something to the contents of the phials which, strung along a festoon of chains, dangled from his scrawny neck.

'To rid the heart of its poisons,' he said, unhooking one and holding it out to Avelina. 'Powder of tormentil.'

Rather than flinch from this approach, as they might have expected, Avelina put her nose to the phial before handing it back.

'Not strong enough for your poisons?' Janie queried wickedly.

Avelina gave her a searching look: 'I know the value of these potions,' she said. 'I have used them.'

She spoke with such unusual authority that Janie was for once reduced to silence.

'A little something for an aching throat?' the herbalist suggested to Janie, not realising that her cracked tones were entirely natural. 'This tincture of dandelion and horehound, perhaps?'

She sniffed at it and pulled a face: 'And what would I need to cure me of *that*?' she grinned.

Ranulph, however, shook his head.

'Dandelion and horehound, certainly,' he said, 'but there's more besides, surely, master herbalist?'

'Ah!' The old man leant closer. 'And what does your witty nose pick out in the potion, my young animal?'

'I smell knapweed,' Ranulph replied simply.

The herbalist's eyes opened in shock.

'Hearty congratulations,' he said at last, holding out his hand. 'I've never known that done before.'

They shook hands, Ranulph beaming all over his face with pleasure.

'My name's Geoffrey, young sir,' the old man said. 'And yours?'

'William.

'Well, William, I think we'll put you further to the test . . .'

He released the stopper from another of his little bottles and held it under Ranulph's nose.

'Herb-robert.'

'Indeed, for disorders of the blood. But that was easy, was it not. Who could mistake old Stinking Bob? Try this one.'

'Willowherb,' Ranulph said, just as quickly.

'Good, good! Now this.'

Ranulph sniffed more carefully this time.

'Sainfoin . . ..' he decided, pausing.

'Yes, yes?'

'. . . and spotted medick.'

'Otherwise known as Calvary clover, do you know, for those

drops of Christ's blood upon its leaves. I tell you friends,' he addressed them all, 'this young man has the rarest of gifts. He has genius. I've never known the like of it before. How would you fancy a job with me, William?'

'Thank you,' Ranulph laughed, 'but I'm well satisfied with the life I have.'

'But how do you earn your bread?'

'We're entertainers. Listen!' And he picked up his recorder and played a snatch of tune.'

'A wasted talent, alas,' Geoffrey lamented, 'your nose.'

He walked with them for another hour, mixing his salesman's patter with the occasional challenge to Ranulph which was always triumphantly met. By the time he bade them a cheerful farewell, Walt had been parted from his money once (a sure remedy for the curse of old age, he was told) and Henry twice over, once for a condition of his own, which he blushingly refused to reveal, and a second time for Avelina, who had become uncharacteristically enthralled by a potion designed to calm the nerves.

'A fool,' Janie said pointedly, 'is soon parted from his money.'

She was sitting up alongside Henry, who held the reins, the others sitting in the back behind them. The waggon lurched and swayed along the dusty road, and nobody spoke for a while. Henry had been slow to recognise Janie's feelings for him, but it was obvious that his gift to Avelina had infuriated her.

'These herbalists are very clever people,' he said, attempting to mollify her.

'At parting fools from their money.'

'With many effective remedies.'

'For curing their own poverty at the expense of fools.'

There was another silence, eventually broken by Avelina.

'Thank you, Henry, for my potion,' she said softly. '*I* believe in its power.'

Janie snorted: 'And there speaks one of the biggest fools!'

She had gone too far, of course, but her spirited pride would never allow her to apologise. She sat glaring into space, her chin thrust out against the world. Avelina's face darkened and her features settled into a permanent frown.

'Fool,' echoed Christopher, liking the word. It seemed to fill his mouth. 'Fooooool.'

'I know what I speak of,' Avelina said.

They camped for the night on a small mound a little way from the road. The sky was clear, and a moon grown almost to fullness drenched the landscape in a soft ivory light. From this spot they could see travellers in either direction, and it would be almost impossible for an assailant to surprise them. Taffy was unhitched from the waggon and tethered to a stake nearby. They ate their supper and watched the stars overhead until tiredness stole into their limbs and it was time to sleep.

'In you get, William,' Henry commanded gently, hoisting him up. 'No nonsense!'

Ranulph shrugged his shoulders and climbed in. It had been decided unanimously that he should always sleep in the protection of the waggon, since he was the target of their pursuers. Janie, Avelina and Walt would share this space, while Henry and Christopher spread themselves underneath, between the wheels. For some time Ranulph had protested that he needed no special treatment, but tonight rebellion came from another source.

'I can't sleep alongside *her*,' Janie said truculently.

The two women had spent the past hours with never a word to one another, and there was a murderous atmosphere between them now.

'No, no,' Henry said helplessly. 'That's unreasonable.'

'I shan't!' Janie declared.

'Then . . .'

But Avelina made the decision for him. She gathered her blankets, pushed her way out of the waggon and jumped down to the ground.

'I'll sleep underneath,' she said.

Henry thought of protesting, but could think of no better solution.

'There's room, isn't there?' she asked, shaking her blankets out.

There was a determined strength in her that he had never seen before.

'Yes, Avelina, of course there's room.'

He created a space between himself and Christopher. Nothing more was said about it. Henry knelt to pray for their deliverance and then the waggon was wrapped in silence. It had been a hard day, and they very quickly fell into a deep sleep.

When they awoke the next morning, however, Avelina had gone.

*

'It's impossible that she was taken by force,' Henry insisted. They had called loudly for some minutes, with no answer but a soft breeze among the trees. 'She lay no more than a hand's breadth from me. Did you hear anything, Christopher? Was anyone here?'

The lad only shook his head, which was still muzzy from a deeper sleep than he had enjoyed for many a long night.

Ranulph had until now said nothing. The others, while they were shouting Avelina's name, had seen him bent low to the ground like a foraging animal following a spoor. He had wandered as far as the forest's edge, and he now returned, sniffing the air.

'Do you smell that sweetness?' he asked.

Walt grinned ruefully, showing his gums: 'My poor old nose lost its powers long ago,' he said. 'Though often enough I'm glad of that.'

'I smell something, I think,' Henry said. 'It's not the foliage or flowers on the trees?'

'No, no, much stronger,' Ranulph assured him. Indeed, it flooded his sensitive nostrils. 'It's a mixture of essences, and I don't recognise them all. There's meadowsweet . . .'

He tried to savour them one by one: 'And that faint apple stench is willowherb . . . and there's poppy . . . and, yes, I sense the plant we call at home enchanter's nightshade.'

Was it this last name which disturbed them? They all felt at once that Avelina had not willingly left them, however hard it was to believe that she had been snatched.

'We must press on quickly,' Brother Walt suddenly blurted, the dagger shaking dangerously in his grasp. Then he added, as if to cover his own lack of courage, 'God told me so in a prayer last night.'

'Pshaw!' Janie guffawed.

'No,' Henry said. 'We must try to find her, aren't we all agreed? We can't possibly leave Avelina here in the forest alone.'

This time Janie remained silent.

'My nose will guide us,' Ranulph said. 'I'm sure she passed between those two ash trees.'

'Then we'll follow her trail,' Henry decided. 'Until the middle of the day, shall we say? If we keep together we'll be safe. Does anyone wish to stay behind?'

Janie's contemptuous answer to a question she must have supposed directed at herself was to snatch a stave from the waggon, to set off down the slope to where the forest began and to begin carving her way into its greenery, sweeping aside low branches and dense bushes with a violence better reserved for their hidden enemy. Or was she, in her secret thoughts, giving Henry a drubbing for caring about that stupid peasant creature with her long silences and her meek and deferential ways?

'Quick, follow her!' Henry called. 'Arm yourselves. Fan out, but don't lose contact.'

He pulled a dagger from his jerkin and ran down the hill in pursuit. Christopher, who during this whole episode had been a silent and confused witness, joined the chase with enthusiasm, running closely behind Ranulph and crying 'Wiwwum wun, wiwwum wun! I catch, I catch!' The rear was brought up by a far less enthusiastic Walt, terrified by the dagger in his own hand let alone that of their enemy. He felt old and foolish, ill-equipped to participate in this mad escapade, with his weak and spindly legs threatening to fold under him at each hard footfall of the descent to the enveloping trees.

*

Once they had been swallowed by the forest, held in its green maw, the search seemed less heady and more fraught with danger. As they shouldered their way through bushes and waded through nettles and bracken, Henry became horribly aware that his brave declaration of loyalty to Avelina had perhaps led them all into danger. Sound was muffled among all that vegetation, and his plea not to lose contact proved difficult to achieve.

Somewhere to his left, and out of sight, Janie filled the air with wild oaths and curses, apparently aimed at the willowy branches which whipped against her face but wide enough in their scattering for Henry to feel their sting. Over to the right Ranulph moved silently, the forest to him a second home. But his silence was irrelevant because Christopher crunched along beside him, whispering loudly the whole time 'What we do, Wiwwum? Where we go, Wiwwum?'

Ranulph, following that sweet smell which was now overlaid by a hundred other fragrances, had the occasional sighting of Walt through the trees to his right. Better, surely, that the old man had stayed in his hermitage, however tedious he found the life. What would be his reward for remaining faithful to Ranulph's cause? To be permanently hunted? To suffer a grim and premature death? Poor Walt! Every branch seemed determined to balk his progress, every root to trip his feet, as he stumbled forward, mumbling incoherently and waving his dagger at the pressing foliage as if the whole of nature were his enemy.

'Tired, Wiwwum. Tired!'

Christopher had ground to a halt.

'Then go back and guard the waggon, old friend. You look after the horse.'

'Feed Taffy, Wiwwum?'

'Yes, Christopher. Feed Taffy. You see the way there – the light through the trees?' The boy nodded his head vigorously. 'Go now, Christopher, and don't lose your way.'

He felt a sense of relief as he heard those clumsy feet crashing back along their path through the forest, though after the incident at Lincoln he had no fears about the lad's capacity to protect himself if need be.

'Walt,' he called. 'Do you think you should go with Christopher? He has the strength of an ox, but I think he could do with the speed of your wits if he finds himself in danger.'

The old man stopped and turned in an instant.

'Must I miss the excitement of the chase?' he demanded, already retracing his steps. 'Oh well, if you insist. Why, how could I put my own pleasure before the safety of our addle-pated friend? Are you sure you don't need me? Right, I'll be back at the waggon when you return. But don't hesitate to call should you need me. I'm armed and ready.'

This whole speech was delivered without a pause, and it was with an almost audible sigh of relief that Walt began to follow Christopher back to the open sunshine and the comfort of the waggon.

Ranulph now relaxed, and the forest began to weave its magic. The fears and anxieties that had so recently held him prisoner fell away, to be replaced by the comforts of nature: the wonderful summery smell of nettles crushed beneath his feet, the cool green light, filtered through a million leaves, the buzz of insects following their strange and timeless ways.

To his left he could still see Henry, and he called to tell him where Walt and Christopher had gone.

'Wait for me!' was the reply.

*

At what point he lost contact with Henry it was hard for him to recall afterwards. He was so intent on following the trail of sweetness that he imagined Henry and Janie must be close behind him. Enough to say that the odour now became much stronger and that, for a second only, he fancied that he saw the movement of loose clothing among the trees some way ahead.

The ground shelved to a small river. He crossed it by a fallen tree trunk, mossy and slippery in the deep shadows. Beyond it, as he climbed away from its rich, clinging mud, the forest thickened. He could no longer hear the others now. This part of the forest seemed darker, colder and utterly silent, as if even the birds refused to sing.

Then he heard a woman's voice: 'William.'

No, he had not imagined it! Somewhere beyond those gnarled oaks . . .

'William,' the voice spoke again. 'This way!'

There was a sudden rush at his feet, but before he could look down, whatever it was had scurried away into the undergrowth.

He shuddered uneasily in the unreal silence. What had happened to make the forest such a hostile place? He had always loved the green solitude of such spots.

He pressed on, determined to overcome his fear. The smell grew stronger still.

'William!'

It seemed to echo in his ears. Was he perhaps hallucinating? The thought passed across his mind again as he pushed his way through the dense vegetation and came across what looked like a green path running between tall trees. It surely *was* a path. He stood for a moment on the edge of it, wondering what it might signify.

And then he saw her.

'Avelina!' he cried.

The girl stood in dappled shadow under a grey-green beech tree. As he came towards her, she smiled, beckoned with a finger and disappeared along the track.

'No, wait! Avelina . . .'

When he caught up with her she said nothing, but held her arms out in front of her as if in supplication. She stood before him, her eyes closed, her body swaying rythmically to and fro as if caught up in something beyond herself. He had seen this same hypnotic trance in animals when hunting or hunted.

'Avelina,' he faltered. 'What is it?'

'Come,' she whispered, her fingers finding his sleeve.

'Yes, yes,' he murmured. The sweet smell seemed to engulf them both. 'Just a little way, then.'

What was this power that had possessed her? Avelina had always appeared so shy, so vulnerable, so unremarkable, yet now she led him on with an authority he could not resist.

'This way,' she breathed. 'Come, this way . . .'

And suddenly it all seemed very familiar: he had followed her in just such a fashion once before.

'No, Avelina!' he shouted desperately. 'No!'

But it was too late. He sniffed at the air. The deed had been done. The betrayal was complete.

16 Missing

Henry and Janie sat inside the waggon, gloomily watching the sudden shower roll the dust of the road into little pellets, then the steadier, heavier rain that followed dissolve the pellets into a thin wet slurry. It drummed on the canvas above their heads. Behind them, wrapped in sacking,, Walt slept noisily. A little way off, under the oak trees, Christopher sat talking to the horse. It was a warm rain and he didn't mind it at all. Soon William would come back and they would all set off together.

Christopher, Henry mused, had the unclouded mind of the true innocent. Three days had passed since Ranulph's disappearance, but it meant nothing to him. He had no notion of time, knew little of cause and effect, and was therefore totally unaffected by the sense of bitter defeat which hung so heavily over his companions. Henry at this moment genuinely envied Christopher his happy stupidity. He himself had spent much time in prayer since Ranulph's disappearance, yet he had the horrible premonition that his supplications to the Almighty had been quite futile. He was unable to believe that he would ever see his friend again.

'So what now?' he asked, close to despair. 'There's no point in carrying on.'

'None at all,' Janie replied tartly, 'when the company's so dull.' It still irked her that Henry failed to feel anything special for her at all, even now that they were thrown together as leaders of their reduced raggle-taggle army. 'It's obvious that we should all go our separate ways again.'

'You think so?'

'Of course! Let's take up where we left off. You go back to your monastery, Walt to his hut, Christopher . . . well, Christopher would go with you.'

'And you?'

'Oh, I can go anywhere,' Janie said confidently. 'It's the open road for me. There'll be players who need a singer.'

Henry shook his head: 'No, we couldn't let you wander off like that. There are too many dangers.'

'Dangers, indeed! I've lived with dangers for too long not to know how to avoid them.'

'That was different. You always had men to protect you – men who were reliable and who didn't take advantage of you.'

'I'd like to have seen them try,' Janie growled. That hoarse little voice of hers broke into a cackle. 'But perhaps you're right. I'll come back to the monastery with you. They must need women to cook and clean.'

The thought of Janie in a monastery brought a smile to Henry's lips, and he very gently put his arm around her shoulder and hugged her to himself.

'No, Janie, a monastery's not for you.'

He paused for some moments before continuing: 'Nor, I think, for me any more. Sometimes things slip away from you. You wake one morning to find yourself a new creature, just as surely as a tadpole becomes a frog or a caterpillar turns into a butterfly. I'm not the Henry that I was when I first knew you, Janie. Then I was full of certainties. Now I know nothing –. I'm just wind-blown grass.'

'Or frog, or butterfly!' she laughed, her face close to his. 'You haven't changed that much, Henry. You still wrap the world in words.'

'Perhaps. But I still see no going back.'

'Then you must go forward.'

'*We* must go forward. I certainly can't leave Christopher, and, as for Walt, well he must make up his own mind, but I've grown used to his company.'

'Grown used to his company! Now there's fine praise for

you!' Walt stirred from his sacking. 'But I suppose I'd better stick around to look after you two. I expect I'll get used to *your* company eventually.'

'Then it's agreed,' Henry said. 'Tomorrow we move forward. Together.'

'But so soon?' Janie asked. She was enjoying their intimate camp, far from the jostling crowds. 'Could they simply be lost? Shouldn't we wait a little longer?'

Henry's eyes searched the fringe of the forest in vain hope that their friends might emerge, smiling and unharmed.

'No,' he said sadly. 'William was wise in the ways of the forest. He would have found his way back if . . .'

But a sudden onset of tears left this thought hanging in the air.

*

Night closed in, and still the rain fell. Sleep did not come easily to any of them. Henry lay beneath the waggon and gazed at the dark sky through the spokes of one of the wheels: somewhere beyond all that darkness were the bright stars and the moon's silver orb, but they were hidden from him now. He tried to hold his eyes shut and pray, but the words froze on his lips: it seemed in these despairing moments that God was lost to him, too. Feeling desolate and forsaken, he lay awake for a long time, falling towards dawn into a troubled and uneasy sleep from which he awoke unrested and still agitated in spirit.

The rain, he saw, had passed, and the drenched grass sparkled under the sun. He crawled from the waggon's shelter to find Janie preparing for the day. She handed him a piece of cheese, and a lump of bread so dry that it had to be dipped into his ale before it was soft enough to eat.

'I've checked the snares,' Janie said. 'Nothing! It'll be a hungry day unless we learn to eat grass like Taffy.'

'Or the goat,' added Henry, finding Hosea's Wife nudging his side and trying to steal his bread.

There came a bellow from the depths of the waggon, and Brother Walt's face emerged, red and angry.

'However hungry we may be,' his thin voice hammered in their ears, 'we shall never eat Hosea's Wife. Not while I live to protect her. Never!'

Henry looked puzzled for a moment, then burst into helpless laughter.

'But I never meant such a thing, Walt,' he protested through his convulsions. 'I was referring to the fact that the goat eats grass, just as the horse does.'

Walt was only partially mollified: 'I heard what I heard,' he said, meaningfully.

They harnessed Taffy to the waggon and packed everything aboard, yet none of them seemed keen to leave. Henry carefully fashioned an arrow of sticks and lay it by the road to indicate the direction in which they were going. Walt fussed with the goat, delaying the moment when she would be tethered to the back of the cart. Christopher, who had suddenly realised that they were about to set off on their journeyings without his beloved friend, seemed to act for them all as he wandered about aimlessly, waving his hands towards the trees and barking 'Wiwwum! Wiwwum!'

'I feel like Judas,' Henry scowled, taking the reins in his hands. 'I betrayed my friend. I led us into that forest.'

Janie took the risk of putting a hand on his: 'Nobody could have stood by a friend more than you did,' she said. 'But now we have our own safety to consider.'

He nodded.

'Yes, you're right of course. But let's try one more call before we go.'

He stood, cupped his hands around his mouth and yelled in

the direction of the forest: 'Halloo!' It echoed around and around. 'Halloo! William! Avelina!'

The words disappeared into the trees. Henry sat down heavily and twitched the reins to set Taffy in motion. He felt as if something had died inside him.

*

It was towards noon that they passed through the village emptied by plague and caught their first sight of the tower. It was a curious structure. Incomplete and now deserted, it stood like a broken tooth on a hill above the village. Something about it seemed to invite exploration.

Christopher was the first to reach the summit and lumber through the open door into the cool stone cavern of its interior. The others followed close behind him, panting from their exertions. They stood in silence for a moment, looking up at the ribbed vaulting of the ceiling, down at the packed earth of its floor.

The room was lit by two small windows set high in the walls. It wasn't until their eyes had adjusted to the gloom that they caught sight of the small door leading to stairs. These stairs curled up, and brought them eventually to a room which made as bright and delightful a contrast to the one below as it would be possible to imagine. It had a boarded floor whose straight planks led to a seated window bay at one end and a large fireplace with carved surround at the other. Sunlight had warmed the dusty air and driven away the dank, musty smell of the chamber below.

From a corner the stairs continued their upward spiral, leading them finally to the sky – or, rather, to an unfinished room whose uneven walls were roofed by that distant ceiling of deep blue flecked with drifting wisps of white cloud. At one end the walls were low enough for them to look down to where their waggon stood, with Taffy and Hosea's Wife champing away contentedly at the grass. Beyond was the deserted village.

'Did the owners of this place die with all the others, do you think?' Walt wondered aloud.

'Before they ever managed to live in it,' was Henry's guess. 'There were no ashes in the fireplace below, and there's no other sign of habitation. They either died or fled the Pestilence, I'd say.'

'But it's a kind of home, nevertheless,' Janie said, clambering up to sit on a flat strip of walling, 'and a safe shelter. What do you say to staying a day or two?'

Henry raised his eyebrows: 'Well,' he considered, 'there's certainly nobody to challenge us for it. It would be a safe haven.'

Walt smiled his agreement.

'My old bones could do with a rest,' he said. 'They've been shaken like a rattle in that cramped cart. Let's stay.'

And so Taffy was harnessed and urged up the rough grass of the hill, and the strangely matched quartet moved into the tower.

*

The surrounding fields yielded crops half returned to the wild, snares provided rabbits and, beneath the hill, on the far side from the village, a pond supplied fat carp and the occasional wildfowl. The bright room, now brushed and besomed and furnished with a few sticks of crudely made furniture, became their home, and each morning they thanked God for his bounty, and each evening they thanked God for his safe deliverance.

They saw few people, and these were mainly passing travellers. None, it seemed, shared their own curiosity, for none deviated from the road and none discovered their existence.

Their first fire in the carved fireplace was lit with great ceremony, for it seemed to mark a settling in. Until that time the food had been cooked by Janie over a fire in the lower chamber. Now they heaped wood into the grate and watched as the blaze lit their faces and filled the room with an orange glow.

It was growing dark outside. Christopher sat contentedly, whittling away at a piece of wood, while the others exchanged stories of their earlier lives. Walt, it was true, seemed a little diffident in this respect, but he finally provided his listeners with such a variety of scenarios that they were clearly woven more with the warp of imagination than the woof of memory. He reddened when Henry and Janie laughed their disbelief.

'You mustn't laugh at an old man,' he rebuked. 'Age deserves respect. I'm too old to remember my youth and, anyway, what does it matter whether these are dreams or reality?'

'Quite right,' agreed Henry. 'We are as much our dreams as we are the outer circumstances of our being.'

'Which makes liars of us all!' Janie added. 'Meanwhile, if you two are going to toss words around, I'll go down and draw us some ale. It's a pity,' she muttered as she took up a pitcher and started down the stairs into the darkness below, 'that nobody pays anyone for word juggling, or you two would make a fortune.'

The ale was what was left of their supply from the waggon. To make it last longer, and perhaps to disguise its sourness, Janie had judiciously thinned it, and it now tasted like little more than lightly flavoured water. The barrel was kept in the corner of the lower chamber, and Janie had to move across the earth floor in almost total darkness in order to find it. Outside she could hear Hosea's Wife shuffling around. The goat had been tethered near to the door in order to act as a guard against any unwanted visitors, but it posed as great a threat to the backsides of the four occupants as to any supposed intruder.

She was about to fill the pitcher when her ears picked up a sound inside the room. It was the sound of breathing, human breathing, and it was very close. She froze. There it was again, by the wall, not a yard away.

'Ha!' she yelled, out of her fear.

The breathing stopped, momentarily, and then there came a rushing past her, a flurry of invisible arms and legs, and the stranger was through the door and out into the night. She saw nothing but his silhouette against the open door and his sudden precipitation forward as his feet entangled themselves on the rope that held the goat.

'Help!' Janie screamed.

Outside she could hear the intruder and the furious goat locked in uneven combat, while upstairs the pounding of footsteps on the boards told her that help was on its way. It seemed an age before Henry appeared, brandishing a firebrand which lit up his face and turned it to that of a demon. Even as he held it towards her, to see that she was unharmed, Christopher plunged past him and out of the door.

'A man!' was all she managed to blurt out.

Henry sprang to the door, only to find their stealthy visitor utterly ensnared at his feet, his ankles entangled in Hosea's Wife's tether, his backside thumped mercilessly by the enraged goat, his neck held in a vice-like grip by a growling Christopher. He lowered the flaming torch to a face grimacing with pain and imminent suffocation.

'God in Heaven above!' he exclaimed.

Christopher at once released his grip and, with a moan, cradled his victim's head in a soft embrace.

'Wiwwum!' he crooned. 'Wiwwum!'

17 Strange Magic

'Such adventures! Things you wouldn't believe! I hardly believe them myself, and yet . . .'

Here Ranulph paused and looked at each of his listeners in turn, his eyes tear-filled.

'Those most unbelievable thing of all is that I should be here with you, able to tell of them.'

He paused to take another draught of the watered ale, his eyes feverish in their excitement. They were in the first-floor room, in a circle, their heads close together. The flames of the fire threw their shadows high on the wall.

'In the depths of the forest,' he told them, 'a net was flung across my face. It was heavy with a perfume richer than incense. It filled my brain with curious fancies.'

His cheeks were flushed in the firelight.

'Come,' smiled Henry, 'you're overwrought, William. The tale can wait.'

'No, no!'

But he paused a while to compose himself and, when at last he began to speak, his words had a strange dream-like quality which, despite their simplicity, conjoured up for every one of them (for even Christopher was touched by this magic, his eyes rolling expressively in their sockets) the weird and wonderful things he spoke of.

He told of meeting Avelina and how she enticed him along the broad green path; of picking out the faint stench of Sourskin only seconds before the cloth fell over his face; of finding himself, the cloth removed, walking along the path, with Avelina to one side and, on the other, a man he had not for some moments recognised.

'Sourskin!' gasped Walt.

'Ah, no, thank heavens. No, it was Geoffrey.'

'The herbalist?' Janie asked. 'The quack who sold poor Henry his expensive potions?'

'That's how I realised who it was. Those phials of his jangled on their chains as he walked. He led us down the path, smiling all the time, chuckling occasionally, rubbing his hands with pleasure. I had no idea what could be making him so merry.'

'You walked freely?' Henry asked.

'Yes, freely. I felt no desire to run. Would you believe that I asked him no questions? In fact I found myself happily whistling. Whistling! And Avelina was singing, I remember, very prettily.'

At this, Janie turned her head and spat loudly into the fire.

'We came eventually to a huge outcrop of rock that rose from the forest floor like the curtain wall of a castle. It appeared to be impassable, but we followed Geoffrey through a narrow cleft in the rock and then, ducking our heads, into a low and crooked passage. The walls seemed to dance with a flickering orange light.

'We soon discovered what caused this strange effect. The passage opened into a massive cave lit by crackling fires. And what their light fell upon . . .'

He paused, examining their faces as if to ensure that they would believe him. They were to imagine the builder of a minster or cathedral in a manically playful mood, perhaps merry with drink; to imagine him ordaining mad columns that pressed up from the floor, or hung from the ceiling, but that frequently had no purpose, tapering to nothing before their journey was complete; to imagine arches, vaults, buttresses in a sort of frozen dance; and to imagine that this builder, this frolic builder, should wish to trap a lake within his walls . . .

'Because at the centre of this chamber was a pool of crystal water. And this strange and wondrous place was where Geoffrey had made his home.'

'And you were his prisoner?' Henry asked, not quite understanding.

'In truth I was, of course. Had I been able to think clearly I should have known that he had trapped me there on Sourskin's behalf – had lured Avelina away as bait. Hadn't I caught a hint of that foul stench? Even now, presumably, Geoffrey's messengers were on their way to Sourskin to report my capture.

'I shudder now to think how close to death I was, but at the time my mind was still trapped by his – what do we call it? His charm? Sorcery? Magic? He's a master of those old powers, Henry, that mother church doesn't tell us about.'

'Inferior powers,' Henry murmured. 'Pagan. You must not trust them.'

'Well, Geoffrey's cave seemed a place of perfect enchantment to me. And most enchanting of all – listen carefully, now – most curious of all were the two deformed creatures who stoked the fires and were busy preparing food for us . . .'

He gazed into the fire, as if uncertain how to continue, as if great care were needed to express himself properly.

'Monsters?' Walt asked, his eyes aglint with interest.

'Monsters, no,' Ranulph resumed at last. 'But these two creatures shared one body.'

'He jests!' cackled Janie, hugging herself with pleasure. She liked a good yarn. 'A two-in-one!'

'Or rather,' Ranulph explained, 'two bodies fastened at the hip and having between them only three legs. Swinke and Swonken were their names – though Geoffrey called them Swinke-Swonken as if they were a single creation. If you and I were to fasten two legs together, Henry, we'd make a sorry sight, but these two skipped around the fires with skillets and pans without the slightest stumble, and the whole time in deep conversation.'

'So they could talk?' Henry pondered. 'They were human?'

'Yes, of course.'

'With human faces?'

'Like yours and mine, Henry – though surrounded by masses of flaxen curls. Intelligent faces.'

'And their dress?'

'Ah, they were clothed very poorly in ill-fitting rags, but they laughed and joked and seemed to enjoy the jobs they were given, however dirty they were.'

'Sound like Devil's spawn to me,' grunted Walt. 'Feed 'em to the dogs!'

'Not so, Brother Walt, not so,' Ranulph protested gently. 'They were roughly treated by Geoffrey, despite their good nature. I'd hate to think that you'd inflict worse punishments on them.

'Besides which,' he grinned, 'the food that they served us was delicious, though I recognised barely a thing on my plate. Avelina and I sat with them and ate hungrily.

'Geoffrey had his own wicker cell within the cave, a gigantic upturned basket, and there he took his food. I never saw the inside of this woven cell, but it was lit inside by tapers that twinkled between the weft of cane like a constellation of stars. I imagined a warm, snug place, doubly protected, as it was, from the wildness of weather, and I was reminded of my drey back in the forest of my childhood.'

As he uttered these words, Ranulph was conscious of that childhood falling away from him. He had seen so much, experienced so much, these last few months. How changed his guardian Grete would find him now!

'That night,' he continued, 'I lay down with a feeling of complete happiness, gazing up at the flickering light on the cave's roof and imagining the shadows to be a troupe of dancing animals, my old friends from the forest come to visit me.'

'And still no thought of escape?' Janie asked.

'Not once. I can't tell you how long I remained in that blissful state. Perhaps it was only for a day or two, but it seemed to last for ever. Geoffrey came and went, always smiling delightedly, but he never made any effort to talk to us.

'I suppose I would very soon have been stuck with Sourskin's blade if it hadn't been for the onset of a fever. One morning I woke with a burning forehead and a sore throat. My breakfast was painful and the food tasteless. Not only that, but my nose was blocked, so that I was unable to smell a thing. I pushed the meal aside and went back to sleep.'

'Sleep,' Henry mused, 'is greater solace to the sick man than food.'

'Quoth the philosopher!' cackled Janie.

Ranulph put a hand on Henry's shoulder.

'When I awoke,' he said, 'it was like coming back to life. During my sleep, sweet dreams had turned to nightmare. I opened my eyes feeling fearful and oppressed. Geoffrey's malevolence, the close and shadowed interior of the cave, the betrayal of Avelina, the deformity of Swinke-Swonken – all these things became horribly apparent to me. In short, the spell was broken. I was free.'

'And so you fled,' suggested Walt.

'At first,' Ranulph said, shaking his head, 'I wanted nothing more than to fall back under the enchantment. So much more pleasant! It was only when I reminded myself that Sourskin was very likely on his way to slit my throat that I stirred myself to thoughts of escape.'

'Leaving Avelina behind?' Janie asked in a neutral tone of voice.

'No. True, I did think of giving Swinke-Swonken and Avelina the slip. After all, I had to move quickly in case my nose cleared and allowed the sweet drugged air into my brain again. But it seemed to me that their senses must have been seduced just as mine were, and that I ought in fairness to take them with me.'

'A Christian act,' Henry nodded contentedly.

'Geoffrey was away from the cave, and the plan had to be carried out at once.'

'Plan?' queried Walt. 'Couldn't you simply run for it?'

'Ah, no, Brother Walt. The difficulty was persuading my companions to forsake the delights of their imprisonment. Avelina was as much in thrall to Geoffrey's concoctions as I had been, and Swinke-Swonken had been forbidden ever to leave the cave. Believe me, it needed a great deal of cunning and persistence on my part.

'I pointed them towards Geoffrey's wicker cell, suggesting that we should garland it with fresh green leaves and flowers gathered from the forest. The herbalist's pleasure, I argued, would far outweigh any anger he felt at being disobeyed.

'I'm not sure that I would have persuaded them if it hadn't been for Avelina, who enthused about the wonders of the forest they hadn't seen for many years. But once we were out into the fresh, cool air among the trees I managed to lead them further and further astray – sliding down a bank here, pointing to some distant imagined flowers there, pushing past branches, wading through bracken. By nightfall we were miles from the cave, heading south.'

'And they were happy to be free?' Henry queried.

The question had the effect of stopping Ranulph's narrative in its tracks. He fell silent for some time, a troubled look on his face.

'Avelina, yes,' he began again, falteringly. 'After a few hours she began to look about her strangely, as if seeing the forest for the first time. I saw tears welling in her eyes. Eventually she clasped my arm, fell to her knees and asked my forgiveness. That made me happy, because I knew that she, too, was free. She was very soon her own self again.

'More's the pity,' muttered Janie.

'Charity, Janie. Charity!' Henry smiled as he laid an admonishing finger against her lips.

'And your two creatures?' Walt asked.

Ranulph frowned.

'They'd been many years under the herbalist's influence,' he said. 'It was painful for them. They began to stumble and lose their balance. We found a grassy bank for a bed that first night, and they moaned and clawed at the ground in their sleep.

'The following morning they woke in a daze, allowing themselves to be led forward again, but speaking very little and appearing to be much weaker than before. And so it has continued . . .'

Henry interrupted Ranulph's story with a raised palm, a worried look on his face.

'Continued? Then where are they, William, if you've freed them? Avelina and this Swinke-Swonken – they're safe?'

Ranulph's face clouded.

'Safe,' he said, 'but in very poor health. I came on ahead to look for you, leaving them to rest the night in a shepherd's cot a little way back. Avelina is, I think, only exhausted. We've travelled a long distance on foot, and at great speed. We've fed on nothing but berries and roots.'

'And your two creatures?'

'Swinke-Swonken are failing fast, Henry.' His face had turned white in the fire's wavering light. 'They're pining for their cave and won't be comforted. I think they've lost the will to live.'

18 New Companions

It was an oddly assorted and awkwardly tongue-tied party which set off for Coventry the next day. The flaxen-haired twins, having survived their night in the shepherd's cot, sat propped on thick sacking at the back of the open waggon, from which vantage point they gazed all about them with a bewilderment that was painful to see. Their flesh was sickly pallid and shrank away from their cheek bones to give them the ghastly look of perpetually swivelling death's-heads. Joined at the hip, they swayed in unison as the cart rocked along.

Ranulph watched his friends' reactions to this strange pair with mounting unease. Janie, to her credit, had held out arms of greeting from the first and had withstood their instinctive frightened rebuff with good grace. It was she who had helped settle them as comfortably as possible on the creaking waggon and who now, walking alongside, threw the occasional cheerful remark in their direction as if to reassure them that they were a welcome part of this ever-increasing travelling band.

The others, however, seemed unable to come to terms with their freakishness. Christopher, of course, could not be blamed either for his initial unearthly howling, the only expression his shock was able to find, or for his later exaggerated gestures of tenderness, fondling each of their heads in turn and babbling 'Shinke-Shonken' over and again until they weakly flapped him away with their matchstick arms.

But shouldn't Henry have found it in him to act naturally with them? His Christian learning told him that they possessed immortal souls, and he had done nothing that was unreasonable or unkind, but it seemed to Ranulph that there was no true warmth in his smiles. This puzzled and saddened him. There were, after all, cripples enough all about them, hideous deformities wherever you turned: it seemed to Ranulph that Swinke-Swonken's affliction, though more curious, was far less disturbing than many another of what Janie referred to, with a chuckle, as 'God's little mistakes'.

Walt, apparently struck dumb by this double apparition, was unable to stop himself staring at them for long periods at a time, a strange grin stretching his face and suggesting sometimes hilarity, sometimes an inexpressible fear. If their eyes met his, he would instantly look away, a nervous whinnying in his throat, his arms jerking in a gesture of confused apology.

As for Avelina, she perhaps felt that any recognition of the twins would only remind everyone of her part in Ranulph's capture. She sat with her back to them, staring ahead with a blank look in her eyes.

The road was much busier now that Coventry was but a day's journeying away, and the people they met seemed rowdier. Ranulph hardly noticed this at first, but as the afternoon dwindled towards evening they seemed to pass increasing numbers of boisterous young men, many of them the worse for drink and much inclined to give their fellow travellers the benefit of their wisdom.

'Tell me,' blurted one, careering towards them, a flaggon in his hand. 'When Adam delved and Eve span . . .' He showed a pair of yellow fangs in an otherwise toothless mouth while he ransacked his memory to complete the rhyme. 'Who was then the gentleman?'

'Be off with you!' Henry ordered angrily, flicking the reins to increase Taffy's speed. 'We want none of that here.'

Ranulph, who had been walking alongside the waggon, jumped up beside him, puzzled.

'A mere drunken lout, Henry' he said. 'We've seen plenty of those. Why's he got you so worked up?'

'Because I know what he talks of.'

They jogged along in silence for a while, but Henry could tell that Ranulph's curiosity had not been stilled.

'Those are followers of John Ball,' he explained at last. 'The devil priest. You've heard of him?

'No. The devil?'

'He seduces the feeble-minded to question those in authority. That's his verse the idiot was spouting just now. Leastways, his followers like to use it. He wants no man to have dominion over another. In his Garden of Eden all men and women are equal. It's a charter for the footloose.'

'He wants there to be no gentlemen?'

'No rank, no respect, no duties or obligations. As if society can function without the power of those whom God has put in authority.'

Ranulph laughed bitterly.

'I know something about those in authority,' he said. 'Am I not on the run from just such a man? Perhaps you believe that Baron Fulke obeys the will of God.'

'No, no! This is a misunderstanding, William. The Baron will have to answer for his crimes at the great judgement seat, and I don't doubt that he will roast in the eternal flames, but this doesn't affect the principle that each man should recognise his degree, and honour those above him.'

'Perhaps so,' Ranulph answered, the little rhyme running through his brain over and over. 'I haven't the learning to argue with you about principles.'

'Our world is being undone by such people,' Henry continued vehemently. 'They find their excuses in famine, the pestilence, the wealth of our church. Everywhere there's discord. Everywhere!'

Ranulph fell silent, unsettled by the strength of Henry's despair. It was enough that his own life should be in constant danger, without the thought that their whole world was on the point of dissolution. He jumped down from the waggon and linked arms with Christopher, who walked with his free hand resting on Taffy's back.

Hungry, Wiwwum,' he said, as if had been waiting to tell somebody for ages.

When they stopped for the night, a little way off the road, Janie suggested that they rehearse their skills for the lucrative performances which awaited them in Coventry.

'There's money in this city,' she told them. 'It's years since I was last here, but I know its streets inside out, and I'll find the best places for our shows.'

Ranulph took up his recorder and began to play a jaunty tune, Janie juggled half a dozen coloured balls and Walt tried rather despairingly to induce Hosea's Wife to jump through a hoop. Henry beat time on a small drum, while Christopher skipped lumberingly between them, clapping his hands to the steady rhythm.

Swinke and Swonken still sat in the waggon. They had spoken not a single word all day, and at times they had closed their eyes (always, it seemed, in unison) and had let their heads slump on their chests for all the world as if they were giving up the ghost. Now, however, as he executed a neat trill on his instrument, Ranulph glanced up and saw to his surprise that both were beating their fists against the side of the waggon in time to the music. And were those faint smiles on their lips?

At supper time, when Avelina served up a thick barley broth, the twins held out their hands for bowls, sucking the dense pottage into their mouths with a noisy urgency.

*

They approached the walls of Coventry the following

afternoon. Days of fine weather had turned the road to dust, which waggon wheels and countless feet now swept into the air as a fine, choking powder.

'My home city,' Janie explained proudly to Swinke and Swonken whose eyes, surely far brighter than they had been the day before, took in the massive gateway before them and, some way off, the spire of a great cathedral.

'A fine place,' they both said at once.

As they jostled with the crowd which funnelled through the large stone gate, a lanky fellow with jaundiced flesh and a disfiguring facial tic lurched close to the waggon, his lips working soundlessly. Henry, who had caught his eye more than once during the past few minutes, swiftly put a hand on his dagger and prepared to draw it from his belt, but the man simply held out a piece of paper.

'From Mark the summoner,' he said.

'Mark?'

'Met you on the road some days past. Says to give you this.'

He thrust the paper into Henry's hand, his features contorting into what might have been either a grin or a gasp of pain, and stepped back into the surging crowd.

'Wants more money, I'll be bound,' Janie said cynically. 'And I daresay he'll get it.'

Henry read the note aloud: 'If you still seek your relic, meet me in Pinchnose Alley two hours after nightfall.'

'Nothing more?' Ranulph asked.

'Nothing.'

They all pondered the message while the waggon swayed ever closer to the gate.

'Ignore it,' Walt said, his chin thrust into the air. 'We know what happens when we trust strangers on the road.'

'But suppose,' Henry countered, 'he can truly help find our relic. Isn't it perhaps worth the risk?'

'Let *me* take the risk,' Ranulph insisted. 'I'm the one who needs it.'

Henry frowned: 'We've long since made a decision on this matter, William. We share the danger. What can you tell us about this Pinchnose Alley, Janie?'

'That it deserves its name!' she laughed. 'It's the area where the tanners work.'

'On the outskirts, then?'

'Yes, it's one of a dozen narrow thoroughfares in the eastern quarter. Evil streets in every way. Honest folk keep clear of them after dark.'

They were passing through the city gate now, and Ranulph found himself offering up a silent prayer that this time they might be successful in their quest.

'I suggest we find a resting place for the night,' Henry said, 'then take stock of our courage.'

*

Did daylight really fade much earlier that evening, or was the apparent swiftness with which the shadows enclosed them merely a mark of his fear?

They had brought the waggon to rest at the edge of a large market square and now arranged their beds in and under it as they had grown accustomed to do. They were a stone's throw from an inn, whose wheatsheaf device swung idly back and forth in a slight breeze. The noise of late revellers might disturb their sleep and their assorted baggage was an obvious temptation for pilferers, but there was a kind of security, nevertheless, in lodging themselves in so public a place. Let Sourskin approach them, he could scarcely hope to conclude his knifework and escape unseen.

A heavy torpor took possession of them. It had been a hard

day on the road, and most were ready for sleep. Old Walt was already away, the breath wheezing in his throat. Swinke and Swonken, laid down with great care on large pads of sheep's wool, were muttering softly to themselves in a language both private and sparse. Christopher, lying between the wheels, yawned loudly, waving the flat of a large hand over his mouth. Henry, his hands pressed together, was busy at his prayers.

Ranulph alone stood by the waggon, restless, his mind turmoiled. Why had he spoken so bravely about risk-taking only a few hours before? Now he felt the fear clutch at his chest, its chill fingers tightening until he could scarcely breathe. He saw the moon glide between the clouds, cold and indifferent. He heard the tiles rattling on the inn roof, a jarring, brittle sound. What he had to do could not be avoided, but he wished it long over, himself far away in a happier time.

From beneath the waggon came a soft woman's voice, breathing words that he did not know, words that he could not be sure were English at all. Stooping, he saw Avelina, her eyes fixed on the scudding moon, wide and bright, her palms pressed away from her as if submitting to some great, invisible force, her mouth moving ecstatically, the strange sounds flocking out like wild birds.

Shivering, he turned away.

*

'You're here, then. Alone?'

Ranulph's hand clasped tightly at his dagger. The voice had come from his left but, turning, he could see nothing but shadow. Above, warehouses pressed their rotting roof timbers against a sky which raced with torn shreds of cloud, but below, nothing, shadow.

'Yes, alone.'

'Courageous!'

'Or stupid!' This was another, a second voice, but it came from the same direction as the first.

'What do you want with me? Step forward like an honest man.'

This was greeted with an audible snigger, but the two men complied, stepping from the darker recesses of shadow until their white faces hovered dimly in the murk like two grinning moons. One Ranulph recognised as the summoner, but the other was unknown to him.

'Is this honest enough, boy *alone*?'

This last word was pronounced with withering sarcasm. Ranulph, confused, glanced around him but could see nobody in the embracing gloom.

'Yes, alone,' he repeated with emphasis.

The summoner looked to his companion: 'Stupid, or slippery-tongued? What say you, my friend?'

'Well, stupidity can't be cured by a sharp knife, that's true enough. Unless, that is, we take his head from his shoulders.'

The summoner grinned cruelly.

'So there's your choice, boy alone. We slice your tongue from your mouth or your head from your shoulders. Unless, perhaps . . .'

Here he turned his head towards the entrance of the alley.

'You can come and join us now!' he shouted to the air. His words echoed dully from the blank walls and fell into silence. 'We mean him no harm!'

Again silence.

'Come!' His voice, when he called again, had an edge of threat. 'Now! Or your friend here will be the worse for it!'

For a few more seconds there was nothing. Then, rising like a spirit from a tumble of broken fence palings that was heaped where the alley began, Janie stepped from her hiding place.

She ran to join Ranulph, taking up a position slightly in front of him, arms akimbo, legs spread wide, looking every inch the protective mother.

The summoner turned to his companion, his grin broadening: 'Who d'you think we're dealing with, the vixen or her cub?'

The other gave a loud peal of laughter in answer as Ranulph angrily pushed Janie to one side and stepped forward.

'I thought I told you to go back to the others!' he hissed at her. 'You've no place here.'

And then, turning to the two men: 'She was merely my guide. It's her city, not mine. I don't know its vile streets, nor what vermin crawl through them.'

He uttered this last with a snarl, grateful that the darkness of the alley hid the tears of humiliation that pricked at his eyes.

'She has no part in this. You must allow her to return to our companions.'

'Oh, must we? And allow her to risk these vile streets and their vermin? I think not. No, she'll stay.'

But suddenly his voice became calmer and more conciliatory: 'We'll do her no harm, boy. You mustn't mind our fun. We didn't lure you here to dispatch you. If we needed such sport there's finer to be had, believe me. Our business is talk.'

'It's a strange place for that kind of business.'

'True, my young rat's tail. Well, there's an alehouse nearby if you'd prefer it. We'll lead the way and risk our backs, though I'd be happier if you gripped that blade a little less ardently.'

Ranulph allowed the dagger to slide back into its sheath. He could not bring himself to look at Janie as they followed the men through a tortuous labyrinth of alleyways and passages. Yet his anger was matched by her own. At one point the passage narrowed to the point of their shoulders touching, and Ranulph was all too aware that she flinched and pulled herself away. The gesture stung him: she had made a fool of him, but her act had been brave and she had sought to protect him. He put a hand behind him to take hers in an act of reconciliation, but she shunned his offer, preferring instead to mutter darkly about the ingratitude of men and their false and ridiculous pride.

Somewhere a dog howled, an eerie sound with the hunger of the wolf still in it.

And then the sound of voices, laughter, singing. A splinter of light fell across their path, and above the light an inn sign rattled in the night wind – a roughly painted angel spreading silvery wings and flapping through a starry sky.

Janie now caught at Ranulph's hand.

'I know this place,' she whispered urgently. 'It's a place of evil repute, a hangout for thieves and cut-throats.'

'Have no fear,' he replied, relieved that her anger seemed to have passed. 'I've a sharp blade, and we've both got fast legs.'

'Ha!' was all she uttered, with a barely concealed contempt for his puffed-up vainglory.

The summoner and his companion swung wide the door of the alehouse and ushered them inside, pressing them to a table pushed into an alcove near the fire. Soon their faces were warmed in its flickering light, while a serving girl slapped full tankards of ale on to the roughly sawn wood of the table. The contents spilled over and spread along the cut grain in thin brown rivulets.

Around them sat, stood, talked, laughed and sang as louche a collection of his fellow beings as Ranulph had ever seen in one gathering, some made merry, some morbid and others violent by the drink that was being tipped into gaping mouths at every table. As the girl left, the summoner dealt her a hearty slap on the backside, but she swatted his hand away without turning her head, only shouting an amiable obscenity at him.

In the far corner of the room two men were pummelling one another, encouraged by a growing group of onlookers. The landlord, a burly man with a lower jaw that would have fitted a horse, took the two brawlers by the neck, to raucous cheers, and tumbled them into the street. Their fight continued as the door slammed shut behind them.

Ranulph turned to the summoner and eyed him carefully. It was clearly the same man that they had met on the road, but with such an altered demeanour that it was impossible to connect the two. This man apparently had none of the calculating greed that had seemed to shape the summoner's former features. Here, instead, was rather a genial, if roguish, countenance, open and laughing and not without a certain handsomeness. His friend's face, by contrast, had been badly scarred by the pox and had more the appearance of a malformed vegetable, animated only by two pale blue eyes that continually flicked to and fro, as if keeping the whole of the surrounding world in play at the same time.

Janie, now that she had no choice but to be here, sat watching the performance of an entertainer who was doing his best to coax tunes from some age-worn bagpipes. Ranulph clamped his tankard to his lips and silently waited, his impatience and uncertainty growing by the second. The summoner having given some considerable time to the loud drinking of his ale, followed this with a loud appreciation of its virtues and a highly dramatic dragging of his sleeve across his mouth to wipe away the clinging froth. Then, having banged the empty tankard on the table and called to the girl for more, he leaned forward, his expression become suddenly conspiratorial.

When his mouth was separated from Ranulph's ear by little more than a few inches he spoke quietly but clearly, seeming to savour each word.

'You're in trouble, Ranulph.'

He started at hearing his name spoken, and some of the ale slurped over the breast of his tunic, but he managed to say nothing.

'I know more about you than anyone ought for comfort. Don't ask me how I've come about that knowing. Suffice it to say that I've been on the road serving my own purposes for as long as you have, if not longer.'

He winked expressively.

'And knowledge is power, eh Ranulph?'

'Blackmail!'

'Blackmail? An ugly word, my young friend. No, not blackmail, I say. An aid to persuasion, perhaps.'

'What do you want of me?'

Ranulph blurted the question, causing heads to swivel in his direction. The summoner leaned back and laughed, as if at a joke, but his eyes spoke differently and they still held on to Ranulph with serious purpose. He waited until the interest had subsided and leaned forward once more.

'What I want of you, before all else, is discretion. Secondly, what I want of you will serve your purposes as handsomely as mine – so listen closely. We can trust her?'

He jerked his head towards Janie and was greeted by a scowl.

'I would trust her with my life.'

The summoner smiled, running his eyes over Janie as if to make out what manner of woman she was.

'Good. Then tell me, Ranulph, what you've heard of John Ball.'

'The devil priest?'

The summoner's grin broadened: 'The very one!'

'That he spreads discontent in the south. And that my friend Henry heartily disapproves of him.'

'And you?'

He shrugged: 'I trust Henry's judgement in many things, but this? I've had enough grief thrust upon me by my betters to wish at least one of them ground beneath the heels of the common people.'

'Ah!'

'But it's of no consequence,' Ranulph added. 'The man I refer to is too far away to be harmed by the likes of John Ball.'

The summoner leant closer.

'By John Ball, perhaps, but there may be others. It's not such a very big land.'

'You mean . . .'

'I mean that if you throw a stone into a pond the ripples will eventually reach the bank. The stone that John Ball casts can be helped to do likewise.'

Ranulph, confused by this hypothetical talk, brough his fist down on the table in frustration.

'What has any of this to do with the relic I seek?' he demanded. 'You promised me information. What of Christ's blood?'

The summoner rolled his eyes and slapped his brow in dramatic despair.

'Can't you see,' he hissed, 'that if what I am talking about comes to pass you'll have no need of Christ's blood, save that magicked from wine by a priest each sabbath? Your foot could be the one to crush your tormentor's throat. Imagine Baron Fulke's face gazing up at you, pleading mercy. Revenge is sweet. Keep that in mind.'

'Baron Fulke?'

How could this man know so much about his circumstances? It unnerved him, made him feel helplessly vulnerable.

'Listen,' the summoner pressed him. 'People are in place the length and breadth of the land, just waiting to move. Now we're in need of messengers, those who will tie York to Chester, Chester to Bristol, Bristol to Exeter . . . Coventry to London. Those who will make of the separate parts one body. Valley of dry bones, eh? And you an Ezekiel!'

He frowned, not understanding the references.

'But why me?'

'You and your companions are travellers already, and so unlikely to arouse suspicion. You're perfect for our purposes. You will work between here and London. The task is not difficult and carries little risk.'

'Little risk! Only the risk of having our heads lopped from our bodies and spiked as traitors!'

The summoner laughed.

'All right, I confess: risk enough. But think of the risk of *not* joining our movement. Why, I could stick you with a dagger right now and find half-a-dozen ready buyers who'd cheerfully ship your body north and claim their reward from Fulke.'

'Blackmail!'

'Persuasion.'

'I must consult my friends before I yea or nay it.'

He felt Janie's breath on his cheek. She had drawn close and was listening intently.

'Since you can hardly afford to nay it,' the summoner continued, 'I hope for your sake that your powers of persuasion match mine. Perhaps you should remind them that they've been knowingly giving comfort and refuge to a criminal.'

Here his face became that of the thin-lipped moralist they had met on the road, and he prodded Ranulph's chest with an extended finger: 'Remind your oh-so-virtuous friend of that!'

Ranulph sat silent for a moment, then turned to Janie.

'How can I tell them?' he asked her, his voice edged with despair. 'What will they say?'

'You mean, what will Henry say,' she replied. 'Whatever it is will be so complicated and long-winded that I shan't understand it. The fact is that you don't have much choice. Perhaps it would be better if the others didn't know. Let's keep it as our secret.'

'No! That would be a betrayal of trust.'

Here the summoner interrupted, resting a hand on Ranulph's arm.

'Just remember,' he said, his eyes fixing Ranulph's like those of a hawk. 'Our cause is just. It needs no apologies. But also remember that before justice is done much blood will have to be spilled. Make sure that it's not yours!'

He rose, threw a coin on the table and beckoned his companion to follow him.

'We'll be here at this time tomorrow,' he said. 'See that you are, too – with some answers.

'I'll be here.'

After they had gone he felt Janie's hand steal into his own and press it: a friend's comfort, useless but more welcome than he was able to say.

*

Henry humphed. Henry muttered. Henry walked around the waggon several times.

'No, absolutely not. Well, perhaps maybe. No, definitely not! It's quite impossible. Immoral, against the order of things, and yet – and yet nothing! Wrong is wrong. There can be no bargain with the devil. But what if? Impossible! But not so. Did Christ Himself not turn the world on its head? No, that's different . . .only one possible answer, surely . . . yes, definitely not!'

He turned to Ranulph, who sat hapless, head in hands, on the seat of the waggon, waiting for his verdict. And now he delivered it, with an unexpected and encouraging smile.

'Why not, indeed? We have come so far that there's no turning back. What's past is past, and we must look to the future. Perhaps this John Ball *is* the future.'

'You don't believe that,' Ranulph said, shaking his head.

Henry shrugged: 'Perhaps not, but I no longer know what I *do* believe. And circumstances are certainly a little pressing.'

Such generosity of spirit brought hot tears to Ranulph's eyes. How was it that this man, a stranger to him only months before, should not only have stood by him through every torment but was now prepared to betray his own profound convictions at whatever risk?

Unable to speak, he merely stood and threw his arms around Henry, hugging him to himself.

19 Scent of Danger

Two days out of Coventry, while they were performing their tricks before an appreciative crowd of travellers, their nostrils picked up the stench of Sourskin.

It was a beautiful day, seemingly without threat, and Ranulph had been rejoicing in the return to health of Swinke and Swonken. Even now they were sitting on the waggon, beaming, their bodies bared to the waist to advertise their strangeness before a bellowing crowd. Surely nothing so freakish had been seen before! Coins were tossed into Avelina's leather bag as she patrolled the fringes of their audience, and all the while Walt scampered ridiculously with the goat, Henry conjured colourful rags from his sleeves and (to stupendous roars) from his nostrils, and Janie's rough-edged voice gave a running commentary as she persuaded these 'kind and honest folk' to part with a little of their money.

Ranulph, playing jaunty tunes on the recorder, was the first to register the foulness wafting in the air. To his sensitive nostrils that unclean odour was unmistakable, and he spun round as he played, half expecting a blade to rip down the length of his spine. But no, his would-be killer had already burrowed deep into that milling throng.

It took the others a little longer to sense his presence, but a few moments later he saw the concern cross Henry's face even as he bowed to the applause, and then Christopher, who had been charged with looking after Taffy, let go the horse's reins and began to bound about, scrabbling at the air with half-clenched fingers and howling with rage and despair. The peppery scent had obviously reminded the poor lad of his heroic tussle with their pursuer back in Lincoln.

'Come,' Henry whispered urgently to Ranulph. 'You smell

it, too? We must gather ourselves together and escape this crowd. There's danger here.'

There was danger everywhere, he thought, as he hitched Taffy to the waggon and watched the members of their party climbing aboard with ill-concealed disgruntlement that Henry should have rounded them up so hurriedly. Sewn into his tunic was a message he carried for the summoner, and which he must hand over to a man who would accost him with a certain form of words.

'Don't forget,' the summoner had told him at their second meeting, 'that no other rubric will do. There will be others who seek this information and will use any means to get it. Rehearse the words.'

'Grimbold knows no master.'

'Good! Those words exactly, and no others. You understand?'

He understood too well. If he escaped skewering on Sourskin's blade he would probably meet his death at the hands of a man who hunted the summoner's secret. Escape that fate, and some blood-thirsty servant of the Crown was likely to run him through for carrying seditious messages. He was threatened on all sides.

Henry, up alongside him as the waggon began to move forward, turned to their friends with an imploring expression on his face.

'Don't ask us to tell you everything,' he said. 'It's better that you don't know. But Sourskin is close by, and there are other dangers which press hard against us. We must make for London at the greatest speed and ensure we keep always on our guard.'

Ranulph, seeing their perplexed faces, felt unable to contain himself.

'This is all my doing,' he said. 'You'd be better off without me. Why put yourselves at so much risk?'

Janie laughed: 'We've heard this lament before, Sweet William! You're stuck with us, I'm afraid. With me, anyway – and I do know something of the dangers Henry speaks of. What say the rest of you?'

Swinke and Swonken, their faces glowing from the hot rays of the sun and their newly-restored vitality, reached out their arms towards Ranulph as if to pull him close.

'You saved our lives,' they said together.

He shrugged: 'You were perfectly happy,' he said, 'before I brought you out of the cave's security into this.'

'Not so,' Swinke said. 'We were drugged by Geoffrey's potions.'

'But happy.'

'Not so,' protested Swonken. 'What do you know of the power of drugs?'

'They becalmed us,' Swinke put in. 'Took away our will. Can that be happiness?'

Janie, noticing that Avelina said nothing, tilted the girl's chin so that their eyes met.

'And you, my deadly nightshade. Are you glad to have escaped that influence?'

Avelina pushed her hand away, her face darkening.

'There are powers you know nothing of,' she muttered. 'Don't ridicule them or they may turn against you.'

'Ha! A threat from a servant of the dark forces! Should I quake in my shoes?'

'Enough, Janie,' Henry warned.

'Enough, be hanged! Let's do away with these weird superstitions! They're of a piece with your priest-worship, Henry, however different they seem. They put the common people in thrall.'

'The common people need to be led,' Henry countered more hotly than he had intended.

'We shall see about that,' Janie glowered. 'The people themselves don't seem to agree with you.'

She nodded towards a straggle of young men with pitchforks, who waved their implements aggressively in the air as they passed, as if about to claim some impossible triumph.

'Perhaps it *won't* be the meek who inherit the earth,' she added provocatively.

Grimbold knows no master, Ranulph mused.

Henry turned away from her to face the road ahead, his ears burning. How was it that she knew exactly how to anger him? And why did he respond to her taunts just as she wished him to?

'And you, Walt,' Janie asked, the mood upon her. 'Are you staying with us whatever the dangers?'

The old man settled into the sacking which supported him in the waggon. It was obvious that he was unwilling to think beyond present comforts, however meagre they might be.

'Whatever the Lord wishes,' he bleated. 'May His will be done, amen.'

'Amen,' repeated Henry, and crossed himself.

*

They urged Taffy forward at an exhausting pace for the rest of the day, pausing only to buy food at wayside stalls and to eat it at a safe place with wide views of the countryside around. Of Sourskin there was neither sight nor smell.

Camped for the night under a clump of trees by a small river, they retired to bed early, chatting in a desultory fashion as tiredness gradually engulfed them. From a little way off came a contented chewing of grass: Taffy was tied to the nearest tree and Hosea's Wife chained to a stake.

'We shall have London in sight by this time tomorrow,' Henry murmured with as much confidence as he could muster.

'And what if we have no success there?' Ranulph asked. 'Shall we search for that relic for ever? Will we always be on the run?'

Henry was silent for a moment.

'No,' he said at last, 'we can't go on like this much longer. Let us pray for success in London. If our hopes should be dashed there, we must reconsider everything.' After a long pause he repeated the last word in a voice heavy with sleep: 'Everything.'

Ranulph, too, was weary, but the thought that a resolution was at hand both excited and disturbed him, and his restless brain kept him awake long after the others had drifted into unconsciousness. What might there be in place of this headlong flight from Sourskin and who knew how many of the Baron's agents? Would he be left alone to meet those horrors face to face, once and for all? He could hardly think so, and yet Henry had said that everything must be reconsidered.

Then he imagined, briefly, a happier turn of events, with the discovery of his relic and his release from the Baron's sport. This reverie, however, was immediately clouded by the thought that such an outcome would inevitably bring about the disbandment of their motley company of travellers, and a great sadness overtook him until he felt the tears pricking at his eyes.

Quite unable to sleep, he rolled from under the waggon and strolled over to Taffy, asleep under his tree. How peaceful to be one of God's creatures whom noone hunted! He stooped to stroke the horse's mane – and immediately felt himself watched.

'Who's there?' he whispered towards the trees.

There was, of course, no reply. He sniffed, but the wind was away from him and gave only the scents of the river: stagnant water where it stalled behind a bend; ancient alders; meadowsweet; an otter on the prowl. Yet he *could* sense a human presence there. He stepped backwards, expecting at any moment the rush of a charging body, the rise and fall of a blade.

'Come out!' he yelled. 'Come out and show yourself!'

He heard a faint snigger from the dark shadow of the trees and then found himself grasped by the shoulders from behind.

'Calm yourself,' Henry said gently, shaking him as if he were in the grip of a nightmare and needed rousing. 'There's noone here.'

'In the trees!'

He was led back to the waggon like a surrendered prisoner, helpless.

'Only your imagination,' Henry soothed him. 'Such a small copse, and we searched it not much more than an hour ago.'

'While there was still some daylight.'

'But the animals haven't stirred. That goat wouldn't allow a trespasser.'

He said nothing more, but lay beneath the waggon, his eyes on the grotesque looming bulk of the trees. When at last he fell asleep, his dreams were loud with disembodied sniggerings.

*

The following day, as Ranulph walked muzzy-headed beside the waggon, Swinke and Swonken began to tell him stories of their early lives.

'There aren't many like us,' Swinke said unnecessarily.

'Because they smother us at birth,' explained Swonken.

'But we were spared because of a dear, kind father.'

'Our mother having died in the shelling of us.'

'And he so stricken with grief that he clung to what little he had.'

'Which was us.'

They seemed able to talk in this double-handed fashion

endlessly, as if each knew not only what the other would say, but where he would break off.

'We were raised in the valley of the River Wye.'

'Close by Tintern Abbey, a most holy place.'

'And where, in our grandfather's time, King Edward the Second stayed when fleeing the army of Queen Isabella, his wife.'

Ranulph, although he was marvellously entertained by their stories (for he knew no history, had never heard of King Edward and Queen Isabella and would previously have found it difficult to credit that such curiously malformed creatures as Swinke and Swonken ever existed), nevertheless kept a careful watch about him, never dropping his guard for a moment.

The road was now far busier. The little knots of travellers had become drifting skeins. Most of the movement was towards London, and most of the people they met were young, noisy and belligerent.

'Eight shillings the cart!' a rubbery-lipped lout shouted, bringing his coarse face close to Brother Walt's. 'Don't pay it!'

'See John Gaunt in hell first!' called another.

Walt flinched: 'What are they saying?' he asked nervously. 'They want money?'

Henry shook his head.

'It's not you they're angry with, Walt, but the poll tax. A shilling a head, haven't you heard, for every man jack in the country.'

'And every woman jill,' growled Janie, 'if we're foolish enough to stay in the one place so they can find us.'

She laughed: 'Pity it's not a leg tax, eh, Swinke-Swonken? That would prove a bargain for you.'

'There'll be trouble over it, I don't doubt,' Henry said. 'Our young King's been ill-advised by his uncle, and the people know it. Do you hear them? These buffoons dare to say they're putting a price on John of Gaunt's head.'

'And seem pretty serious about it,' Ranulph observed.

'What, this pathetic rabble? Ha!'

Dust rose from the scorched earth as they trundled on, the afternoon sun breathing hot against the backs of their necks. Christopher trawled a leather bottle from the bottom of the waggon, took a deep draught of water and handed it to Ranulph.

'Dwink!' he bawled happily. 'Dwink, Wiwwum!'

When it reached Swinke, he tipped the bottle to his lips, swigged mightily and passed it to his twin.

'After our father died,' he said, resuming a story he had left off some time before, 'we had to earn our living as best we could.'

'Although,' Swonken started up immediately, spilling water down his chin, 'we had no training for anything at all.'

'So we found work on a large estate.'

'It being harvest time.'

'And we were the best pickers of beans that ever there were.'

'Thanks to the fact we could walk between the rows . . .'

Here Swonken paused, and the pair of them finished together: 'Picking on either side!'

Further tales of their early work experiences were here cut short by Janie, who stood up in the waggon, waved a triumphant arm and shouted at the top of her voice.

'London!'

*

At first they could see nothing at all. Taffy's head dipped and rose, dipped and rose in front of them against a flat and featureless horizon.

'The smoke,' Janie grinned, amused by their incomprehension. 'Can't you see it against the sky?'

No, for some minutes more they could not, but Janie had been this way before.

'First the smoke from the cooking fires,' she explained. 'Then – just you wait – it's a miracle!'

And there *was* something magical about the sudden appearance of that great city. The distant haze had undeniably translated itself into smoke when, in a single second it seemed, a vast scattering of buildings sprung up across the flat plain, stretching east to west not far short of a mile.

'That's London?' Avelina asked, in tones which suggested that she feared the answer. The sight clearly awed her to the point of terror. 'All that?'

'And more,' Janie nodded. 'It runs down to the great river Thames and then beyond. We're far from it yet.'

The distance was, indeed, deceptive. An hour later they could make out some of the detail on the larger buildings (a church tower here, a campanile there), but the road still stretched long before them.

'I've an introduction to the Master of a Dominican friary just outside the city walls,' Henry said. 'We'll go there together, William, and hope for encouraging news of your relic.'

'I know the place,' Janie told him. 'Another hour, perhaps two, and we'll be there.'

Ranulph tried to suppress the hope that welled inside him. Had he not known disappointments enough not to confuse desire with reality? Despite himself, however, he began to imagine his mission accomplished, for the alternative was too terrible to contemplate.

'In London,' Janie said happily, 'I shall buy some fine clothes. Skirts and girdles and shoes!'

'And I a prayer roll I've longed dreamed of owning,' Henry threw in. 'What about you, Walt?'

'A comfortable pillow,' the old man chuckled, 'on which I

shall sleep for a week without interruption.'

Then they all began to fantasise wildly about the wonders they would discover in England's greatest city – all except Ranulph, who sat with his head between his knees as Taffy drew them closer and closer, his head dipping and rising, dipping and rising.

*

'God bless my soul!' the Master roared with scarcely containable mirth, his large belly rising and falling. 'You really expected to find such a thing here? What a splendid notion!'

Ranulph and Henry fell silent, feeling chastened and very stupid. Through an arch they could see brothers in white habits and black cloaks slowly pacing a stone floor. A thin bell rang.

'I don't say that there's not a drop of Christ's blood to be found anywhere in Christendom. How should I know? But what gave you the idea you could afford such a thing, eh? This is a private enterprise? It's not financed by the Pope himself?'

Recognising their discomfiture, he inclined his head towards them in a gesture of sympathy, then turned on his heel, beckoning them to follow.

'Come! This way! I'll show you a relic.'

They crossed a courtyard, walked a length of cloister and entered the friary church, a cavernous building designed for preaching to the local populace. Attached to the foot of a crucifix on one wall was a short length of cloth.

'There!' exclaimed the Master, raising a fat hand towards it. 'A part of the shroud in which our Lord's body was wrapped after the crucifixion. How much do you think that cost?'

'Obviously, sir,' Henry faltered, 'a very great amount.'

'A fortune! It was, of course, given to us by a wealthy benefactor who is well remembered in our prayers. I tell you, we could run the friary for five years on what that relic cost.'

He laughed: 'Now you tell me what you would offer for a drop of our Lord's precious blood!'

Ranulph tugged Henry's arm, anxious that his friend should not bear the full brunt of their humiliation.

'We see all too clearly how foolish we've been,' he said, the words tumbling unguarded from his lips. 'Now that you've had your sport belittling us we'll be on our way.'

Henry blanched to hear such bluntness of speech, but the Master merely raised a finger to silence him.

'Hush, my son,' he admonished. 'I've no wish to upset you. Forgive my robust humour. I'd truly love to help you if I could.'

He beamed: 'And haven't you asked to see Christ's blood at the most appropriate time? Tomorrow is the feast of Corpus Christi. We keep the vigil tonight.'

The Master ushered them almost tenderly from the church, an arm around each of their shoulders.

'You must stay the night with us here,' he said firmly. 'And my considered advice to you is to turn on your heels in the morning and return whence you came. London is in turmoil. The rabble is on the march in vast numbers from Kent and Essex. We receive dreadful news almost hourly.'

'We must enter the gates, sir,' Henry said.

'Don't you understand, my son? Every honest man is threatened here. The very King himself!'

'We understand,' Henry nodded. 'But we have a duty.'

'Ah well, a duty cannot be shirked. But stay the night with us first. The light is already fading. You rest with us and we'll see that you're well fed before you leave in the morning.'

Henry winced.

'But there are eight of us, sir,' he said deferentially.

'No matter, no matter! I've seen your company from a distance, but we've plenty of room here. Bring them in!'

'From a distance, but . . .'

'There's something amiss with your friends?' the Master enquired with a chuckle. 'Where are you from?'

'Myself, sir, from Holy Island.' He reached into a pocket. 'I have a letter of introduction which I had no time to show you.'

'Ah, Brother Edgar, is it not?' the Master smiled, taking the paper. 'A fine man! And you, boy?'

'From the same part of the country,' Ranulph said. 'In the demesne of Baron Fulke.'

'Is that so?'

The Master finished reading his letter, then read it again, slowly, all the time humming contentedly.

'Yes, a fine man,' he repeated at last. 'A very fine man. And the Baron was your lord, boy, eh?'

'And still is,' Henry interjected. 'Which is the very root of our problem.'

The Master shook his head.

'No, no,' he said. 'Not *still is*. You've been on the road a long time, I suppose. The news has outrun you.'

'News?' they both asked together.

The Master looked carefully at Ranulph for a moment, as if he feared that what he had to say might disturb him.

'Your Baron Fulke,' he said, 'is dead.'

20 The Streets of London

Ranulph knows no master!

The words, having once formed themselves in his brain, dashed about it with all the frenzy of a tormented bear straining at its tether to swat blindly at its howling persecutors.

Fulke is dead. Now Ranulph knows no master!

Why was it that the notion brought terror in equal measure with relief?

While his friends gathered in the refectory for a simple but welcome meal, Ranulph paced the friary grounds alone. How could it be that his enemy was dead? He knew that the abbott words must be true – that the baron had been fatally struck in the neck by an arrow while hunting, though whether by accident or design nobody was able to say – but he could not *feel* that it was true. He had been hunted so strenuously and for so long that his freedom seemed impossible to accept.

The great arc of sky was slowly deepening to the rich tinge that precedes the ultramarine of night. Stars began to appear, stitching tiny pinpricks of brightness in the gathering darkness.

Somewhere a shepherd played a pipe, the thin reedy sound almost lost in the huge silence that surrounded it. His sheep, ghostly white forms in the middle distance, grew ever more insubstantial as a faint mist rose from the pasture to seep into the thickening gloom.

Lucky Ranulph knows no master!

Climbing a small mound, he threw himself upon the grass and closed his arms over his ears as if he could drown the relentless, cocksure chanting inside his head.

Below, where London spread before him, the starlight was echoed by the lanterns and tapers which flickered at a thousand windows. He lay back, his nostrils saturated with the smell of the grass and the rich brown earth beneath it. A star fell, and his eyes followed its swift progress to earth.

He felt at this moment, and with such an intensity that his arms reached involuntarily into the darkness above his head as if to the mother he had never known, that he must go home. He yearned for his northern forest. He longed to be curled up beneath the root of the fallen tree or, hidden in his secret drey, to watch the raucous hunters coursing by.

It was then that he understood his dread.

Ranulph shall be master now!

No, he would not hear it. He closed his eyes and drummed his fists against the springy turf until they ached. How could this thing be? He was a humble, ignorant peasant. He was a frightened, hunted creature. He was a clumsy performer in a makeshift travelling troupe. Those might not be glorious roles, but he recognised himself in them. They fitted. He was Ranulph the survivor, Ranulph live-by-your-wits, Ranulph the nose!

When, at last, he opened his eyes, he saw that the trembling flares of London had been transformed to orange flames. It was some moments before he realised that fires were raging in several parts of the great city. Were they ceremonial fires? And did his ears pick up, across the townscape, a murmuration of clamorous voices?

Above his head there burned a steadier glow. A large orange moon had risen in the heavens, and the friary walls were tinged with its reflected glory. Inside, his friends would be finishing their meal, rejoicing that their trials were over.

Ah, how fortunate to be Henry, soon to find himself embraced by Mother Church! How wonderful to be Janie, never happier than when travelling! How blessed to be Christopher, knowing nothing of the past and caring nothing for the future!

He allowed his heavy legs to carry him down the slope towards them, his eyes filled with tears.

*

As they passed through its gates in the fresh morning light of a fine June day, did the great city of London disappoint them? Ranulph remembered what an old woodman had once told him: 'A forest, no matter how it stretches, be it from here to the furthest ocean, only ever seems as big as the nearest trees.'

Now, as the houses pressed in on them from either side, he knew this to be true, for they were very soon locked into London's labyrinthine streets and passageways with no clue as to how far the metropolis stretched. It was so much like the other cities that they had passed through, so much like Lincoln, so much like Coventry – perhaps louder, perhaps rougher, perhaps pushier (though this may have been his fearful fancy) but basically so much alike.

And yet there *was* something else. A curious vibration seemed to pulse through the air. It leaped from the eyes of those who looked at them, from the bodies of those who brushed against them. Each in turn felt the excitement, but it was Henry who spoke of it first. It was mid-morning, and they sat round the table of an otherwise empty alehouse, feeling the need to rest their feet and gather their wits.

'Is it my imagination,' he asked, 'or is this place a beehive that's been stirred by a stick? Everyone's a-buzz! Even Swinke-Swonken pass almost unnoticed here, the people are so preoccupied.'

The twins smiled, and their heads nodded in happy agreement: anonymity was a luxury they were rarely afforded. It disappeared soon enough, in any case, for the landlord arrived to gaze upon them with jaundiced eyes that peered from a face whose skull seemed several sizes too small for the skin that covered it. His pendulous jowls quivered as he spoke.

'What the devil's that?' he demanded, pointing an accusing thumb towards the hapless twins.

Henry, seeking to brighten that gloomy countenance, beamed his most friendly of smiles.

'Just another of God's mysteries – like you and me, brother.'

'Looks more like one of His jokes, and a poor one at that. Still, London's full of weird people at present. I don't understand any of 'em, but if their money's all right I suppose I shouldn't grumble. What'll it be?'

Ranulph, grinning, whispered into Avelina's ear: 'Little wonder it's quiet in here with such a Lord of Mirth to greet you. Let's hope his ale is better than his company.'

Their order taken, the landlord turned to go, but Janie tugged at his sleeve.

'Tell me, grandad,' she asked. 'What's the matter with this place. People down here are jumpier than frogs around a lily pond.'

He gazed at her in disbelief.

'You know nothing of last night's horrors? No, I can tell that you don't. Well they've broken open the Marshalsea for a start.'

'The Marshalsea?' Ranulph queried.

'The prison, addle-pate! At Southwark, which is just across the river. The men from Kent have set free the criminals so that we've all to fear for our necks. And the men of Essex have ransacked the Archbishop's palace at Lambeth and put his property to the torch. They've spent the night in the fields outside the city, but nothing's going to stop them. The world's gone mad.'

'This is the work of John Ball?' Henry asked.

The innkeeper nodded, almost bringing his face to destruction.

'Aye, him and a few too many others. They've stirred people up aplenty with their damning of all those in authority. Even the King is threatened, if rumours are to be believed.'

'But *are* rumours to be believed?' queried Walt, clearly worried by this new threat to his peaceful future. A feeble hand reached under the table to stroke Hosea's Wife, the one warm certainty he knew in life.

The landlord fixed him with his right eye, closing his left in a strange gesture of emphasis.

'In my experience,' he said, 'the blacker the rumour the more likely it is to come about. Bright rumours, they fizzle away into nothing, but the black ones . . . No, take my word – trouble's coming.'

'Not that trouble ever took away a man's thirst,' Henry suggested brightly.

'Well, that's true enough, by the precious blood of Christ.' He crossed himself and turned away to fetch their jugs and tankards, calling back over his shoulder: 'But I see dark hours ahead, my friends, dark hours ahead.'

While they waited for their drinks, Janie took a penny whistle from her pocket and began to play a merry little tune she had picked up from a pedlar along the way. It would normally have brought a sparkle to their eyes and a general tapping of feet, but for some reason it did not. Had the landlord's gloom taken possession of them all?

'Tell me, sir,' Henry asked when he returned. 'How shall we find Cheapside.'

The landlord set his tray down heavily, so that the ale sloshed and spilled.

'Cheapside, is it? What honest man ever wanted Cheapside?'

'Honest entertainers, sir, and we hear there are rich pickings to be had there.'

They listened to the landlord's grudging directions carefully, for at Cheapside they were to find their connection: 'Just play there,' they had been told, 'and you will be found.' If events were moving as swiftly as the landlord suggested, they had little time to waste.

'Connections must be made,' the summoner had said. 'A chain with a broken link half-way is but half a chain.'

The landlord gave his last few directions, added a dire warning and abandoned them, the while pursing his lips and kissing the air in a gesture as free of meaning as his closed left eye had been.

Walt supped his ale thoughtfully.

'I don't understand any of this,' he said. 'If Baron Fulke is dead, as the good abbot said he was, then surely your troubles are over, boy. We return, you take over at the castle and we all serve you faithfully' – a little smiled played about his thin and cracked old man's lips – 'while you remember the debt of gratitude you owe us.

'This rebellion, this power-to-the-peasants nonsense, will ill serve us. Let's forget Cheapside and head north while we can.'

Ranulph shook his head: 'It's not quite so simple,' he said. 'We have other business to complete first, as Henry and Janie know too well.'

Henry nodded: 'We have a message to deliver, Brother Walt, and I believe we would create greater risks for ourselves by turning now. We are being watched, and not only by Sourskin and his brood. But take heart: this task will soon be accomplished.'

'And then,' Janie chuckled, patting Walt's bald pate so that he shrank away in outrage, 'we shall be on the open road once more! Isn't that so?'

Her cheerfulness was immediately stifled by the mournful expression she witnessed on Ranulph's face.

'Isn't that so?' she demanded again.

'A new life!' encouraged Henry.

But Ranulph's face only darkened further.

'Don't you understand?' he said. 'Nothing's changed. Someone else will have seized the Baron's vacant chair. Someone else will be sleeping in his bed. Someone else will be swaggering and bullying in the way of the powerful. You can't doubt that, surely. Why should they wait for me?'

And then, so quietly as to be almost under his breath, he added: 'A plague on all those who would rule others.'

'I'll drink to that,' said Janie.

'Why Wiwwum unhappy?' Christopher asked, his face clouded with confusion.

'He's not unhappy, old addlepate,' Henry said briskly, ruffling his hair. 'He's just being thoughtful.'

'No. Wiwwum unhappy.'

Ranulph managed a weak smile: 'It's all right, Christopher. How could I be unhappy with friends like you? I was only thinking of what has been and of what might have been – just mourning a past that is forever lost to me. There's no going back.'

'And the girl whose token you carry?' Henry asked a little mischievously. 'This Elizabeth?'

Avelina and Janie both allowed curiosity to flicker across their faces.

'Oh yes, the girl,' Janie smiled slyly. 'Such a fine lady's name! What about the girl?'

'And the token?' Avelina asked, knowing nothing of it.

Ranulph's finger drew patterns in the spilt ale on the table top,

'Just like a dream,' he said at last. 'Like a dream you wake from, that's all.'

It was Henry who broke the mood.

'Come on, drink up!' he chided. 'Let's save our talk – we've Cheapside to find.'

'And may the Lord protect us,' whinnied Walt as they trooped out into the bright daylight and hitched Taffy to the waggon.

*

Gathering an audience with their opening antics had never been such a problem. The few people who were persuaded to turn from their business in the bustle and jostle of Cheapside seemed guided more by antipathy than curiosity. Even the dramatic appearance of Swinke-Swonken from beneath the voluminous cloak which kept much of their peculiarity hidden (a revelation that had never before failed to provoke loud cries of amazement), was here greeted with nothing but a few grunts of disbelief and an alarmed outburst from a thin woman in rags who gave every indication of being deranged.

'Snow in summer!' she shouted. 'Last night a moon that wept blood! Now this! Omens all! Destruction! The last days! Our Lord is coming with a sword to strike down the wicked!'

Henry, afraid lest her ranting should turn the mood of their small audience ugly, raised his voice above hers.

'Simple trickery! We are but entertainers, come from afar to part you from your cares and troubles for but a short while, and from a few of your paltry coins for rather longer.'

The joke fell on deaf ears in all but one instance – a man of indeterminate age, who showed his appreciation with a smile made lop-sided by a mighty scar that ran from above his left ear to the right of his chin.

Janie, who was about to burst into the loud singing of a bawdy ballad, grinned back at him, fascinated by a face that had evidently once been handsome and was now, if nothing else, distinctive and interesting. Where the sword (for it was surely a sword) had sliced through the lips they now curled back to one side of his mouth, so that even when he had ceased to smile his teeth were clearly visible in a shocking, fixed parody of mirth.

It was to this face that Janie now sang her song, and the vigour of it, and the way that the words fired their arrows of wit in quick succession, soon brought new spectators to the small space they had managed to find between the busy market stalls.

> *Cut your stick, old greybeard,[xit]*
> *I've sappier stems to try.*
> *A visit to the coppice*
> *Will keep me in supply . . .*

Encouraged by this growing response, the troupe continued with their act, but as Hoseas's Wife felled the assembled line like nine-pins many of the watchers drifted away, pointedly ignoring the bag that Avelina had begun to take round. They were the poorest takings ever, three coins only – and all of them from the hand of the man with the scarred face, who spoke to Avelina as in a sing-song voice as he dropped them into the bag.

'Tell your friends that Grimbold salutes them and thanks them for a timely performance.'

Avelina relayed the message, and Ranulph beckoned the man to join them.

'Who do you serve, sir?' he asked.

'Grimbold knows no master,' the man replied through his distorted grin.

'We have business to do,' Ranulph said in a hushed voice. 'We must find somewhere more private.'

The man contorted his visage into a grimace: 'There is nowhere more private,' he insisted, 'than a busy London thoroughfare where everone is about his own task with no care for the business of others. Just hand me the message and I'll be on my way.'

He extended a hand from which Ranulph instinctively flinched, for he detected upon it a faint, but unmistakable, smell. It was the smell of pepper.

'Wait, my friend,' he said. 'The message is sewn into my tunic. I can't tear it out in full daylight without creating some suspicion, even here in London. No, let's over to the shadows of that alleyway and do our business there.'

Was Henry watching them? Would he follow? Ranulph could only hope as much as he approached the alley.

'Hurry!' scarface urged him, laying a hand on his shoulder as if to prevent him escaping.

Ranulph reached into his tunic. What emerged was not the message, but rather a knife whose gleaming blade, a second later, rested against the man's throat.

'Henry!' he called, not daring to look behind.

'Yes, I'm here. What is it?'

'Take his arms, Henry. He belongs to Sourskin.'

'You're sure?' Henry asked, pinioning the man's arms behind him. There was no resistance.

'He'll tell you so,' Ranulph spoke through clenched teeth. He pressed the knife forward until a bead of blood glistened on the wildly throbbing throat and his eyes opened wide with terror.

'Mercy!' he cried. 'I mean you no harm!'

Janie, who had followed close behind, offered Henry her scarf and the man's hands were soon securely tied behind his back. Henry now took his hair and, tugging it back, exposed the throat more openly to Ranulph's knife.

'Where is he?' Ranulph hissed. 'Quickly, or I'll saw your head from your shoulders with the greatest of pleasure.'

'That's it,' Janie urged. 'Spike him!'

'Dear God,' murmured Henry, his eyes rolling in disbelief. Janie, however, was not to be denied.

'Let me at him!' she cried. 'I'll teach him to smile at me and then play the scoundrel!'

It was perhaps the fierceness of her expression which finally did the trick.

'I'll tell!' their prisoner gasped.

'Where is he?' Ranulph demanded again.

'Here, in London.'

'Close by?'

He grunted: 'Close enough'

'Can he see us now? Is he watching us?'

'No.'

'Then . . .'

'He has a room in an inn near to the river. I am to take the message to him.'

'We shall take it together.'

'No!' the man almost screamed. 'He'll kill me!'

'Perhaps,' Ranulph nodded, 'but I'm the one with a knife at your throat, and if you don't take us there I shall certainly kill you. Now – lead on!'

*

Long and low-beamed, it was more a gallery than a room. Sourskin gazed venomously at his four unwelcome visitors, Christopher having tagged along behind Ranulph, Henry and Janie and refused to go back.

'So we meet again, boy.'

He sat at the far end of the room before a window that gave on to the grey swirl of the Thames. Ranulph said nothing, but his eyes narrowed, and he still held the knife that had pressed against scarface's throat.

'You seem to have the advantage this time,' Sourskin said, a dreadful leering smile on his lips. 'Never mind. As we are no longer adversaries it matters little.'

'Not adversaries!' Ranulph exploded. 'Why, I've come to kill you!'

'Oh, I think not.' Sourskin gave a short laugh. 'We fight for a common cause. We're allies.'

'Don't banter words with him,' Janie urged, but the others motioned her to silence, anxious to fathom Sourskin's meaning.

'How did our friend the summoner put it? A link in the chain. Yes, that's what I am. You have, somewhere upon you, a message. I alone know its destination.'

Henry stepped forward.

'That message about Grimbold knowing no master,' he said. 'I can't believe that it was ever entrusted to this creature here.' (He inclined his head in the direction of the man with the scar, who stood silently to one side of Sourskin, clearly frightened for his life). 'He's not of the summoner's party. Neither are you.'

Sourskin threw up his hands.

'Why, of course not. The original messenger is dead.'

'Killed by you!' Ranulph accused.

'So be it. The stark fact is that he's dead. The summoner, too, of course. Sang like a lark while he still had the breath. Now I alone have the means and the knowledge to bring this business to a satisfactory conclusion – or I shall have once you hand me that piece of paper.'

'And why should we?' Ranulph asked. 'What interest is it of ours?'

'May I inform you,' Sourskin replied, 'that at this very moment there's an army of peasants marching on London. Perhaps I misunderstand you, but my intelligence suggests that you're greatly in sympathy with this chaotic rebellion.'

'We're no rebels,' Henry threw in, his voice faltering as he thought how unsure he now was about opinions he had held to for a lifetime.

'Listen to me,' Sourksin urged, his voice suddenly become conciliatory. 'Let us talk frankly. Of course it was for some time my intention to seize this boy and take him, dead or alive, to Baron Fulke. We all have to earn our bread in one way or another, and that kind of thing is very much in my line.'

Now he addressed Ranulph directly: 'With Fulke's death, which I'm sure you must know of, you were of no further use to me. But this plot of the summoner's, this grand scheme for the overthrow of things – why, I can turn that very well to my advantage. There's money in it.'

'What has one scrap of paper to do with that?' Ranulph asked, curious despite himself.

'It's an unlocker of doors, boy. It's an alert to people up and down the country to prepare themselves. When the peasants reach London the King and his advisers will be much preoccupied. That message you carry will foment a rising so great that they'll never contain it.'

'Then let them get on with it,' Janie declared airily. 'It's nothing to do with us.'

'The timing's crucial,' Sourskin said. 'If this mob strikes too soon every rebel will be picked off one by one. I alone have the means to coordinate the uprising, because I alone know the destination of that piece of paper. So come – let me have it, boy.'

Ranulph backed away, the knife useless in his slack hand. Much as he abominated Sourskin, he was horribly confused about his attitude to the rebellion and the confusion made him vulnerable.

'Come, hand it over!'

Sourskin shook the knife from his fingers and, grasping his shoulder with great force, pushed him to the ground. His free hand swiftly ran through Ranulph's clothing, hunting for the vital message. That stench was almost overpowering.

'Enough,' Henry protested, stooping ineffectually above them. 'Leave him alone.'

'Ah!' grinned Sourskin. 'I have it!'

'Wiwwum!'

Did Christopher remember his meeting with Sourskin in Lincoln? Did he believe that Sourskin intended Ranulph harm? Whatever the cause, he now lumbered forward, his lips mumbling something incomprehensible, and he swung his huge fist ferociously through the air, felling Sourskin like a tree put to the axe.

'Wiwwum!' he sobbed, enfolding his friend in a suffocating embrace. 'Wiwwum happy now?' he almost pleaded.

They all looked down on the stricken body, silent and appalled. None of them found it possible to utter the word, but the angle of the head to the body left no doubt whatsoever that Sourskin was dead.

21 Mob Rule

Even as they left the room where Sourskin lay, they heard raised voices in the street below. The mob was upon London, and the citizens were passing the news excitedly through the thoroughfares.

'The rebels have taken London Bridge!'

'Death to all churchmen!'

'Hurrah for John Ball!'

Some looked fearful and sought to find shuttered safety within their houses, while others whooped with joy and set off to welcome the invaders.

'This way, Henry!' Ranulph beckoned, attempting to force a way through a street wild with confusion. Christopher clung to him, his eyes still red from weeping, making progress difficult – though no more difficult than that of Walt, who struggled along with Hosea's Wife behind him on all too long a tether.

Henry drove the waggon, urging Taffy onwards. Janie sat beside him, with Avelina and Swinke-Swonken in behind.

'This is hopeless!' Henry shouted above the hubbub that surrounded them. 'We'll have to find somewhere until the streets clear.'

They came to an inn, and Ranulph grabbed Taffy's harness, tugging the horse towards an arched opening that led to a courtyard with stabling.

'In here!' he cried. 'Are we all together?'

They were, but their troubles were by no means over. The landlord, who had already bolted his front door and closed his shutters, tried to prevent them entering at the back.

'You can't stay here,' he told them. 'I'm locking up.'

His wife, her face white and strained, stood a few paces behind him, wringing her hands.

'Lock up by all means, my friend,' Henry said in his most reassuring voice, 'but we intend to stay inside.

'Don't worry,' he added. 'We mean you no harm. You may be glad of our presence before the night is through.'

Swinke-Swonken were already down from the waggon and practically skipping inside, preceded only by Hosea's Wife, which had tugged itself free of Walt's tiring grasp. The innkeeper shrugged as the rest followed, then slammed the door behind them and dropped a heavy bar across it.

'You've the means to pay for your board?' he asked sullenly.

'Of course, my friend,' Henry smiled, hugely relieved to be safely inside and off the teeming street. 'Here, take some in advance.'

'And fetch some pottage,' Ranulph added. 'We're hungry.'

Where, he immediately asked himself, had this strange self-assertion come from? Could it, just possibly, be anything to do with a life that beckoned him from afar? No, he refused to consider such a thing.

'If you please,' he added swiftly.

*

Long hours passed, during which the commotion outside steadily increased, with frequent beatings upon the door which the innkeeper steadfastly ignored. There was a smell of burning in the air, and every so often a neighbour or passer-by would press his face to the one narrow, unshuttered window and recount the terrible doings of the day before being carried away by the swirl of the crowd.

'They've burned the Savoy to the ground!' yelled one of these fleeting visitors.

The innkeeper, who sat facing the door as if to protect it, turned his head towards them.

'John of Gaunt's palace,' he said. He was growing accustomed to being the interpreter for these incomers who knew nothing of his city. 'They hate John of Gaunt. Can't say I've much fellow feeling for the man myself.'

'And the hospital of Clerkenwell,' shouted their informant, his voice growing fainter as he was swept off his feet and borne away.

As the light began to fade, so the news seemed to grow steadily darker.

'The Fleet is broken open!' a woman's voice wailed.

'They've taken the prison, Kate?' the innkeeper demanded urgently of the wall.

'Aye, and set all the miscreants free. There's blood on the streets!'

'The King's under seige in the Tower!' threw in someone else. 'Wat Tyler has an army of thousands outside. They'll have him yet!'

The innkeeper turned in his chair.

'Not young King Richard,' he muttered to his knees. 'There's no man should think to slight a King. God bless his holy soul.'

He rose, and stumbled into a back room where they could hear him pouring ale into a jug. His wife now appeared with lighted tapers that threw strange shadows all about them.

'We ought to decide a plan of action,' Henry said in a determined fashion which brought all the others about him.

'Escape,' declared Walt. 'That's all we need to think about. We can't stay here.'

'At least we're safe,' countered Henry.

'Until they burn the house around our ears.'

'Fire!' exclaimed Christopher. 'Smell fire!'

Avelina started up, a look of dread on her face, but Ranulph put a hand on hers.

'No,' he said. 'That's just the smell of distant flames. I would know if this building was ablaze.'

The innkeeper reemerged with a tray on which were three jugs of ale.

'I want no part of this trouble,' he told them. 'Here in the city we arrange our affairs to suit ourselves. I don't ask what happens out there in the country. If there are lords that treat their people badly they should be brought to task for it, but there are dangerous men about who seek to warp men's minds. We don't need these John Balls and Wat Tylers. There's enough evil in the world without them making more of it. That's what I think, leastwise.'

With that he distributed the drinks and sank back in his chair while the mob continued to bustle by outside.

'What I meant,' Henry resumed, 'was that we must decide what to do once we're away from here. And that's chiefly for you to decide, Ranulph.'

He started.

'William,' he corrected.

'No,' Henry insisted. 'The danger is past now, and you can take your proper name again. He's Ranulph,' he revealed to their companions. 'Ranulph, heir to a large estate in the north. I, at any rate, shall call you Ranulph.'

'Wiwwum,' said Christopher.

'And Christopher we shall excuse,' Henry laughed.

He brought his face close to Ranulph's: 'What will you do?'

Ranulph raised the drink to his mouth so that he should not have to answer for some moments. They watched him in silence.

'I can never,' he said at last, 'be the person I once was. Everything has changed. I've seen so much more of the world, and I've learned so much.'

'Very true,' Henry said. 'I've seen you change before my eyes. But that doesn't answer the question.'

'And I've also seen,' Ranulph continued, 'that the whole world is changing. All this commotion outside – it's not just a matter of a few hotheads setting fire to some grand buildings, is it? You've witnessed it as well as I, Henry, on our travels. The people will no longer tolerate the cruelties of their masters. They want to be free.'

'Perhaps they don't realise what freedom will demand of them.'

'I don't know about that, Henry. All I know is that I understand that feeling. I was an ill-treated peasant myself, remember. How could I go back and lord it over my own serfs as it gave Baron Fulke such pleasure to do?'

'And what's the alternative?'

'To go where this rebellion leads, I suppose. To refuse to be a prisoner of the past.'

They sat silently over their drinks for some minutes.

'Besides,' Ranulph said eventually, 'I don't wish to lose the friends I've made.'

He looked around him now, his eyes slowly travelling from the large and drooling Christopher, to saucy Janie, to wizened old Walt, even now petting his stupid goat, to strange Avelina with her secret knowledge, to Swinke-Swonken, sprightly in their new-found health, finally to dear, faithful Henry. He felt very close to tears.

'Perhaps you wouldn't lose us too easily,' Janie grinned. 'I quite fancy travelling the great north road. There are good pickings these summer months.'

'I'd accept a small living,' Brother Walt offered graciously.

There was a new sound outside – the sound of a bell and a loud shouting. They all moved quickly towards the wall.

'Just think on one thing,' Henry counselled Ranulph earnestly. 'Not every lord is a Fulke. You wouldn't have to behave like that.'

The innkeeper had a finger to his lips as he strained to listen at the small open window.

'They're crying death to the lawyers,' he said.

The bell rang again, and then the shouting came much louder. They could all hear it now.

'. . . that all lawyers, and every official of the Chancery and the Exchequer, shall be delivered up for execution. We shall have their heads! And all those who can write a writ or a letter. The order is that all these vermin shall deliver themselves, or be delivered, to the Tower!'

'Pray God,' the innkeeper said softly when the crier had passed on, 'that our King remains safe in the Tower.'

'Amen!' trembled his wife, and the tankard she held in her hand shook violently and spilled ale on the floor.

*

They slept fitfully that night, constantly awoken by shrieks, moans and bangings which might have been near or far. Henry would have been away at first light, and Walt gave him ample support, but the innkeeper himself persuaded them to stay a while longer.

'See what's on the streets first,' he warned them. 'I know these folk. Their passions have been roused to fury. You'd have little protection from a wild knife along an early morning alley.'

'We'll have word of what's happening soon enough,' his wife added, friendlier for having shared their company in troubled times.

So they waited, had breakfast and waited a little more. The street outside was quieter now. The vehemence of the night before had given way to a brittle tension. The king, they learned at midmorning, had travelled to Mile End with his powerful barons to meet the rebel leader, Wat Tyler.

'May God protect him,' breathed the innkeeper.

The King, an excited neighbour informed them towards noon, had agreed to Tyler's demands that there be an end to serfdom, that no man should serve another unless of his own free will and that land should be rented to labourers at a rate of fourpence an acre.

'If only we could *all* choose our own rates,' commented the innkeeper's wife with a scowl.

By early afternoon they had a more detailed report from Mile End. It had further been granted that the rebels should seize all traitors who opposed the King and his law. At this, the innkeeper spat juicily upon the floor.

'Which means,' he said, 'any poor soul they choose to condemn. I should be on my way, my friends – and don't look behind!'

They gathered their few belongings together, harnessed Taffy to the waggon and made their farewells of an emotional innkeeper's wife who suddenly revealed a hidden store of affection by reaching out both hands to ruffle Swinke-Swonken's curly locks.

'Remember us,' she trebled, and she waved a handkerchief until they were out of sight.

It had been their intention to make straight for the north gate, but they were very soon forced to accept a disturbing reality: once they reached the city's main thoroughfares they were caught up in a seething, violent mass of humanity, and they could go only where it carried them.

'I'll guide Taffy through the crowd,' Ranulph shouted above the din, and he jumped down from the waggon and took the lead rein. The poor horse's eyes were wide with fright, and Ranulph had to stroke his mane and coax him along.

None of them, not even Janie, had ever been to London before, and they gazed about them with mixed awe and fright.

Swept southwards, they were puzzled to see in the mid-distance, beyond the last houses, a billowing of vast sheets which seemed suspended in the air.

'Ships!' Janie exclaimed as they drew closer, and almost immediately they saw the water slapping at the timbers of large quays where the woollen cloth exporters kept their boats. The road widened here for a stretch, and Ranulph tugged and strained at Taffy's harness to pull them out of the swirl of traffic which would otherwise have dragged them eastwards along the riverbank.

'We'll rest here,' he called, and he ran round to put chocks under the wheels.

From the vantage of the waggon they saw wonderful things. Close by, to their right, the great bridge of London, heavy with shops and houses, straddled the mighty Thames on nineteen massive arches. Even as they watched, a large merchant ship began to nose its way through. To their left, not half a mile away, an impressive stone building commanded the river from a hill on its northern bank.

'What's that palace, friend?' Henry called out to an old man who limped painfully past the waggon.

'Palace? Why, that's the Tower of London. Impregnable.' He chuckled as he went on his way, calling back joyfully: 'Or *was* – Wat Tyler's men have taken it!'

They huddled together in the waggon, resigned to their immobility.

'We shan't be away today,' Henry said. 'Not while this madness lasts.'

'And it's not a time for music-making,' Janie conceded, ducking as a passing lout swung a long wooden staff all too close to her head. 'There's not an ounce of merriment in these folk.'

'Hungry!' Christopher started up. 'Hungry!'

Swinke-Swonken reached into a large sack and distributed bread to all the company. It was past its best, but they chewed it thankfully enough.

'We shall be lucky to eat ever again,' Walt bleated, self-pity getting the better of him.

There was a smell of salt in the air as the Thames began to run upstream from the sea. Heavily-laden ships setting off for far off countries laboured sluggishly against the tide. At about four in the afternoon the human tide turned, too. Now the crowd pressed in from the east and surged towards the bridge, its mood uglier than before, its roar even wilder.

'Death to all lawyers!' cried a tall, bony man who waved above his head an engraved silver sword which must have been snatched from a rich man's house.

'Death to all lawyers!' the crowd chorused.

'John Ball hath rung thy bell!'

And again they followed him: 'John Ball hath rung thy bell!'

These cursing, panting, sweating peasants pressed close to the waggon, and some of them struck it with their fists or with stout sticks as they passed.

'Death to all traitors!' the cry went up.

Then Ranulph saw, bobbing high above the crowd, something his mind at first refused to believe that he saw. It was a human head spiked on a pole. His stomach heaved and he turned away.

'Dear Mother of God!' he heard Henry gasp.

'Mercy!' cried Janie, and she leant across to Christopher and covered his head with her arms so that he should not see.

But there were more, and they could not be avoided. The ecstatic rebels, fresh from sacking the Tower and beheading their most hated enemies, were parading their trophies to the citizens of London with ghoulish rapture.

'Dance for us, Master Simon!' they crowed, as the head of

the Archbishop of Canterbury was rhythmically hoisted and lowered, its blind eyes wide and staring.

'A penny for your thoughts, John Legge!' one man cried, pointing jubilantly at the next head to pass by.

'You gave us the poll tax,' another exulted, 'and now you're properly polled yourself!'

As this army of serfs who would be serfs no longer jostled clamorously towards London Bridge, it was obvious that the great and mighty of church and state were not its only victims.

'Death to the foreigners!' came the collective shout as a cluster of heads jogged by.

'Filthy Flemings!' someone yelled.

'Lousy Lombards!'

Ranulph, who had climbed to sit on the seat beside Janie, spoke over her head to Henry.

'Try not to look so disapproving,' he urged him, 'or we shall have our skulls paraded alongside theirs.'

'But this is horrific, bestial!'

'Look happy, Henry, whatever you feel.'

Henry, unable to feign pleasure at the carnage about him, simply lowered his head and clenched his fists, his heart pounding. Walt, Avelina and the twins had taken the precaution of lying down in the waggon, and Ranulph now urged Henry to do the same.

'I'll pull the covers over you.'

'I've no wish to skulk in there,' Henry protested.

'For the safety of us all,' Ranulph almost commanded him. 'They're killing anyone out of the ordinary. You're perched up here with the look of a pained bishop on your face. And you're an educated man, Henry. You can write letters. Get out of sight!'

Henry complied, allowing himself to be concealed in the waggon. Ranulph sat on the driving seat with Janie on one side and Christopher on the other.

'Let's all look happy,' Janie chirped rather unconvincingly, and she slipped her hand into his.

The raucous procession boiled past them for a full hour more, began at last to simmer and then, very slowly, to cool. As the afternoon became early evening knots of marauding rebels still swirled in and out of view, loud and threatening, but the blood-letting and the rioting had moved elsewhere.

'Perhaps tomorrow,' Henry said, having emerged from hiding with the others, 'we shall be on our way.'

'Possibly,' Ranulph replied. 'But I don't think this business is over yet.'

He took Christopher with him to find food and drink for themselves and the animals, thinking all the while how strange it was that he should have escaped death at the hands of Baron Fulke only to fall into another danger every bit as real. That danger was personified, on his return, by a gang of four peasants who had approached the waggon and were even now taunting a flustered and distressed Henry. They had him surrounded.

'That's fine talking,' one of them was saying. 'What kind of work do you do, master?'

'I'm an entertainer.'

'You could entertain *us*, master, I'd guarantee. Like to dance, would you?'

Here a dagger appeared and was prodded at Henry's chest, so that he had to skip away from it.

'A fine dance, eh boys?'

'But I don't think he's an entertainer,' another of them said. 'Sounds like a lawyer to me.'

He said the word with heavy menace.

'Oh, a lawyer, is it?'

Christopher began to shoulder his way towards them, but Ranulph held him back.

'We're entertainers,' he said, 'as my friend told you. 'We work as hard as you, and for no more money.'

The four now swung round towards him.

'You don't till the soil,' one of them accused him. 'You don't have that look about you.'

'There's more work than labouring.'

'You don't get up a sweat, I'll be bound. Is this another lawyer, friends?'

'Do I sound like a lawyer?'

'You talk like a northerner,' said one who had so far remained silent. 'You're not a Londoner, and you're not from Kent or Essex.'

'A kind of foreigner, is he?'

Where this interrogation was leading it was all too easy to see, but before it could be pursued any further Avelina swayed forward, a glazed expression in her eyes.

'Abrasadabra,' she murmured.

'What's this?' the most aggressive of the peasants demanded. 'Witchcraft?'

Avelina approached him and slowly raised her hand. In it they saw a small cloth sac, which she held under his nose.

'We are sufferers all,' she intoned, 'who need healing.'

He sniffed at the pouch, then took it from her.

'What is it?' he asked, still holding it to his nostrils. 'Some sort of magic, eh?'

'Only the magic that there is in nature.'

The peasant took himself off for a few moments, inhaling deeply, and when he returned there was a gentleness about him, a profound calm.

'You have more of this?' he asked her.

In reply she turned, glided to the waggon and returned with three more sacs.

'It will work for two days,' she said.

'And you can make more?'

'When the moon is young.'

The peasant nodded, leading his companions away: 'We'll be back, mistress. We'll pay well for this.'

Avelina closed her eyes, sank to her knees and seemed to fall into a deep trance where she knelt.

'Let them come back,' Janie whispered scornfully. 'They won't find us here.'

As darkness fell new fires sprang up in the city. There was a continous commotion of raised voices, and from time to time the most hideous cries were carried to their ears.

Having devised a watch, so that one of the party should always be on guard, they settled down for the night as best as they could.

'May God in his mercy spare us all,' Henry prayed.

The silhouetted head of the Archbishop of Canterbury, erected in triumph above London Bridge, appeared to nod Amen.

*

'To Smithfield!'

Ranulph was awoken by a cry which was taken up on all sides. They had spent the night surrounded by members of Wat Tyler's raggle-taggle army who, their sport temporarily over, had sunk to the ground wherever tiredness had taken them.

'Stir yourself,' one of these bleary-eyed warriors now accosted him. 'We meet the King at Smithfield today.'

'To Smithfield!' another yelled, brandishing a fist. 'For justice!'

Avoiding Smithfield was, they discovered, as impossible as reaching the north gate the day before. Despite their resolve, they were once again sucked into the same streets as the mob the moment they started off.

'At least we're heading north,' Ranulph smiled wearily.

'Who knows what we're heading for?' was Walt's ominous reply as he stroked Hosea's Wife in the back of the waggon.

The sun shone fiercely overhead, and the heat stoked the passions of the rampant warriors who flocked towards Smithfield and destiny. Some spoke with relish of the violence they had perpetrated the night before, while others rehearsed the suffering which was yet to be inflicted on those traitors who had so far escaped.

Arriving at the large field in which the meeting had been arranged, they saw that Tyler's army, many thousands strong, had drawn itself up in battle formation to one side.

'This is our chance to get away,' Henry said, and he pulled sharply on the reins, taking the waggon towards the far side of the field. At this moment, however, a new rush of peasants arrived, blocking their way, and the horse instinctively swerved and picked up pace.

'Woah, Taffy!' Henry called, losing control. 'Come back!'

When they at last came to a halt, with Taffy furiously shaking his mane and snorting his discontent, they found themselves in an embarrassingly exposed position. The peasant army was arrayed to their left, with a man who could only be Wat Tyler himself mounted on a little horse less than twenty yards away. Directly ahead of them, and a good deal closer, a bevy of gorgeously attired gentlemen sat astride taller, sleeker mounts, accompanied by a lad not much older than Ranulph and far more frail.

'The King,' breathed Henry, and he reached to the top of his head to take off a cap which he found,to his consternation he was not wearing.

'That's King Richard?' Ranulph asked, dumbfounded. 'So young?'

'Fourteen years old,' whispered Henry, aware that their voices could easily reach the royal party. 'And the man next to him, in the cloak, must be William Walworth. He's the Mayor of London.'

Taffy, his mood recovered, began to chew the grass. Walt lowered Hosea's Wife to the ground and fastened her rope to a wheel. The sun rose higher in the sky. More peasants were still arriving to swell the ranks of their grimy army, but Tyler must now have decided that the hour was ripe, for he spurred his horse forward and brought himself up close to the King.

'We demand,' he shouted, far louder than he needed for the King's hearing alone, 'an end to all bishoprics. You grant it?'

The young King nodded: 'We grant it.'

'And an end to all lordships.'

'We grant it. All but the lordship of the King.'

'Your majesty.'

Was this said sarcastically or with deference? Ranulph found the question impossible to answer. Tyler was fired with zeal, and the excitement gave his behaviour a frenzied edge.

'All estates of the church must be confiscated.' He turned his horse, trotted away and returned. 'Do you grant that?'

'We do.'

'And that all the commons who stand here with me today shall be pardoned.'

'Granted.'

'And freed!'

Here there was a roar from the peasants closest to Tyler, who had been able to follow the negotiations. The King nodded his agreement and his lips moved, but it was impossible to hear the words.

Now Tyler circled the royal party and made a gesture to one of the royal servants.

'Ale. I must have ale!'

The drink was fetched, and Tyler first swigged some down, then rinsed his mouth and spat upon the ground.

'Your majesty,' he offered, holding out the cup.

The young King made no move to take it. He was not accustomed to drink from a vessel soiled by another man, and his breeding would not allow it. In the silence that followed Walworth spurred his horse forward and placed a hand on the hilt of his sword. His words, spoken with such venom that he stood up in his stirrups, echoed around Smithfield.

'You insolent worm, Tyler!' he cried, pulling out the sword. 'You stinking wretch!'

Did he mean to use the weapon or was this a mere flourish? In the event, Hosea's Wife presented him with an irresistible temptation. Ranulph became aware that the goat had slipped its tether only a second before it sprang at the rear of Tyler's horse. The peasant leader himself seemed to sense the attack at the very same moment, for he turned his head – and was immediately felled by a meaty blow from the mayor's sword.

'Ah, my beloved!' wailed Walt.

Christopher, imagining the incident to be a variation on their usual act, clapped his hands above his head and began to moan in appreciation.

An arrow sailed over their heads, then another. With a terrifying yelling and growling, Tyler's army began to advance on the royal party in order to avenge their stricken leader.

'Under the waggon!' Ranulph shouted, swiftly leaping over the side.

And then a miracle happened. The young King, as if oblivious of his vulnerability, trotted towards the oncoming army and raised a hand to stop them. One lad alone – and he stopped them.

'Sirs,' Ranulph heard him call, 'will you kill your King? I am your captain. Follow me to Clerkenwell.'

The front rank of peasants faltered. Those closest to the King bent their knees. Those further behind, having been checked in their stride, demanded to know what was decided and, with instant meekness, followed on. The field began to clear.

'They honour their King,' Henry said in a satisfied tone as they all sat, bemused, on the waggon.

'And that stupid deference is their undoing,' Janie countered. 'That's the end of their revolt, believe me. They've thrown it all away.'

It was still morning. The day held hours enough for travelling. Ranulph, taking the reins and shaking Taffy alert, felt Henry's quizzical gaze upon him.

'I'm going home,' he said.

Epilogue

The four horses cantered through the forest clearing, their riders' faces flushed with the thrill of the chase and stung by a keen October wind. The sun, a silver orb in a cold blue sky, hung just above the eastern horizon. The leafless trees rattled as they passed.

'To the left, where the ground rises!'

They swung round, climbing swiftly, and one of the riders loosed an arrow which sang through the air and embedded itself in a birch trunk. Their dogs surged in front of them, baying.

'Now right again!'

They plunged through undergrowth, leapt a fallen oak and came out of the trees on to a high plateau. Below them lay a castle, with a river running close by. There was no sign of their quarry. The defeated huntsmen reined in their horses and caught their breath.

'You haven't overlooked, sire,' panted a middle-aged man who wore the dress of a superior servant, 'the hour of the wedding?'

'Who could forget?'

A stranger to the area would have been surprised to discover that the great lord he addressed with the customary respect was a lad of no more than fifteen.

'And that the bishop will at this moment be breakfasting, sire.'

'Rot the bishop!'

The horses' breathing turned to steam which formed wispy patterns in the thin air.

'The bishop should know his place,' Ranulph added, with the hint of a smile in his eyes. 'And in these parts, at least, it's below the level of a baron.'

'And the lady,' persisted the servant, 'will be waiting, too.'

'Ah, yes. The lady.'

That was clearly a different matter, for Ranulph now turned his horse's head, and they began to trot back the way they had come.

'If the lady is yet up,' he added. 'We made an early start.'

Young Baron Ranulph wore his black cloak and breeches as if he had been a lord all his life. He rode with similar aplomb, too, although he had never so much as sat astride a horse before returning to his northern estate in triumph a little more than a year ago.

'Just a moment,' he called suddenly, stopping by a tall tree and craning his neck to inspect it.

'Sire?'

They watched, puzzled, as he dismounted, strode to the trunk and, light as a squirrel, leapt into the branches. A few seconds later he was looking down upon them from a small platform a few feet above their heads.

'My drey!' he grinned. 'Would you have guessed?'

He jumped down, swung into the saddle and, a strange, bemused expression on his face, led them on through the forest until they saw the castle before them once again. Ranulph had fallen silent. It was the first time he had revisited his old hideaway, and he had felt a heavy sadness steal over him as he gazed down from it. That was the child Ranulph's drey, not his. He had no business there. Great lords never climbed trees. They were the huntsmen, not those who looked furtively upon the nobles at their sport. It could never mean the same to him again: his innocence had disappeared along with his suffering.

'Wiwwum!'

He was greeted at the gate by a burly Christopher grown yet more stout on the good food that was never in short supply at the castle. There were no complaints of hunger now.

'Come, Christopher,' Ranulph smiled, leaving a groom to lead his horse away. 'You can help me prepare for the wedding. You'd like that?'

'Good!' the idiot lad enthused, wrapping an arm around him as nobody else would think, or dare, to do. 'Good, Wiwwum!'

They staggered, like a version of Swinke-Swonken, into the courtyard, then through an arched doorway and along a narrow stone passage towards the baronial apartments. Ranulph could never follow this route, however many times in a day, without thinking of the time he was brought here by the castle steward – the *former* castle steward – and accused of attacking the lady Elizabeth.

The church bells began to ring, reminding him that he had, indeed, returned from the hunt only just in time. But was a baron not allowed some licence? And he had, of course, someone to prepare his clothes for him.

That someone now emerged from his apartment, her huge frame filling the doorway, her gesticulations leaving him in no doubt that she been waiting some considerable time and was not a little angry.

'Sorry, Grete!' he sang, holding his hands together in mock supplication so that his one-time guardian should understand his meaning, too. 'I shall get dressed immediately.'

He had discovered a ruthlessness in himself when he returned to inherit the castle and its lands. It was a pleasing ruthlessness, since he knew that treating his enemies gently would have brought about his immediate downfall, but it was unusual in being completely bloodless. Ranulph had seen enough blood-letting to last him a lifetime.

No, he had banished those who had plotted to have him killed, that was all. Fulke's retainers and his other close followers had been similarly dispatched, to be replaced by people he knew and trusted. Let Grete wave her fists about as if she would hammer him into the ground, he knew from her protection in the hard times that she was loyal and loving.

'What do you think to this crimson gown, Christopher?'

'Red, Wiwwum.'

'Yes,' he laughed, 'the reddest crimson there ever was. As red as the fair lady's mouth, I'll warrant.'

He slipped into a new pair of leather boots and was at last ready for the great occasion. They retraced their footsteps along the corridor, flinched from the bright sun which struck their eyes as they stepped into the courtyard and quickly passed through an archway which brought them to a grassy area in front of the church. The wedding guests were already gathered here, their bright clothes dazzling in the sunlight. Further away, at a respectful distance and half hidden by the comfortable shade of a cluster of tall oak trees, knots of peasants stood in their best drab costumes like a crowd at a peep-show.

The bishop stepped forward to make his greeting.

'Your scrivener tells me that you were present when that felon Wat Tyler met his end at Smithfield. A joyous moment, was it not?'

'A significant moment,' Ranulph replied. He knew that the bishop suspected him of beliefs dangerous to the wellbeing of the church. 'It brought the rising to an end.'

'Indeed. And your scrivener himself, so he informs me, played a vital role in the event. Isn't that so, old fellow?

'Vital,' beamed Walt, who held Hosea's Wife on a short rein, remembering her fancy for prelates. 'I set the goat on that Wat Tyler.'

'Of course,' grinned Ranulph. 'You played a hero's part.'

'And who knows,' the bishop added, anxious to fire his warning shot across the young baron's bows, 'what might have come to pass had Tyler not perished then. Perhaps the overthrow of the King and all who rule his kingdom with him.'

He slowly turned his head, allowing his eyes to fall upon Christopher.

'And the creation of a world in which the lowly would never again know their place.'

Now he glanced sideways at a young woman whose natural bashfulness contrasted with the splendour of the beautiful yellow gown she wore.

'A world in which the true faith gave way to witchcraft and the Devil's works.'

Ranulph laughed: 'Avelina is no witch, I can assure you. She is our herbalist, and you won't find a better.'

'A world,' the bishop continued, as if he were giving a sermon that could not be interrupted, 'in which unnatural things symbolised the overthrow of the natural order ordained by God.'

Ranulph, who had decided to treat these cautionary remarks lightly, nevertheless found anger welling inside him as he saw the bishop's gaze fall meaningfully upon two of his friends who chatted brightly close by.

'Swinke and Swonken are God's creatures, too,' he said shortly.

'But . . .'

'As,' he added swiftly, 'are the peasants who work my fields. If I choose to pay them better than your average lord that is my own concern.'

'Ah, indeed,' the bishop blustered, nonplussed. 'But . . .'

Here the church bells mercifully intervened, clanging more furiously than ever. It was time to go in. The bishop led the way, with Ranulph and Christopher a pace behind. Once inside, they turned to face the porch.

'Janie,' Christopher exclaimed, first pointing, then widening his eyes and spreading a large hand across his mouth in an expression of joyful amazement.

Ranulph smiled: 'She's very beautiful,' he said.

She was, in fact, as they had never seen her before, her hair piled high and studded with jewels, her white dress long, flowing and wonderfully brocaded. But her eyes were regular Janie-bright, and her lips were quite as red as ever.

'Booful!' Christopher echoed.

And now Henry was by her side and taking her hand in his, his eyes merry with happiness.

'My children,' began the bishop, stepping forward.

Ranulph himself felt as if he had never been happier. Not only was his dear friend, his wise counsellor, Henry pledged to be his right-hand man in running this vast estate, but now, in marrying Janie, he had ensured that every one of their travelling band should remain together. With this union of two hearts their journey had come to an end.

And his own affairs of the heart? There had been little time of late to think of them, but now he put a hand into his pocket and took out the fragment of brooch he had carried with him through all his troubles. In his imagination he saw the two halves brought together again to form a perfect sphere, deep crimson like a bead of blood.

Perhaps, he mused, the missing piece was a precious relic he was destined yet to find.